The Life to Come

The Life to Come

stories

Tim Lees

LASTIC
PRESS

For my mother and father

Acknowledgements

My debts of gratitude are now too large either to repay or list in full, so I'll keep this short. Pride of place must go to Andy Cox for initial publication of many of these pieces, and for a commendation I'd like carved upon my tombstone (preferably in the very distant future). Thanks to Trevor Denyer for likewise giving a couple of stories their first home. Andrew Hook, of course, deserves credit and thanks not only for this collection, but for the whole Elastic Press line, helping keep alive a form about which mainstream publishers no longer seem to care: the short story. In addition, I would like to thank the many people who advised me, wittingly and otherwise, through the writing of these pieces; my friends for their continuing indulgence; and, for this and much more, my parents. Without whom.

Table of contents

The God House

Waiting for her in Reception, as he had so many times, or roaming through the House itself, Muldoon soon came to recognise the types and dispositions of the other visitors. The bulk were simply sightseers, of course, or there on business: priests, technicians, clerks... They didn't interest him. But there were others whose intentions seemed more personal, and more significant; yet also, more obscure.

These were the ones he called 'devouts'.

Always solitary, often shabby or unkempt, they ranged the halls like ragged ghosts, unwilling or unable to move on. He knew that many took illicit drugs to heighten their religious sense, or practised brutal deprivations, going without food or sleep for days on end, in their attempts to merge with the divine. A few had predilections for specific galleries or areas. Some chanted to themselves, or railed at unseen presences; and once, he watched a woman – young, but scarecrow-thin – perform a wild, ecstatic dance before her chosen deity, flinging her body back and forth, as if a fire burned in her flesh. These people, far more than the gods themselves, seemed to epitomise the place for him, to give it character and meaning. What were they looking for? What did they want?

He wondered, too, about his own motives for being there. A few months back, if anybody had asked, he might have told them he was simply waiting for a friend; nothing more complex or sinister than that.

1

But now, he couldn't be so sure.

Each day he went, he got there earlier, spent longer in the galleries, felt less and less inclined to leave. Even his rendezvous with J. seemed almost like a chore some nights, a forced return to normal life; and, though the feeling always passed, it left him with a vague unease, a sense of hollowness inside... And one more thing he couldn't talk to her about.

At first, he'd seen it as a kind of transference: since J. worked at the House, then, by exploring it, he was uncovering another aspect of her life – a part of her he'd never otherwise have known, or understood.

The trouble was that she disdained the place. She'd no more love for it than if she'd worked on an assembly line – and rather less regard for many of her co-workers. If she'd imagined he identified her with her job, in even such a vague, tangential way, she'd probably have been appalled.

Her bitterness surprised and worried him. It was a side of her he'd never managed to accommodate. It distanced her, it went against his expectations; and – in some strange way – it helped provoke his love.

*

She worked hard, she said. But not from choice. Some nights he found her irritable, tensed up with the pressures of the day. She needed time to rest; to come back to herself, she said. They'd drive out to a quiet bar to drink and watch TV until she felt like moving on.

She'd got a job, he hadn't, and he tried to make allowances for that.

Yet it was difficult. He felt uncertain with her, as he'd seldom done with other girls. She could be touchy, over-sensitive; some nights her lips would press together with a kind of buried rage, her face grow hard and angular. There was a way she held her shoulders that alerted him... A danger sign. On nights like that, he'd sit beside her, curbing his impatience, trying to keep a distance from her moods. He'd let her take the lead, decide the time to talk, or eat, or drive off somewhere else.

In consequence he worried about looking passive, weak. Or saying the wrong thing. Making the wrong moves. Misinterpreting...

He worried – worried, all the time.

2

With J., he seldom felt relaxed or natural. He couldn't deal with her. He always had to plan out strategies, make efforts to impress – forever choosing between one act and another as to which would show him in the better light.

He knew this kind of insecurity was close to love. And yet it never made him happy, and he never tried to talk to her about it; neither of them, really, was particularly *verbal* about things. Some days he'd make up speeches that began, "When I'm with you, I feel..." but they were too embarrassing, too awkward, like a foreign language. And they held a risk. Supposing she rebuffed him? Told him he was asking far too much? So long as he kept quiet, he could hope. And hope was something that he didn't want to lose. So he'd steer the conversation onto lighter themes, tell jokes, trade gossip... Ask about her work.

Despite the popular prestige associated with the House, her job was ill-paid and demanding, and her prospects limited, she said. The good positions were all sewn up – it was who you knew, or who you slept with; that's how you got on. She loathed the sense of intrigue that encumbered everything, the self-importance of the priests, the negligence of admin staff, the sheer high-handedness of the Electric Company, who nowadays called all the shots.

She rarely went into the galleries. Once, it's true, she'd visited them regularly – but that was just a phase she'd been through, nothing more. These days when she clocked off she simply wanted to get out, as far away as possible. "That place takes too much of my bloody time anyway," she said.

So he was left to wander and explore alone, like any of the other solitary pilgrims. He knew that, physically, he was starting to resemble them: losing weight, his clothes a little shabbier each week, a little further out of style.

He wondered whether this would matter, whether it diminished him in J.'s eyes.

Everything, these days, seemed to come back to her.

*

The God House was immensely old. It had been built far to the north of ancient settlements, but gradually the city had crept up around it, sprawling over the surrounding countryside, with tower blocks, industrial estates, hotels, parks, garages – the full remorseless landslide of modernity. The God House nestled in it like a fossil in a limestone wall.

Nearly twenty miles across, and twice as long, a quick glance might have taken it for some intrusive feature of the landscape, an old volcanic bastion or terminal moraine, as yet unrounded by the weather. Birds and vegetation colonised its roofs. On certain days, huge clouds clung to the taller spires, moored there like zeppelins, blocking out the sun. The God House had a climate all its own, both temporal and spiritual. Few lived beneath its walls from choice. The vast estates to north and west were ghetto towns, notorious for violence, crime, and strange religious cults... What influence the House held there was still a matter for debate.

As for Muldoon, like most people he seldom thought about the slums; he kept away from them, and kept his mind on other things.

The chief of which, just now, was trying to find his way around the House's maze-like inner rooms.

Few maps were accurate. The guidebook gave him only the most generalised of outlines; older maps were even less precise. The size and labyrinthine nature of the place inevitably leant itself to errors, and the errors leant themselves, in turn, to superstition. Common legends claimed the House was somehow infinite in its extent, contained within a finite world; or that its galleries would shift and change continually, to thwart even the best-prepared explorer.

Such stories, he was sure, were nonsense.

Rather, the House was just what it appeared to be: a vast and complex structure, physically massive and imbued with great religious strength, designed entirely for the purpose of confining and reducing forces which, during primeval times, had had free play across the world. As such, its function was entirely practical. Its later uses, as a temple, a museum, and, more recently, a means of generating power for the city, could be regarded as subsidiary.

*

Inside the halls, the gods were ranged like creatures in a zoo. Each filled its own domain the way that light fills up a room, extending to the furthest limits of confinement. Shields and barriers divided them, one from another, keeping each from the attentions of its neighbours; and visitors, from the attentions of them all.

Nevertheless, few came before the gods without feeling their influence. Certain emotions, certain concepts or associations rose before the mind... Occasionally warm, affirmative and life-giving; more often, distant and unsettling, like the hints of revelation glimpsed on psychoactive drugs. There was a sense of something great, world-altering, just out of reach, there on the fringes of the mind. Yet every time, the revelation failed to come; the feeling vanished, leaving just a tantalising residue, a might-have-been.

In some cases, the contemplation of the gods produced dissociation, melancholy, inconsolable awareness of mortality and loss. In former times, when pilgrims had arrived in droves, the over-zealous used to fling themselves upon their chosen deities, intent on immolation; sometimes hundreds dying in a single day.

The world had grown more secular since then.

. *

Though each god was unique, the gods resembled one another closely, much as animals who share a mode of life resemble one another. If asked to list the qualities of godhood Muldoon might have replied: absolute constancy; infinite patience; power; loneliness; unknowability. Although he knew the gods – by virtue of their nature – must surely have contained all things.

Sometimes their faces could be glimpsed, like dim reflections in a pool. Such images were far from human, yet, stared at for long enough, they seemed to bear a tenuous connection to humanity, much as a beast's face does to a man's.

Some thinkers had proposed the possibility that, after such long association, while mankind had not grown noticeably more divine, the gods might well have grown a little more like men.

*

J. worked in Archives, easily the biggest section of the Admin block. Its records went back three millennia and more. Here, for example, the utterances of the gods had been recorded in gigantic ledgers, which the priests still pored over in search of meaning. One part of her job – a small part, too, squeezed in between her other duties – was to transfer all these records to computer disc. It was a job she stood no chance of finishing.

Some nights her fingers ached so much she soaked them in a mix

5

of water, lemon juice and herbs, until the tips would shrivel up like prunes. It was an old family recipe, she said. She came from a long line of typists, pianists, and keyboard operatives of every kind. Her family, she joked, were noted for their manual dexterity.

He begged her: "Proof?"

She teased him: "Later. Maybe. If you're lucky."

He'd known her just three weeks by then.

Those were the easy days of their relationship; the easiest they'd ever be.

*

A tour party had seized possession of the western halls. Their guide, a brisk young woman in a skirt-suit, ushered her clients with that mix of flattery and bullying the House Wardens seemed to have taken for their own distinctive style. Her face was thick with make up. In the dim light, it became a mask, a palimpsest of signs, all giant smiles and imprecations. When she lectured, her abrupt, school-ma'am-ish voice would rise to counteract the slightest inattention in her group. She was impatient. Questions might be brushed aside, or answered in the briefest way. From time to time, sharp flash bulbs popped, leaving their afterglow to float in Muldoon's fuddled eyes. He loathed these crowds, resented them as if their presence there was almost sacrilegious; bumptious, noisy trespassers, who had no real right to share the place with him.

Off in the darkness, then, he saw the boy.

Dressed in a tightly-buttoned gabardine, hands folded at his groin, his face was now so pale it seemed to float among the shadows like a white balloon. Muldoon had seen him other times, on other days; and now, they swapped a look, each sharing his contempt for the intruders.

Muldoon moved closer, drawn by curiosity. The boy was surely a devout – if only marginally so – and Muldoon experienced a sudden urge to talk, to question him, to try and understand.

He wondered whether he, too, might be considered a devout, though of a rather different kind...

*

"You feel them sometimes," J. had told him. "Even in the offices. They're not confined. Well, not like people say they are, at any rate."

It was a Sunday morning. They'd made love, drunk coffee, smoked

6

their morning cigarettes; from her window, far away, the chief spires of the House were faintly visible, framed by a trio of decaying tower blocks. Now they looked tiny, almost insignificant; and yet his eyes were drawn to them, time and again.

J. talked. She lay back, head on one side, coiling a lock of hair around her fingertip.

"You're sitting there, and suddenly, it's like there's someone looking at you, right? Over your shoulder. You can feel it. Or... not looking, really. More, just sort of *there*. It really frightened me, at first. But you get used to it. They don't do any harm."

"Scary." He stroked her belly, outlined with a fingertip the curve and hollow of her navel, the pale down on her soft, brown skin.

"Not really. Not these days." She lay motionless, eyes on the ceiling. "And you get chills, sometimes, as well. I mean, the offices are air-conditioned, there's no real reason. But it happens. They're just snooping around, that's all. I don't care, anyway."

He ran his fingers lower, traced a small mole on her hip; he brushed the fringes of her pubic hair.

"What do you care about?"

She stirred, then gently caught his hand and pinioned it. "Well, to be honest, what I care about right now is having breakfast. Hmm?" She raised his hand up to her lips, kissed it in what seemed a sisterly kind of a way, and laid it on his chest. "Sorry," she said. "You know?"

*

He'd come into a chamber so vast that the far walls vanished into mist and darkness, and the ceiling could be guessed at only from the spread of the supporting columns in the shadows high above. He heard the tick of dripping water; underfoot were smooth, round pebbles, as if once – God knows how long ago – a river or a stream had flowed there.

He might have been the first person to enter in a thousand years.

Above him, in the centre of the hall, the god hung, tall as a cathedral, ancient and implacable; it had assumed a form, though not a human one. Instead, a complex of great arches rose up, intertwined and twisted like the limbs of some enormous squid, frozen to sudden immobility; it had a wild, near-architectural grace, and a pervasive air of sentience – even of watchfulness – that spread to every corner of the hall.

7

He couldn't breathe.

The arches dribbled water, and their flanks were pocked by scales and crusts like half-shed skin, or fluted in peculiar, tangled patterns; huge round sockets gaped at him like cavern mouths.

His belly shrank; the sweat ran cold across his brow.

He felt his thoughts begin to dim and fade, like stars dissolving in the night... His mind already wilting under pressure of the god's. And this, as well – he realised – was a part of what the House could offer him: putting an end to all the clutter and minutiae of his life, the cheap illusions of his own self-worth... Leaving him naked, burned out; empty as a ghost.

Hours later, he was back outside, under a gloomy, moisture-laden sky.

Waiting for J.

*

Some nights he felt them, crowding through his dreams, disguised as friends and former lovers, school teachers, ex-workmates – people he'd not thought about in years. Their lips moved and their hands gesticulated urgently. Their eyes sought his... What message were they trying to impart? What news?

Or was it all simply a crude bid for attention, like a child crying out, 'Look at me!'?

He woke up drained these days. He seldom ate. He puffed on cigarettes for nourishment, and drank great vats of hot, black coffee, trying to keep himself awake.

He suffered dizzy spells.

On rare occasions – yet still frequently enough to worry him – he woke from brief, perplexing fugues, to find himself on unfamiliar streets, no notion where he'd been or what he'd done... As if he'd fallen for a while into the time-scale of the gods, with neither flow nor sequentiality... Time locked in ice.

He was convinced the House held the solution to his problems. All he had to do was tease it out, somehow, as if it were a puzzle waiting explanation. Like the children's games he'd played when he was young.

*

"See this." The boy undid his cuffs, carefully folding back his sleeves.

8

He held his arms out. For a moment, in the dim light, Muldoon saw nothing. Then he realised what he'd first taken for hair along the boy's thin forearms was, in fact, a fine cross-hatch of scars, most of them old and faded, but a few still clear and fresh.

He looked up at the boy's face. Shadows fell across it like a furtive domino.

"They need a proof," the boy was saying. "So they'll trust you... right? They need a sacrifice..."

He sounded rational, a bit impatient, like a tutor with a backward pupil. Muldoon's disgust and fascination mingled. He was waiting now, uncertain of himself. He watched the boy pull down his sleeves and button them fastidiously round his wrists.

"You have to give to them. Or else they can't give back."

The boy moved forward, out into the light. His face was pale and thin, the jaw too heavy, the cheeks wasted and sunk. Dark skin had bagged beneath his eyes. Muldoon felt sure the boy was ill. He reached out, offering a hand. The boy stepped back abruptly.

"Don't you fucking dare," he warned. "Don't put your fucking hands on me."

He'd taken Muldoon's gesture for a sexual advance (perhaps what he'd been secretly in need of all along, Muldoon would wonder afterwards). Quick as a weasel he turned, and in a moment vanished in the shadows of the colonnade. Muldoon called out. He wanted to explain, only his voice was caught up by the echoes of the gallery. It sounded thin and insincere. He had been innocent, and yet his words were full of guilt.

*

Muldoon felt tired. He'd walked a long way, eight or nine miles since the early morning. He settled on a low stone bench to rest. This was an empty hall, lit by a few small lights around the walls, and one thin shaft of sun that cut the air above his head.

Today the galleries were full of workmen. Little gangs of them had dogged his travels, busy shoring up the walls, replacing cables, checking out the wiring; re-adjusting settings under the inspection hatches set into the floors.

He'd watched them rig a new god to the grid. As fittings were attached and sluices opened, ripples had flashed back and forth across the god-stuff like a sudden shock of fear; and only when the final switch was thrown had it appeared to calm, then fall into a languor which resembled – to Muldoon's eyes, anyway – the sickly sleep of anaesthesia.

He'd stayed there till the workmen packed their tools away, unwound their yellow warning tape and loaded everything onto a little, battery-powered trolley. They'd paid him just the briefest glance, given a quick, dismissive nod to one another; he guessed they'd labelled him, the way that he'd once labelled visitors there. Dismissed him as irrelevant to them. Irrelevant – and slightly ludicrous, as well?

He found J., later, perching on the wall beside the car park, eyes narrow, forehead creased.

"What bloody time do you call this?" she asked, tapping her watch.

He gave a slight shrug, helpless to explain himself.

"I, you know, I got lost..."

"Got *lost*?" she said. "You *got lost*? Kids get lost," she told him. "*Little* kids. You know?"

*

Philosophers and theologians visited, bringing with them strange equipment: meters, gauges, counters, measuring devices of all kinds. He knew that many still believed theology could be refined, becoming an exact science, as chemistry and physics once were; offering a yardstick for all other disciplines.

Muldoon was sceptical. The theologians, for a start, seemed hardly adequate to such a task. Long years stuck in religious colleges had emphasised their oddities, these feathery old men with their peculiar tics and mannerisms. Often, they were physically unusual – too short, too tall, too angular, myopic, stuttering, or otherwise impaired. Even the younger ones were strange, half-mad with their peculiar schemes and theorems. They seemed to dread all human contact. Often a simple question, even a greeting, would be met by an insistent turning of the head, as from a source of pain. Such creatures, thought Muldoon, could no more live outside the rarefied world of the church than fly.

Philosophers, generically, had quite a different character.

Careerists to a man, robust, aggressively competitive, the lower ranks of House staff came to dread their visits. They demanded and complained, protested at the least delay, walked round like bantam

10

cocks, convinced – despite their calling – that appearances were everything, that glossy surfaces led automatically to glossy reputations, lucrative consultancies, promotions and the like.

Far worse, a few of these high-flyers took an interest in the women of the House, including J., and (though she was open in her denigration of them) Muldoon could never feel at ease, imagining her in their company. Such men were wealthy, powerful, dynamic; accomplished talkers, liars, con artists... He didn't trust her not to fall for one of them.

She'd shown him products of their work sometimes. Their theses were incomprehensible, larded with jargon and insistent bows to others of their trade, with whom they wished to curry favour. It seemed a miracle they even bothered visiting the House at all. They showed no signs of understanding it; no wish to, either, thought Muldoon, with a peculiar, comforting awareness of his own superiority.

*

Yet whatever virtues he might still possess, it seemed that J. no longer noticed them.

"Let's put your collar straight," she said, tugging his shirt so violently he feared he'd lose a button. He sat there, passive, while she wrestled with him, and he heard the breath hiss through her teeth.

"What's wrong with you?" she said. "What's happened to you, recently?"

"What's wrong with me?" Yet surely, it was she whose life was out of whack, constantly fidgeting with matters that had no real consequence; the kind of trivia he found it hard to even think of any more. Why bother how he looked, or what he said, or did? Or who he talked to? What he ate? The gods made everything irrelevant. For some while, after he'd been close to them, it seemed perspectives changed, reversed themselves, and what was near lost all significance, all meaning. Only their greatness, and their vastness, seemed important.

He was puzzled to remember how, he too, had been like her, wrapped up in all the minor, unimportant details of his life.

Her voice came to him, grating on his consciousness. He realised she'd been talking for a long time. Now she railed at him, as angry as he'd ever seen her, even when she spoke about her job.

"You don't have any goals," she said. "You don't *do* anything – "

The tired sound gnawed his brain. She listed all his faults, his indolence, his carelessness, his lack of thought for others... She was trying to provoke him, make him argue – maybe trying to end things, there and then.

He put his coat on and walked out.

It was only later the confusion came. Should he have stayed, and tried to calm her down? What made her act like this so suddenly? A migraine? Bad day at work?

Back home, he waited for the phone to ring.

He tidied up his room. He swept the floor, shifted the furniture and cleaned the carpet. He took a stack of newspapers and crammed them in the bin. Then, though it was late at night, he filled a bowl with water and began to wipe the woodwork down, cleaning the smudges from around the door handle and light switch. He took his clothes out of the wardrobe, folded them, and put them back.

He went to bed consumed with rage. He couldn't manage to believe the night's events.

*

Days passed.

She didn't call.

There came a time when it occurred to him that maybe something irreversible had happened, something more inside himself than in the outside world.

He shut his eyes, trying to conjure up her face. Even to picture her would have been some kind of assurance, some link to the past. Yet nothing came. He would have recognised her anywhere, he knew, but now, away from her, he couldn't place the details, couldn't see the colour of her eyes, the shape and texture of her forehead... The soft, firm muscles of her mouth.

I can't go back to her, he thought, and started sobbing without really knowing why... He felt he'd travelled too far out, beyond the world of normal people, normal human interactions. He'd no right to talk to her, to even think of her. No right to talk to anybody, anymore.

All that he had left now were the gods.

He felt them most at night. A whisper, or a sudden chill... And it was true, the thing she'd said: they weren't confined. Each time he'd left the House, he'd taken a small piece of them away, lodged in his mind. A germ, a spark... A virus of divinity.

Their voices purred at him.

It was a choice. An either/or. People were petty, awkward, unpredictable. Only the gods remained the same. No new thoughts came to them, no old thoughts died away... Stasis. Absolute. Perfection.

A wind beat at the windowpane. It roused him, stirring some forgotten instinct in his head. He was surprised how cold the room felt suddenly, although the sun still shone outside. He moved a few steps, clutching a blanket round himself for warmth. His limbs were stiff. 'It's like a room where someone's died,' he thought. He clattered tea spoons on the sink unit; they made a tiny, hollow sound. He looked out at the street.

What were those people doing there?

He tapped the glass. He called to them. They didn't hear. They weren't aware of him; it was as if he'd lost all resonance, as if he could have yelled into their faces, and still met the same response.

The sense of distance frightened him.

One day, he thought, I'll reach out for a cup or spoon and see my hand pass straight through. And then I won't be there. Not any more.

Afraid to be alone, he went outside. It was the scents he noticed most: the smell of recent rain, the traffic fumes, the odour of damp privet from a local park. He walked. The streets were wet. Fat pigeons scattered lazily before him, bloated from their pickings at the market place.

Each day, he walked.

He had to be with people, even if he didn't speak to them; he needed their proximity, as if, by watching them, he'd be reminded of who he was.

The third morning he came across an old couple, loaded with shopping bags. They smoked a single cigarette and passed it back and forth between them, taking just a few drags each; somehow the tenderness of this, the sharing touched him in a way that he could not resist.

He bought a pack of cigarettes, smoked two or three in quick succession, then lit another, and phoned J.

13

*

He found the boy again. Now he'd grown thinner still, if possible. He seemed fixated with a single hall; whatever power its deities possessed, he wandered helplessly between them, like a small boat, drifting with the tides. He took no interest in Muldoon. The brief attunement that they'd felt was gone. Muldoon was just another onlooker, a person of no possible significance.

He'd heard the gods' call, then rejected it.

Muldoon, nevertheless, peered at the young man's face, as if at an alternate version of himself. The hunger there was animal, and all-absorbing... One day, he felt, the young man's skull would surely burst from all the pressure it contained. Still, there was a look about him – filled with such intentness, and such concentration – that even now Muldoon could almost envy him. His life was simple, anyway; it had just one aim, one goal, no matter how destructive it might prove.

Could I have saved him? Muldoon asked himself. *Should I have tried?*

Unable, even now, to talk about his own experience, he talked about the boy instead; he speculated on his past, offered a dreary list of circumstances, echoing his own: no family nearby, no job, mistrust of others, difficulties making friends...

"No ties," Muldoon explained. "Nothing to hold him here – like, in the real world. That's the thing..."

"The *real* world?"

"*This* world – you know? With men and women – " He was animated, making gestures with his hands, as if to drag the words out of the air. "That's why – religious people, monks, hermits – that's why they live *alone*, you know?"

She shook her head. Of course they lived alone, she thought. You wouldn't call them hermits, otherwise, would you?

She sipped her coffee, lit a cigarette.

"I think they're pitiful," she said. "They're worse than drug addicts. You see them coming back, day after day... Someone should do something. It isn't right."

She glanced out of the window. Dark clouds hung over the House, distorted by the pressure shifts into a flowing, step-like form.

Their presence marred a sheer blue sky.

14

He told her: "No. It's not addiction. More like... going to a foreign country, and forgetting your way home."

J. shrugged, dragged on her cigarette. He always had to go one better, didn't he? Always had a smarter explanation, something only *he'd* been able to work out. Like Sherlock bloody Holmes...

And yet she was amused, rather than angry, and she reached across the table, and she clasped his hand. There were a lot worse things in life, when all was said and done. A lot worse.

And worse people, too.

"Let's go out for a drive," she said. "Into the country. Somewhere new."

"Just one more cig," he said, and lit up. "This," he told her, "*this* is what you call addiction..."

*

Strange rumours had been circulating recently about the gods.

They had begun as idle talk, bar gossip, jokes. Now nobody considered them in such a light and careless fashion. Even when they went unsaid, their implications seemed to underlie all other topics of debate, and add an edginess, a shiver of anxiety to even the most casual exchange.

For years, the gods had given power to the city. Few people doubted their omnipotence. Commerce and industry had grown without restraint, convinced they held a reservoir that could be drained indefinitely; always expanding with the markets, and with every wave of new technology that came along.

But now, it seemed the gods had been misjudged. Quite likely, they were finite beings, like ourselves; creatures whose lives and strengths, though vast, were hardly without end.

The rumours spoke of certain galleries, certain enclosures, which just ten years earlier had each contained a major deity.

Today, those sites were empty.

A tremor of suppressed alarm ran through the city. People took to turning lights off, showering instead of having baths. They ate cold lunches. Anything, no matter how absurd, that might conserve the power.

No-one knew the truth. The House officials, naturally, denied the tales, but they persisted, nonetheless.

15

Muldoon asked J. one morning, as they lay in bed, whether she'd any notion what was really going on.

She gave a brief, dismissive snort.

"That," she said, "is probably the last thing we'd be told. And anyway," she added, "what the hell. I'm going to change my job. I've had enough. And then we can forget about the gods. *Forever*, right?"

He doubted things would be so simple. And yet, for now, he felt the same as she did; a pleasant, unaccustomed luxury: he didn't give a damn.

The gods, in any case, would be there for a long time yet.

And they knew how to wait.

Starlight

"That man," my Mother once remarked – meaning my Uncle Edward – "is a *plain embarrassment*."

But family was family, and he was one of us, no matter what he did; as a result, I think, his influence on me went more or less unnoticed for a good few years, at least until the damage had been well and truly done. By then (so I believe) there were quite real fears I might follow in my Uncle's less than reputable footsteps.

But, alas! While I was every bit as profligate, I lacked even a spark of his extraordinary genius. My life, instead, has been a catalogue of small, prosaic failures: bad investments, foolish marriages, and countless ready opportunities passed up in hope of something brighter, later on. Indeed, if I had better ways of making money, then I'd hardly be here now, tapping my story on a borrowed typewriter. My bank accounts are gone, my rooms are bare, and, if I might risk a note of pathos here, my childhood seems the only thing of value left to sell.

These days it strikes me as remarkable my parents even let me near my Uncle Edward, much less permitted all those long, indulgent holidays I actually spent with him. Both Mum and Dad were sticklers for propriety; true members of the British bourgeoisie, they took the values of their age and class and hugged them to their bosoms like the Word of God. Above all else, they dreaded seeming 'common' or 'uncouth' – just as they loathed those folk they felt had somehow 'got above themselves'. The balance was precarious, and I, like any child, seemed destined to upset it every chance I got. A dropped 'h' or a grubby sleeve, a hint of schoolboy slang – these things were acts of treachery in a persistent but unstated version of the class war which, although I scarcely understood it, I accepted as a normal and inevitable part of life.

Each morning as I left for school my uniform would be inspected with a truly military rigour. Dad would don his spectacles, straighten my collar, probe my Windsor knot with open scepticism... The best that I could hope for was a grudging nod. I cleaned my shoes so many times I'm told I even made the motions in my sleep – unending little circles, finger tucked into a corner of the sheet... Not that my parents were the least bit cruel or unconcerned for me – the very opposite! I'd often hear my Mother boast how much I valued cleanliness, how neat I was, and certainly my nightly twitchings never worried her, the way they might a modern parent. They were signs of diligence, no more. Even my future would be spotless, all mapped out for me, following Dad's career in loss adjustment...

I still wonder, sometimes, how things might have gone if I'd agreed to all their plans. Would I have been rich? Successful? Happy? Who can tell?

At any rate, when I was eight or nine (as story tellers say), Fate lent a hand. Two events contrived to push me towards Uncle Edward: first, a series of debilitating asthma seizures, for which the doctor recommended country air; second, and far more intriguingly, a number of 'corruption' cases in the local parks.

I listened eagerly for news of these, aware just from my parents' tone of voice that there was something fascinating and mysterious involved; yet something I could never ever ask about. Even the dictionary – so enlightening on words like 'penis', 'harlot', 'haemorrhoids' – gave only the suggestions of 'decay' and 'moral depredation', shying from the details.

Mum and Dad were much alarmed. The city wasn't safe for somebody as young and as impressionable as I – especially through the long, unstructured weeks of holiday. They had my health to think of, too. I needed somewhere clean, secure – out in the country, say...

Of course, it wasn't Uncle Edward's name that sprang to mind.

Certainly not. But Edward's wife was Kate, my Mother's sister; and Aunt Kate, at least, was held to be reliable, dependable and sure.

So I was placed aboard a train at Paddington, to be collected, two or three hours later, like some noisy and enthusiastic parcel, at a little station in the West Country; from which time on, it seemed to me, all normal life came to an end. Indeed, in some ways I might say that I'm still waiting for it to resume.

*

My Uncle was a shortish, stocky man, bald since his twenties. In the time I knew him, he changed little; the hair he had went grey, his movements became stiffer, and in later years, he was inclined to peevishness and bouts of temper. Yet, at heart, he would remain the same indomitable and eccentric spirit who (he claimed) had roamed through China and Tibet, and been the friend of great African chiefs and medicine men... Well, I may have had my doubts about a few of Uncle's stories, but I never voiced them; I liked listening too much, and didn't care to spoil things, either for myself, or him!

His house was large, set on a hill in rather shambling grounds, just out of town. Approaching from the station, I'd watch eagerly to catch my first glimpse of its chimneys, poking up above the trees. Sometimes, the sight brought unexpected novelties: a giant radio mast, swaying in the wind; a copper-coloured gadget like a sextant gleaming on the gable-end; and once, a good half of the roof blown off, in one of Uncle's less well-judged experiments. He always had some kind of project on the go – more often, two or three. The bulk were innocent. A few, less so. I well recall his bid to film his dreams, his fascination with the power of clocks; the symphony he wrote by simply spattering the score with ink – each page, he claimed, the essence of a single microsecond, caught in time. (The local bandmaster, a sombre Methodist, had other words for it). The Dadaists would have been proud of him, for sure! But most of all, I think back to a single winter visit that I made. New Year, perhaps? Or later – say, a February half term? I had a brand new bike, and rode beside it in the guard's van all the way from London, reluctant to abandon it for even half a minute. How I dreamed of the adventures that I'd have, cycling the long and solitary miles round Uncle's home...

Yet this was not to be. A heavy snow had fallen, blanketing the countryside. I was allowed down town, but my Aunt considered longer trips dangerous, and she forbade them. Oh, I loved the snow – I built a snowman on the front lawn, right above the road – but equally, each day, I longed for it to disappear.

Till, bit by bit, I learned about my Uncle's latest scheme, and then my bike was soon forgotten, propped up in my Aunt Kate's pantry, out of sight and – almost – out of mind.

I'd heard before how he believed the stars to be alive, great beings swimming through the depths of space as whales do through the sea; or else, perhaps, the fragments of a single, vaster entity, all scattered now – the relics of a great primordial God ("In which case," he remarked, "the basic nature of the Universe is one of loneliness, division, loss...")

He had a habit of expounding on such matters at the tea table, much to my Aunt's annoyance. But if she seemed put out, then he'd evoke the Great and Good in his defence: "As Aristotle made quite clear..." "It was Voltaire who first proposed..." He was not, I think, particularly accurate in his citations from such folk; at any rate, it seemed they all agreed with him!

"The Universe is a gigantic living, breathing thing," he claimed, waving a half-eaten ham sandwich at us both. "Think of the implications, then. Consider them. For instance – if the stars are all alive, then what then are we? What are the planets? What, I might ask, is this fine *sandwich jambon*?"

He took another bite, chewed thoughtfully, then fixed me with his eager, javelin gaze.

"Faeces," he said at last. "We are no more – no less – than faeces from the stars."

"*Edward*!" My Aunt was genuinely shocked.

"A stellar dung..."

"Now that is *quite* enough!"

My Uncle put his head on one side, shrugged, but made no effort to apologise.

"Just Science, dear. A little Science lesson for the boy..."

My Aunt indulged my Uncle's Science as another woman might have tolerated pigeon-fancying, or any similarly doubtful male pursuit. His Science was all well and good, kept in its proper place –

for preference, as far from her as possible.

But Uncle wasn't finished with me yet. After the meal, with Aunt Kate busy in the kitchen, he tipped his head for me to follow him. The living quarters of the house were all my Aunt's, and bore her hallmarks: cosy, comfortable, safe. The attic was my Uncle's realm. A fold-down stair connected them, so rickety it took me all my nerve to climb; but then, as Dad would surely have agreed, nothing worthwhile in life was ever gained without a little mild discomfort.

And the attic – ah. The attic was another world.

The debris of my Uncle's past enthusiasms crowded it, the shelves piled high with rolled-up charts, coiled magnets, microscopes, bottles of tinted glass; and there, in one corner, the mounted skeleton of an appalling monster: a great biped with a long neck and a ball-shaped, needle-toothed, demanding head, almost on a level with my own... It would be years before I realised that the thing was fake, a fish's skull fixed to the neck of some poor flightless bird. Yet, as a child, I thought it the most terrifying creature I had ever seen.

This time, there was a new device. Clumsily balanced on a sawhorse, bolstered with a pile of bricks, I took it for a telescope – a big reflector, with the eyepiece at the side; but when I rushed across and peered into the lens, I saw no stars and planets – only blackness, void.

"Tsk – boy – "

He motioned me to sit. I stood before him, one foot treading on the other, while he filled his pipe; and then he talked to me, the way he always did, not as a child, but as a protégé, a student, someone in this fickle world whom he could trust.

He lit a match. I batted at the smoke, making it dance this way and that.

"And what," he asked, "do you suppose a *distillate* might be, eh?"

I shook my head. He talked some more about the stars, tracing their relative positions with a finger on the tabletop. He talked of brightness, spectral type, blue O-stars ("crotchety and proud"), cool M-stars ("slugabeds"), bright G-stars, yellow like the sun; he talked of supergiants, dwarfs and doubles, binaries bound up in turbulence by clouds of fiery gas ("No different in their way to Earthly marriage, I might postulate...").

21

"And if a star's alive – " smoke drifted from his lips " – is it alive like you and me? Or in a different way?"

"Like – no, different – no – "

"Does it have lungs, a brain, and kidneys? Does it have a spleen? Does it have – testicles?" He peered at me. I made a prune-face, trying not to laugh. "Which parts are living? All of it? Or only some of it?"

I shrugged. He spoke about the speed of light, the long, long journey of a single photon on its way to Earth. He quoted figures at me, strange names he said were Arabic, because the Arabs were the greatest of astronomers in history...

"And by the time the light comes down to us, it's so diffuse, it's almost nothing, hm? It's spread too thin. The thing you'd have to do – assuming that you wanted to – is *concentrate* it, yes?"

"..."

"Distil it, like a fine liqueur. That's what. Refine the... sheer *quintessence* of it. There's a word for you. Remember that."

He tapped his pipe, peered in the bowl, then put it in the pocket of his cardigan. He gestured me towards the telescope again.

The eyepiece made a cold ring on my skin. Behind me, Uncle switched the room lights off. I stared, but even so, I couldn't see.

"Go on, go on," he grunted. "Pay attention – and look harder!"

So I tried again. And realised, suddenly: this was no ordinary telescope, designed to look out at the stars; instead, through some extraordinary web of lenses, prisms and what-have-you, it was meant to *draw the stars' light down to Earth*, to hold it and condense it, drop by drop. I stared into the blackness. It seemed as if I balanced on the lip of some great abyss then, till I could hardly tell if I was looking up or down, or else, indeed, if I'd already fallen and was tumbling through that empty, unlit void...

Till presently, I saw a light.

I thought my eyes were playing tricks on me at first. Only it came again, and stronger: silver, twinkling, slowly gaining magnitude. It seemed to swim out of the dark, and yet it wasn't constant, like a lamplight; there were moments when it winked out, flickered and dispersed, then slowly gathered itself up again. For moments it seemed shapeless, like a little phosphorescent worm or fish. But then, as it came closer, I began to make out limbs, a torso, and, at last – a head.

22

"But it's a man!" I cried.

"Not quite, my boy..."

Nevertheless, this was enough for me: here, in this tube, my Uncle had distilled a living being, a homunculus, an imp of starlight. I watched it, rolling in its inky medium. It pulled its legs in, hunched its shoulders, furled itself into a small, fluorescent ball; then stretched, impatiently, its body twisting like elastic, thinner and thinner...

"Middle star, Orion's belt. Pretty fellow, eh? Taken a good few months to grow 'im that big. Don't know what I'll do if he gets bigger..."

"Is it alive?"

"Alive? Well, if you like. Bit of a question, really. Is it alive? Are we?"

He put the main light back on. I blinked. He covered up the eyepiece with a little metal cap. "In case," he said. Then he was taking out his pipe, re-lighting it, and off onto another tack: the properties of magnets and their beneficial influence on human health. "Sadly neglected in the modern world," he said.

*

Over the next few days the temperature went up. The snow turned into slush, and then to endless, dirty rivers running down the roadsides. Shod in wellingtons, I dragged my bike out from the pantry and sailed off, imagining myself some bold adventurer, set for a wild new land... The world itself had lost all its familiar summer shapes, grown stranger, less hospitable; the trees upon the river bank were stark and bare, the waters where I'd fished for minnows, scarcely months before, become a rushing, broad grey torrent. I lingered on the hump-backed bridge, watching the river surge beneath. A chill wind cut the air. Huge, glassy lakes spread in the fields, suggesting some weird, post-disaster world...

I cycled on. There was a cottage, so low down it seemed half sunk into the mud. A woman called me. She knew my name, the way that people do in small towns. She gave me milk and soggy biscuits.

"You'll be staying with young Katherine Bledsoe, then," she said, though it was odd to hear my Aunt described as 'young'.

"And Uncle Edward," I put in.

"Ah, well..." She gave a slight, unhappy shrug. "Young Katherine's quite a decent sort, mind you."

I had the good sense not to mention my less creditable relative again.

*

I thought that it was thunder woke me, trailing from the waking world into my dreams; but then I must have dozed once more, because the next I knew, someone was shaking me, and fiercely whispering my name. I smelt my Uncle's strong tobacco, and the faint, mushroomy odour of his cardigan.

"Don't talk, don't talk. Can you dress in the dark? Your warmest clothes!"

I hardly needed prompting about warm clothes. Mine were folded neatly on the chair, as Mum always insisted. Quickly, I pulled them on, and then together, blind as bats, we crept downstairs. I knew about the fourth stair, with its tricky, high-pitched squeak, and the sixth stair, which creaked even louder; I stepped over them. But Uncle, clumsy in the way that adults are, blundered sublimely onto both.

There was a single, frozen moment. Then my Aunt's voice cawed: "Ed-*waaard*!"

He stopped, cleared his throat, then in a pallid imitation of his normal voice, stammered: "One m-minute, dear. Just going for a drink of water..."

To me, he breathed, "We'll need your bike. Be quick!"

I felt my way along the hall, into the pantry. Aunt Kate was quizzing him. I heard my name. I lugged the bike into the hall. My Uncle shoved the front door open and a shock of ice-cold air caught at my face. My Aunt's voice echoed in a ghostly wail: "You *can*not take the boy outside at this hour – "

Then we were racing down the front drive, both of us. I leapt onto my bike. My Uncle wrenched the gate open, we plunged through; and yet something had gone wrong, somehow. All round us, there was deep, pitch darkness, an opacity of night...

The streetlights had gone out.

My Uncle hesitated, peering right and left. He sniffed the air, and then he pointed. "This way," he cried – in tones that I could never disobey.

"What's happening? What's up?"

I was too thrilled to think straight; nonetheless, in some dim corner of my mind, there nagged the thought of Auntie Kate's displeasure, and I hoped that, when the time came, he'd produce a good enough excuse to get us off the hook.

My Uncle cut a wild, outlandish figure, out there in the dark. He seemed to wear a cloak like a magician, though I realised soon enough it was his heavy woollen dressing gown, thrown on over a cardigan and baggy pants. He still had slippers on his feet – not very practical for such a damp, cold night. They flip-flopped as he walked. Sometimes he slithered on the icy ground, and leaned on me for safety. But he'd no time to go home and change. He made that very clear.

"Go, boy, go! And tell me what you see!"

He thumped my shoulder.

"Wha – ?"

"Go *on*!"

I was his scout. I rushed ahead, down to the corner and then back again.

"Yes? Yes?" he wheezed.

"Nothing," I told him. "No-one there. Lights out – "

"We're on its trail then! Come along!"

Gasping for breath, he told his story. There'd been an accident, he said, a dreadful accident (although he never told me how it happened); the condensing tube had toppled from its moorings, crashed down on the floor, and cracked from end to end. Such shoddy workmanship! Such poor materials! (And surely not my Uncle's fault, when all was said and done?) Suddenly freed, the imp had jumped up, like a genie from a bottle, and Uncle grabbed for it. It slithered from his grasp; it squeezed between his fingers just like soap, and ran off dancing round the room. He swatted at it, knocking books and bottles flying, but the creature merely skipped away. It even seemed to laugh – to put its gleaming hands upon its hips and rock with mirth. Then suddenly it flew into the air, fastened to the light bulb and embraced it like a baby at its mother's breast. The workshop vanished into darkness. Uncle stumbled, barked his shins. Only the imp shone, brilliant as ever, though it cast no light; rather, said my Uncle, it *enclosed* the light, hogging it greedily. And then, before he'd had the chance to recollect

25

himself, it tumbled from its perch, bounced off the floor and struck the window, where – instead of stopping – it merely strained a moment, then pushed its way straight through the glass, without leaving a scratch.

My Uncle, trying to recall his wits, began to fiddle with the light switch, frantically; but every particle of light had vanished from the house. He had to wait until the moonlight poured in and refilled it, like a murky pool, before he managed to negotiate the steps and find his way down to my room.

"I do believe," he said, "I do believe it's *feeding* on the light!"

We raced round town like mad things for the next few hours. Often, he'd send me skittering up side-roads, cycling off on crazy errands, trying to anticipate the creature's path. I saw no sign of it. The sky was luminous with stars, a million tiny points, spilling their living rays upon the Earth; while all around, the world was black and cold, the merest cinder, floating in a void...

My temples ached. My legs were tired. The air seemed to pulsate around my head, throbbing to a rhythm like a beaten drum, *boom, boom, boom...*

At last, completely out of breath, I stopped beside the market square. I wished that I was back in bed. Our great adventure had begun to pall on me, I must admit...

And then I saw something.

A faint, uncertain glimmering, up near the Post Office... The lights of High Street made a string of baubles stretching up the hill; baubles, which, even as I watched them, flickered, dimmed, and then – like toppling dominos – went out.

I spun the bike around and pedalled back to Uncle, fast as I could go. I found him leaning on a bollard at the top of Richmond Street, apparently exhausted. He stared up at the sky, muttering, as if in pain: "Oh, Betelgeuse, oh Albemuth... Antares, star of Scorpio..."

"Uncle – "

His voice had a peculiar, sing-song lilt, as if in incantation, and his eyes were almost shut.

"Castor, all broken parts, you great *ménage*..."

"Uncle. I saw the lights go out!"

"Rigel and... Hm?"

26

"The lights," I gasped, waving my arms.

His plan was simple, outlined in a moment: I would cycle round, using the side streets, come up behind the creature, frighten it, and drive it straight into his grasp. While he – well, what would he do, then? I asked.

"Oh. Ah." He shrugged, lifting his hands. "I'll think of something, I suppose..."

He didn't sound particularly self-assured.

*

I cycled off. One of my pants legs had been soaked from riding through a puddle; my naked fingers now felt frozen to the handlebars. My wheels began to slide and slither under me.

And for the first time, then, I felt afraid.

The air was soundless. Nothing moved. Blind windows stared at me; the houses here were dark and empty-seeming, and I couldn't match them with the jolly day-time buildings that I knew stood in their place.

I came out on the High Street just as planned, swung round and headed for the Post Office. I might have been the last person on Earth. I looked for Uncle, but he wasn't there. The moon had gone, thick shadows clung to everything... Then suddenly – a blinding light.

Man-shaped, and moving.

Moving *towards me*!

Yet the perspectives were all wrong. The creature seemed much closer than it should have been, so close it almost filled my vision. Or else –

My eyes adjusted, like a rapid shift of gears while cycling.

This was no tiny sprite, no harmless little imp such as I'd seen back in the workroom. Now it towered over me; its head was on a level with the first floor windows, and it seemed to waft and ripple, like a flame; strange traceries, as intricate as veins, ran up and down its body in a rush of fire. Its form would oscillate and flicker till my eyes began to ache. I blinked, I shook my head... Where was Uncle Edward? The old familiar street had been transformed into a roaring channel, a great mouth that seemed to suck me in, compelling me towards that remnant of a star, that freak of life engendered in my Uncle's attic rooms.

And I remembered his instructions, but I think I only followed them through sheer paralysis of will. I gripped the handlebars, steadied myself – then pedalled full tilt for the thing, ringing my bell like Billy-O and shouting at the full stretch of my lungs!

I expected – even then – expected it to flee.

Instead – *it came straight at me*!

The next moments were a jumble. I felt as if a whirlwind caught me up. A long, thin arm of light reached out; it seemed to stretch and stretch. A bluish glow swept through the world; then everything was upside down, the rooftops swirled, I saw the telegraph wires, the flash of a reflection in an upstairs room – I landed, *thwack* –

My first thought was for my bike. Had it been damaged? Was it safe?

I picked myself up, awkwardly. The bike lay on its side, six feet away. Across the street, I saw my Uncle, crouching on the ground, wrestling with a dense, dark mass. His body pressed on it, he seemed to wrap himself around it, grunting with the strain.

Then, struggling still, he gathered up the whole thing in his arms and hugged it to his chest.

He grinned at me.

I realised what he'd done – he'd caught the creature in his dressing gown. The heavy, dark material was practically impermeable to light. It was a wonderful, *ad hoc* solution, and it made him look so proud, I thought his cheeks would burst from smiling.

I was wet and dirty and my knee was grazed; but the bike was quite undamaged, and so I grinned, too. We headed home in a delightful haze of self-congratulation. My Uncle clutched the bundle tight. Sometimes it seemed to heave and jump against his chest, so that he gasped a little with the effort and clung tighter.

"Is it heavy?" I enquired.

"Oh no." He sputtered, like a schoolboy giggling in a class. "Oh no, no. I'd say – it's very *light*..."

We both laughed, helplessly. He told me of his epic struggles: "It was after you – it didn't see me hiding in the doorway – and I leapt out, *yah*! Spun my dressing gown up high, a trick I learnt out in Malaysia, hunting flying foxes there – and then – "

But he was over-confident. Or maybe he'd forgotten how the footpaths were, that chill, damp night. One minute, he was right beside me; next, he'd gone. I looked around and saw him, flat on his back, arms waving helplessly; the gown unfolded great black wings and from its midst a silver dart shot high into the air, hung for a moment, then, spinning on its axis like a corkscrew, whisked itself into the sky.

I stood, my head back, watching it grow smaller, smaller, dwindling till I couldn't find it anywhere among the great star fields that arched over our heads.

*

We were both punished, Edward and myself.

I was confined to bed, next day. Aunt Kate was sure I'd catch a chill. She railed about the terrible condition of my clothes; she threatened to inform my mother, a threat which, luckily, she never carried out.

As for my Uncle: there are subtle punishments in marriage. Then, they were unknown to me; today, all too familiar. Relations at the dinner table cooled to freezing point. He tried to please her, poured her tea, inquired after her every whim; she made it clear, however, she had little time for him. He disappeared into the potting shed for long hours with his pipe. He couldn't face his lab, he said; his best experiment was ruined. To have achieved so much, then lost it all... It was more than any man should have to bear.

A mood of deep dejection settled on him for the remnant of my stay. While Auntie Kate, in time, forgave us both, nothing could shift the gloom from Edward's soul. One day, not long before I left, I found him sitting on the front step with his pipe in hand, surveying the considerable view, down into town and off towards the distant hills... It was a bright day, almost spring-like, and the sky was dusted by a feather-weight of cloud, sketching its patterns on the blue. But Uncle Edward only stared with sick and joyless incapacity. His shoulders slumped. His free hand hung between his thighs like loose, dead meat.

He looked out at the world, and then I heard him speak, more to himself than me.

"Star-shit," he said distinctly. "Nothing else. That's all we are. Just star-shit..."

I was amazed; embarrassed; yet delighted, too! I'd never heard a grown-up swear before, excepting barrow boys and other common

29

sorts my family had little business with. I had assumed it was a childhood vice, confined to school, with its great wealth of secret languages and codes. I was astonished at my Uncle's clear familiarity with our vocabulary – though, to be sure, he'd used it in his own, uniquely Edward-ish capacity.

At that point, I confess, my admiration for him knew no bounds.

Head Crimes

She says, "He's trying to poison me," her voice so tiny now it's like a little girl's.

I tell her, "Mum, that's daft, Mum," but she sighs, and shakes her head, and looks up at the ceiling; we can hear him sometimes, working in the room above, or going to the bathroom where he keeps the paint.

"It's true," she says. "He's putting something in the milk. He thinks I haven't seen him, but I have."

"People don't *do* that, Mum!"

"You're young. You wouldn't know." She shows me how she keeps a 'secret' bottle down behind the sofa, where he can't get hold of it. "I go out to the shops each morning early," she confides, though anyone can see it isn't fresh; the bottle's got a thick, white rind around the top, and there's an odour to it, mingling with the smell of paint. "One more expense," she says. "But what else can I do? I've seen these people on the news. They find someone... a woman on her own, like me... It's a compulsion with them. They can't help themselves."

"You've seen it on *Columbo*, not the news," I say.

She split up with her boyfriend, Colin, three weeks back. I ask her if she wants to talk about it, but she waves her hand dismissively. I tell her she's just overwrought, she's let things get on top of her, I say, and witter on about 'projection' and 'transferred anxiety', though

31

normally I hate that kind of pop psychology – it always looks so great in books, and sounds so stupid when you say it.

Not that she's listening, anyway. She stares down at her hands and fidgets and won't look at me. Her parting's like a chalk stripe in her hair.

It's later – much, much later – she tells me, quietly, "I only loved one man in all my life, and now he's gone."

I think she means my Dad, only I can't be sure.

*

The days close early, this time of the year. By four, we're sitting in the dark, and neither of us makes a move to put the light on.

There's a *tap-tap* at the door.

She shoots a glance at me. I start to rise – I want to see this lunatic, this would-be murderer – but she's too quick. Already she's up and out the room ahead of me, shutting me in. I listen to their voices in the hall. His speech is soft, inflected – Irish, possibly, or Scots. I pray she won't start shouting or accusing him, and yet I hear her laugh, her friendly, cooee-style goodbye. The front door shuts. That's one more trouble gone, I think, another problem over with. I rush up to the window, glimpse him for a second or two, climbing into his van. He's younger than I'd thought, dark, curly-haired... But not a monster, not a thug. The engine starts. He drives away.

My mother comes back, smiling now.

"Well then," she says. "I'll put the dinner on in half a tick."

"I can't stay, Mum. I've got a lot to do."

"I won't eat on my own. It isn't worth the fuss. But if you're staying, I'll make us something nice."

I tell her, "Mum," I say, "I can't believe a word of this. Not any of it."

She hasn't heard. That's how she acts.

"Your favourite," she tells me. "Stir-fry. Just the way you like it, hm?"

*

It's nearly eight when I get home. I stopped for cigs, then bought a half bottle of gin on impulse, just to keep them company. I'm good, most weeks, I ration out the bad habits, just one at once... Then other times, they gang up.

32

And that's tonight. The scent of booze, the stink of fags, the aftertaste of mother's stir-fry, mixing round inside, like memories you can't shake off.

Two years ago it was the postman, spying on her through the letterbox. Before that, gangs of kids, chanting her name outside the house, or following her to the shops and back. Though maybe that was true. And there were other things. We watched a programme on the sex killer, Fred West. She made me sit through it, right to the end. Let's switch it off, I said. What's on the other side? You don't want to see this, do you? Is there a film on? Yes? "I met him," she said, very quietly. "I met him," she said, louder now. "He asked me to his house."

I didn't answer her. It chilled me though, it chilled me to the bone.

The doc says it's a coping mechanism. Better she externalise her fears like this rather than blame herself. It's healthier, he said, more positive; a sign she's getting well. But I said, blame herself for *what*?

Tonight I drink. I smoke. Then when I'm ready, I call Dad.

He lives in Southport now. The line's so bad, it's more like calling East Berlin. I ask him how he is. He wants to talk about the club he goes to Friday nights, some scandal over money; I interrupt, and tell him about Mum.

"She's lonely. Can't you just pop over some time? Just for a while? At least give her a ring?"

"She's lonely. Always she is lonely. We are apart since ten years now. Why do you ask me?"

"Eight years. It's eight years, Dad."

He says something in German, and I take a breath.

"I think she's ill," I say. "You know? She's hired this bloke to decorate the house, only she's scared of him. She's saying weird things..."

"She has hired a decorator? How has she hired a decorator?"

"I don't know. I think she saw an ad somewhere. But, Dad – "

"She tells me she is penniless. And now she has a decorator!"

"This man – " I say.

"Listen. Your mother, all her life, she wants things that she cannot have. There is no money – oh, so what, she says. We have it anyway. You do not know this, but it's one big reason we broke up. One big reason. If she is ill, she needs a doctor, not a decorator. That is what."

33

I plead with him. He mutters and complains, but in the end, I know he'll do it.

"Alright," he says. "Tomorrow, then. I phone."

"Thanks, Dad."

There's a small sound like a belch from the receiver. It's a habit he's acquired of late, a way of rounding off his conversations. I don't think that he even knows he's doing it.

*

There must have been a moment when it dawned on me my parents' marriage had been neither made in Heaven nor ordained by God. That there was no predestined plan. What it resembled, rather, was some rogue atomic particle, produced under conditions so anomalous, so rare, that its decay was almost guaranteed, right from the start.

My father came from Bremen, Germany. Well, more or less. In 40 years, he's never lost his accent, never learned to pass as local. I suppose he tried. He must have done. He couldn't pick it up. When I was young, I dreaded speech days, open days, school fetes – anything that brought him into contact with my friends. He felt at ease with kids. He liked them, reckoned they liked him, as well, when actually they giggled and made *sieg heil* signs behind his back.

He'd never had a childhood of his own. He'd lost it to the war, to Hitler, or the allied occupation – blame who you want. He wouldn't talk about it. Anything I knew, I'd got from Mum, or from the history books. By proxy, anyway.

You wonder how you live with somebody so long and still not know them, still not know their past. But you don't question it. When he was there, that's all there was – the now, the present tense, the day to day minutiae of our lives. Dad saying, *lay the table. Do the washing up. You want an ice cream*? The rest, we didn't ask about. Though once or twice he'd bring his box down from the attic, rummage through his souvenirs, inspecting this or that: old sepia postcards (castles, rivers, laughing girls), a cartridge case, an empty pack of Lucky Strikes, the contents traded long ago for God knows what; and at the bottom, two things to mark him for the hero that as kids we knew he had to be: a dented mess tin, and a Luger pistol, wrapped in oilcloth, so heavy I could hardly lift it,

34

much less point the thing. "Will it shoot?" He shrugged, or shook his head, a vague kind of a gesture, then he took them all away.

They were objects. Like things in a museum. Nothing linked them, nothing personal, no reminiscences, no stories, nothing much at all.

I knew he'd fought. A soldier on the Russian front, a boy. I thought I knew. His relatives were all in Eastern Europe somewhere. Everything about him pointed East. The town of Bremen hardly figured, from what I could see. A handy place to leave, maybe. A good place to be from.

"He got in trouble," Mum said once. That was her first hint, sketchy, tentative, perhaps not even formed inside her own head yet. "He couldn't stay."

Trouble? I said. I was twenty-five, my father's past as blank as ever, except that now, like all forbidden things, it fascinated me. I felt I'd got a right to know.

"It wasn't easy," she said then. "Even for normal people... Sometimes, well, they had to do things... you know. They didn't want to do. To get enough to eat."

Black market, then? I asked her. Theft? What? Politics? What then?

"No, no. I don't think so. He doesn't say. Don't ask him, please. Don't say we talked."

My father's life is mine as well, in part, and from the moment I could talk I could say *bitte, danke, Liebchen* (his pet name for me); at home, we spoke an odd, half-German patois, a private language unlike that of any other family I knew. My mother's name was 'Mutti', father was 'Papa'. I made efforts later, changed them consciously to 'Mum' and 'Dad'. I wanted to belong, to join the wider world.

Dad wasn't garrulous. My Mum, he said, could "talk the left leg off a donkey," but he'd much rather sit back, watch TV, or read the paper, black-rimmed glasses on his nose.

I think now that his accent proved as awkward and embarrassing for him as, in different ways, it did for me. And where in later years he could communicate with ease – his odd pronunciation and eccentric turns of phrase endearing, quirky more than weird –

back when he first arrived, he was a foreigner, a German; and that meant the Enemy.

He'd come here as a rep for some new Deutschland enterprise. Munitions works converted to make razor blades. Or something like that. I try to picture him, lost in a strange and often hostile country, roaming door to door with cases full of samples, smiling at the retailers, at children, anyone at all, trying to win their confidence. He'd tell them he was Polish, sometimes, says my Mum. It made things easier that way.

His loneliness must have been terrible.

"He was such a poor boy then," she says. "He didn't know a soul. Not one. And he was thin... You could have put your fingers round his arm. Like that, see? Dreadful, dreadful..."

My English grandmother began to cook him meals. My mother's dad was dead. She was sixteen, several years his junior. They ate together every night, unless his work took him away. He shared her meals, and then he started bringing presents: nylons, chocolate, bananas... It's common knowledge where that leads.

Only after the divorce she told me, as if picking up some old, forgotten conversation: "Those camps. Those awful camps. They put them all in Poland, you know, not in Germany. The Germans wouldn't have them near."

"Concentration camps...?"

"That's where he was. That's what he did. During the war. Guarding them. That's what..." Her voice trailed off.

"Come on," I said. "He was a soldier. You said that. You've always told me that. Since I was small."

"And now you're grown up, and you can hear the truth."

"Come on," I said again. My voice starting to shake.

"He couldn't fight. He was too young to fight. Of course he was. He couldn't be a soldier. So they gave him other things to do. Old men, boys... They gave them guns. They made them guards."

"But – "

I put it down to bitterness. She wanted life to match the way she felt, to justify her misery. She wanted something we could all be truly angry and upset about.

Except she wasn't crazy then. She wasn't mad. Just sane enough to make me wonder, anyway, and make sure neither of us mentioned it again.

*

I was five years old before it struck me I had a German name. I hadn't realised Diedz was any different from Smith, or Green, or Jones. It even had an English sound. But written down... Well, it confused people. My teachers couldn't get it right. Then I was Mary Gundel *Dids*, or *Deds*, and even, sometimes, *Mary Gundel Dies*. The class was full of Greggs and Hills and Greenhalghs. Not even a Patel or Sulliman to even up the score. The knowledge I was foreign came on slowly, bit by bit, like finding out you've some appalling, terminal disease, just when you've never felt more fit and healthy in your life.

You think you know what racism's about? Try growing up in England in the 60s with a German dad. The War still fresh in everybody's mind, but turned into a kind of music hall act now, proclaiming the supremacy of all things English... Victor's spoils. TV looked like a crime against humanity, some nights, only we never noticed it. And cinema was worse: *The Great Escape, The Dam Busters, The Cruel Sea...* In my brother's comic, each week mighty Captain Hurricane would foil another evil Jerry scheme, and weedy Nazis fled into the distance, yelling *"Himmel!" "Donner und Blitzen!"*, springs and stars and shivers of confusion radiating round their heads.

At first it all seemed simple, clear, face value stuff. The good people were good, the bad people were bad. The bad people just happened to be Germans.

It didn't seem to bother Dad, but I was lost. It felt like cheering two opposing hockey teams, you couldn't do it. And we never saw my father's family. I wondered now if they were blond-haired sadists wearing leather coats, or bullet-headed thugs.

My father didn't match these people. He was mild, and easily discomfited. He never hit us, didn't shout, though he'd a way of looking that could make us cringe. He got upset on days his newspaper was late. Or if it rained while he was waiting for the bus. I couldn't see him part of anybody's war machine, ever. Not my Dad.

And yet he'd fought. Even today, that's something that he's never spoken of, not once. And if he didn't fight, the nagging feeling, maybe

37

he did something worse, and that's why he's kept quiet all these years. Mum's fantasies might not be fantasies at all. Not all of them, at any rate.

When I was young, I had two friends from down the street, two boys. They played at soldiers. Bam bam bam! Kill the Jerries, kill the Krauts! I told them, "*Kraut* means cabbage. *Kraut* is not a person, it's a green. A *Kraut* is something that you eat." They argued with me, but I wouldn't own up I was wrong, so they just stood there, aimed their fists, and shot me dead.

*

I read about the Russian front once. 1943. The soldiers got so hungry that they chewed the leather from their boots to keep from starving. And I kept on thinking about that, all the time that I was eating salad nicoise, sole bonne femme or nasi goring: *they chewed the leather from their boots*. The kind of detail journalists just drop in casually, no explanations, worst of all, no names. Who? I wanted to ask. Who? Which soldiers? Which? Any named Diedz?

*

The first time Mum was ill she locked herself inside the house and wouldn't come out for a month. She piled the furniture against the doors. She drew the curtains and put barricades against the windows, making an island for herself, bare floor surrounded by a wall. The neighbours thought she'd gone away. She ate up all the food out of the freezer. Then she starved. I was in London, then, and it was over when I heard. Dad phoned. He said she was in hospital. I thought he meant she'd got a virus or a broken leg. It's not just English people who go in for euphemisms.

"It's alright," he reassured me. "Nervous trouble, that is all... A little rest for her."

He'd already moved out by then. He lived with Kate, the woman from the coach hire firm. I hated her for years. I hated him, almost. You don't forgive people for trying to live their own lives first. Especially not your Mum or Dad.

We think our families belong to us. We think they're ours by rights, like property. Maybe that's part of growing up: learning they're not.

*

The phone rings in the middle of the night. It's Mum. She says she couldn't sleep for worrying about me. Am I alright? Have I been eating well? I tell her what I had for lunch and dinner. She's silent for a long time, then, as if considering.

"I don't like you living on your own," she says. "You hear so many stories, these days... Young girls... Well, I just don't like to say. But you know what I mean."

"Mum. I've lived alone for fifteen years. I think I've learned the ropes by now."

"And not just girls," she's saying. "Women, too – women my age. No wonder I get worried... Perhaps you've got a boyfriend to look after you?" There's a little optimism in her tone. "Somebody nice?"

"I think I've gone off men. Till further notice, anyway."

Another pause, and I imagine I can hear her frowning, hear the muscles shifting and contracting in her brow.

"You're young still," she advises me. "You won't be young for long. You don't get second chances out of life. And it gets harder later. Everything gets harder."

"I'll be fine."

She doesn't speak then. I say, "Look, Mum. It's 1.15. I'm in bed. What did you want?"

"I want to talk to you." She sounds surprised. "We haven't had a talk for ages."

It's like when children try to lie and don't know how.

"We'll talk tomorrow," I suggest. "I'll call you from the office – right?"

She doesn't answer. So I prompt, "Tomorrow, then?"

More silence. Then, "I don't know where I'll be tomorrow. I don't know – " She clicks her tongue. "Perhaps I won't be here..."

I know that this is meant to sound in some way sinister, only I won't give in. Still sounding cheerful, I say, "Right, OK, I'll call you in the evening then."

"No – no. You see, *he'll* be here. That's the thing. *He's* coming round."

"Who's coming round?"

"You know." She won't pronounce his name.

"Your decorator? Mum, you're not still bothered about that, are you?"

I tell her, "If you can't get on with him, for God sake, fire him. Pay him off, get someone else."

She sighs, letting me know that this is somehow not a possibility.

"You don't have to be rude to him," I say. "Invent a reason – tell him that you've changed your mind, you only want the upstairs doing now. Tell him anything."

"He looks at me. He looks at me peculiarly. He's got these little squinty eyes..." She pauses, gathering herself for something. Then she says, "Can't you come round? If you were here, I'd feel alright. It wouldn't worry me..."

"Mum," I say. I don't know which of us is parent, which is child. "I've got to go to work tomorrow. It's important! Can't you go and see Aunt Joan or somebody? I can't go taking days off, just like that."

"You don't know what he's like," she says. "I'm so afraid..."

Her voice is dwindling on the far end of the phone. It sounds like water going down the sink, fading away.

Next day I visit her.

*

He's in the kitchen, drinking tea, slouched with his backside on the counter-top. I've never seen him close before, just glimpsed him, that one time. He's 25 or so, hair curly, grey with plaster dust. He's got a streak of white paint just above one eye. His clothes are paint-stained, too. He wears a darkish T-shirt and a pair of Levi's, patched at knee and crotch. He lifts his mug to toast me, and he smiles.

"You must be Mary."

I like the way he loafs there, his body has a nice, relaxed sort of a curve to it. His arms are muscley. But he'll have to watch the beer; already, there's a slight bulge in his T-shirt, hinting at a belly just a few years off. Not too bad, yet, though.

He's alright, I think.

We chat for several minutes. And there's nothing wrong with him. No psychopathic tendencies, no squinty eyes, nothing you'd ever think was sinister at all. He turns away from me to light a cigarette and then I run my gaze over him, thinking, here's this evening's fantasy, at any rate.

My mother talks to me all afternoon. She acts so cheerful that I'm almost angry now. She tells me all the gossip, talks about the neighbours that I've never met, and girls she says I was at school with, though I don't remember any of them. One's in the police. Another's at the bank. A third's got children, one with spinabifida, they don't think it'll live.

"Why did you ask me here?" I say.

She glances round, suddenly irritable, and flaps her hand for quiet. "Not now," she says.

"I think I need an explanation. I phoned work and told them I was sick. I lied. But you don't need me here. You haven't any problems..."

"Later," she insists, severely. And she's still my mother, after all, so I shut up and eat my biscuits like a good girl, and I watch her as she reaches down behind the sofa cushion and brings out the gun. And smiles: the sweetest, loveliest, most motherly of smiles.

The thing's too heavy in her old, arthritic hands. She cradles it, the way you would a kitten or a tiny child. My father's gun. It looks much smaller now, after so many years, although I know it's got to be the same. I'd just assumed he took it with him when he left. But maybe she took it, instead. "You see? I'm quite safe now."

I smile and nod like I'm agreeing, and I wonder how to take it from her, gently, so she won't get too upset; and wonder if it's loaded, and how stupid it'll be to end up getting shot by my own Mum.

"Think you should put it down now, eh, Mum? Eh?"

And I remember something else I read, another piece of cod-psychology. How none of us really grows up, how we just play the same old games all our lives, from childhood on: cops and robbers, Brits and Jerries, mums and dads... How underneath, we're all just ten years old.

But I think, ten. That's pushing it. I'd give us eight, or seven. Six, maybe. Or less.

The Life to Come

Don't talk about the future. Don't even think of it. The more you think, the stronger it becomes, the more it pushes back towards us, gifts us with its rubble and detritus... It's not even *our* future in any case. We all made sure of that. Or thought we did. We thought we did...

*

The phone rang, one a.m. Hannah's voice.

"...this alien," she said.

She didn't really sound upset at first, more like the times she'd called me when her washer'd sprung a leak or she'd had trouble with her boss, something like that; controlled, and calm, and rational.

At first.

"It isn't moving much," she said. "Just sort of sitting there, just looking, you know? And it won't let me go near. I don't know what to do..."

"You tell it to get out."

"It isn't like that, John. I don't know what might happen. It's... it's, well, it's sort of scary. You know?"

"Look," I said. "You get a big stick and you poke it till it goes, alright? Simple."

"It's not like that..."

I heard her sighing on the far end of the phone. She said, "I'd

43

really very much appreciate it if you came round. Please John."

She always used my name at times like this – times when she wanted something and I didn't want to give. Like an official, undeniable request.

"I'm going to bed. I've had a few beers, too. I don't know if I'm safe to drive."

"Please John. Get a taxi. I'll pay."

"What's it doing now?"

"I don't know. I can't see. I'm not at home. I'm in the phone box on the corner. I was worried... It was acting funny – you know?"

I told her I'd come by tomorrow, first thing. It wasn't what she wanted though. I tried to say, look, just forget it, call the cops, call someone else, call anyone. But I felt guilty. There were things between us, and I owed her favours; and it looked like this was when she called them in.

"Alright," I said. "I'll come."

She didn't comment on my tone of voice. She just had time to start to thank me, then her money ran out and the line went dead.

*

My clothes were in the laundry basket but I pulled them out and put them on. I wasn't bothered how I looked or smelled. I thought I'd risk the car. If I could sort it in an hour or so, or less, with luck. If I could get back home to bed...

She was waiting in the street for me. As soon as I got near, she ran into the road and flagged me down, as if she thought I'd have forgotten where she lived. She wore a baggy jumper and red jeans. Her hair had been pinned up but it was starting to come loose, stray locks hanging unevenly on one side of her face.

"Thank God," she said.

"I don't see why you couldn't have got someone else." I was grumpy now; all through the journey, I'd been brooding. "What about the neighbours?"

"They're away. Except for Rob, and he's asleep..."

"It didn't dawn on you that I might be asleep as well?"

"Oh, John," she said. "Don't be like that."

I wouldn't look at her. I just said, "Let's get it over with," and headed up the drive.

44

Her flat was on the ground floor: two rooms, kitchen, bathroom. I waited while she fiddled with the lock, tapping my foot. She got the door open. We went inside –

And I could *smell* the thing. It was an ugly smell, bringing to mind old grease-caked frying pans and something harsh, electric, like the smell of dodgems at the funfair, part organic, part...

She asked me, "Are you going in?"

I turned the door handle, and slowly, slowly, peered into the front room.

It was there, alright.

Big as a small man or a ten-year-old child, perhaps. I'd never seen the like of it, not even heard of such a thing. It squatted on the writing desk, its knees up to its chin and elbows jutting ominously. What might have been its head swivelled around and looked at me.

I felt the heat off Hannah's body, pressing on me from behind.

"Well?" she whispered. She was hoarse, and I could see why.

"Well," I said.

The room wasn't disturbed – not much. Some books were scattered on the floor, the TV had been shifted round at a peculiar angle, but the place hadn't been wrecked, not like you heard about sometimes.

I slipped out, pushing Hannah back behind me, and I gently shut the inner door.

She waited while I lit a cigarette. I needed one. I went into the hall and took a few drags. Then I looked round for a weapon. The best thing I could manage was the pump on Hannah's bike.

I took it off. She looked at me.

"It hasn't got a flat tyre. That's not why it's here."

"Hold this." I handed her the cigarette.

I went back in the lounge. We stared at one another then, the thing and me. It had a black, insectile carapace, and in between the joints and sutures there were moist, sticky membranes, glistening in the light of Hannah's standard lamp. I told myself it didn't look that tough. I reckoned you could crack that armour pretty easily, given a hammer, or a pickaxe, or a gun.

I held the bicycle pump up, as threateningly as I could.

And stepped into the room.

45

I crept around the corner of the sofa, till there was nothing between me and it except a few scant feet of carpet, and we stood there, looking at each other.

And the creature moved.

It shuffled slightly, started to emit a rapid clicking noise from some part of its body. Very gingerly, I took another step. The clicking became faster, higher pitched. It sounded like a Geiger counter going mad; a swarm of angry, gravel-voiced bees.

Then the thing reared up. Black flanges opened in its casing. A kind of ruff appeared around its neck.

I backed off, faster than was really dignified.

She told me, "That's what it was doing earlier. That's when I went and called you."

The creature put its head on one side. Slowly, the noise dropped down, and died.

"It's probably just a defence display," I said. "It's probably as scared of us as we are of it."

But there'd been something specially unpleasant in it, something in the smell, and I kept thinking: venom, acid, claws, fangs – germs...

"Why don't you call the cops?" I said.

"I did. They said it wasn't urgent. They said they're busy. They said if it's still here tomorrow – "

"Bloody brilliant."

She gestured to the living room again. "John – " she begged.

I hefted up the bike pump. But no, I wasn't going back inside. I had a bad feeling, a very bad feeling, and I didn't care to test it out.

"We'll lock the door," I said. "It's not really doing much harm. We'll lock it in and sort things out tomorrow."

"I can't stay here. Not with that – "

"I'll take you back to mine. We'll phone someone tomorrow, someone who can deal with it, OK?"

I said to get her valuables. She came back with a toothbrush, credit cards, a stack of CDs: whale noises, jungle sounds, *Voices of the Tundra...* Jesus Christ, I thought.

"They help me to relax," she said.

"Alright, alright."

I put them in the car and we drove home.

*

There was activity out on the streets. Another breach, perhaps: police sirens, alarms ringing... An old Toyota shot a red light, barging straight in front of me. I slammed the brakes on, blared the horn in fury. I was nervous now, after my *tête-à-tête* with Hannah's beastie.

First thing I did when I got home was pour us both a good Bush Mills to calm us down. Then we had the usual embarrassment about the bed and who slept where, and I wound up with a blanket on the couch.

I don't think either of us got much sleep that night.

*

I'd heard the stories.

First it was the drugs the kids were using – weird new chemicals that suddenly appeared and swept across the culture like a wave, only to vanish without trace; then software of a kind we'd only dreamed about, a million miles from Microsoft...

A California UFO cult found fragments of an unknown metal at a site in the Mojave desert. Some of the pieces found their way into more reputable hands, and just for once they didn't disappear, or turn out to be shreds of some crashed truck or weather balloon. What they were exactly – even their composition – no-one seemed to know. Strange lights were now a regular occurrence in the sky. Watches and clocks behaved erratically, stopping dead or running backwards at a frantic pace. Physicists across the globe reported inexplicable anomalies in the activity of sub-atomic particles; a temporary shifting of the spectrum in a small town outside Amiens in France rendered the reds almost invisible, revealing curious new colours in the ultra-violet range. A giant silver bridge was seen, spanning the Bering Straits, dismissed by many as an Arctic mirage, though clearly visible from space. It did not, apparently, touch either shore...

Things hit nearer home as well.

One morning I'd come into work, opened the filing cabinet, and found –

It was a gauntlet. Five-fingered, silver, with a faint black streak, presumably a burn, across the knuckles. Inside, it had been padded with a soft, lilac material, like silk, but probably man-made. A metal

47

strip around the wrist made one half of a seal of some kind. This wasn't flimsy or high-fashion. This was tough and strong – a work glove, that was obvious.

I held it up, and asked if it belonged to anyone. When that failed, I asked what it was.

"An oven mitt?"

"Your fancy dress?"

"A special glove for hitching in the dark...?"

The jokes got feeble pretty quickly, though. We all knew what it was. It went with silver suits and fish-bowl helmets and the kind of people who said 'Take me to your leader,' when they turned up on your doorstep in the middle of the night. The sort of thing that only Dan Dare could look trendy in.

I was with Hannah still, back then. It was our 'trial marriage' phase, when we'd decided to attempt to live together, just to see how we got on. And if it worked, I'd quit my flat, move in with her, and... Well, it seemed a good idea. Just for a while.

It started out OK. We had a lot of fun, just playing house: buying some pictures for the front room, nipping down the deli for a little treat to swallow with the evening beer... And then, the growing tetchiness, the disappointment we both felt we'd a duty to conceal. And lots and lots and *lots* of television.

Nowadays, I wonder just how many marriages have been – well, 'saved' isn't the word – *perpetuated* by the all-embracing drone of that big box parked in the corner of the room?

Not ours, anyway.

We watched the news, the documentaries. We heard about the debris being found around the world. Because that's what it was. Not the Second Coming. Not an invasion. Rather... detritus. Fragments. Odds and ends.

A leak in the continuum. These little bits of rubbish from the future, dribbling back towards us, like the swill thrown off an ocean liner; all sorts of discards, broken things... Even the bridge that didn't reach the land. Almost the kind of things we'd read about since we were kids. Almost, only – not quite.

I couldn't follow all the explanation. I couldn't follow because Hannah said, loud in my ear, "That's daft. If that's the future, then it's going to be there anyway, like, in a few years. Isn't it? So we just wait and then – "

"*Listen*," I said.

She'd used that high, complaining tone, and even though she'd used it on the TV presenter, I still reacted like she'd used it against me.

"But if – " she started off again.

We had a row. Our second, or our third? It wasn't the decider, just another nail banged in the coffin of our married bliss, and three or four days later I packed up and went back home. I'd always had this notion of how great it ought to be, living with someone, having a partner, raising a family even... But Jesus Christ, how good it felt back in my own place! No-one to interfere, no-one to pester about washing up, or shopping, or forbidding me to pick my toe-nails (a habit which she claimed could make her physically sick to see).

All that was months ago.

And here I was, driving her back.

*

There was a crude half-barrier blocking the street – a couple of old oil drums filled with concrete and a plank across them. I drove round.

The house looked quiet. In fact, it looked exactly as it always had, except for a peculiar misting of the downstairs window. We both sat and watched it for a few moments. Then I turned the engine off.

She said, "I can't go in."

"You live here, don't you?"

She grasped my arm. "Go and have a look first, will you? Go and have a look."

I sighed. Her hand increased its pressure. So I shook my head, resigned myself, and got out of the car.

Even from the driveway I could tell that there was something wrong. At first I thought the window had been smashed – crazed, but not yet shattered, the way car windscreens break on impact; but as I drew near, I realised there was something sticking to it, something on the inner surface – some kind of thread-like substance, covering the lower surface of the panes.

I hesitated for a moment. I felt some of Hannah's trepidation. Then, reminded she was watching, I went on.

The glass was laced, smeared with something. I picked a clear spot, cautiously approached and peered inside. The view was pretty limited. I couldn't see the creature, anyway. But now the whole room was transformed. It looked like some sort of a nest, the inside of a big cocoon. Whatever Hannah might have hoped for her possessions, this wasn't good news. I could just make out her stereo, there on the top shelf, dribbled with what looked horribly like bird-lime, and the book shelves hung with ropes and globules of the stuff; a big, white mass where the sofa should have been. I moved up closer, put my eye against the glass and –

Splat!

I jerked back, lost my balance, tottered several steps, tripped and fell into the flowerbed. I wasn't hurt; but the peep-hole I'd been staring through was covered by an oozing gobbet of white goo.

So. Still in residence, it seemed. And sensitive on privacy, as well.

Somebody coughed. Not Hannah, though. A man. I turned round slowly. He was youngish, with limp, fair hair and one of those enormous, oily-coloured anoraks favoured by council workers who spend time outdoors. In one hand was a clipboard. In the other, his ID. I couldn't get my eyes to focus on it.

"Have to warn you, sir. Breach area. Entry forbidden. Your house, is it?"

"No," I said. "It's – " I nodded, just as Hannah came up.

She was fidgety. She clenched her fists, unclenched them; our official friend, biro in hand, kept asking her for details, who she was, how long she'd lived there, what she'd seen...

"Get more and more of these," he told us. "Live uns. Ugly buggers, too, a lot of 'em. 'Scuse language, miss. Advise you both, stay well away until it's sorted, that's what. We've got a team for it, like, but they're busy right now, see? Big breach, it was. Bloody big. Might be a few days yet. We had a case in – "

"Days!" she said. "But all my stuff's in there – my clothes – my books – my – "

I pulled a face. "I think it's set up home," I said.

"Oh, God – "

"I would advise," said the official, "that you find somewhere to stay the next few days. Perhaps your boyfriend here – "

"He is *not* my boyfriend!" she snapped. "And how can I stay

50

anywhere? I haven't any clothes, I haven't even got a bloody toothbrush, and I haven't – "

"There's a crisis helpline number I can – "

But her glance soon cut him short.

She looked up at the window. Tears filled her eyes. She put a fist up to her forehead. And then she said, "It's in the front room. Not the back. It's in the front room. So I can go and pick my other stuff up, anyway."

"I really don't advise – " He tapped the clipboard. "We got rulings, miss. Besides... could be dangerous, you know? Should be a warning sign by rights, to warn people, and – "

"Yes," she said, "that is what warning signs do, isn't it?"

"Come on," I told him. "Just give us a minute, can't you? Be a sport."

He wanted to say no. He did. But Hannah looked at him. He hesitated. Then he said, "I've got another house to check on down the way. I'll go and have a look at that. I won't be long."

So we went in. She seemed to hesitate, uncertain what she wanted; me, I flung open the wardrobe, unhooked the hangers, bundled everything outside.

"Not that," she said. "I don't want that. That's old."

"Can't stick around." I threw the stuff out bodily. She told me later she could picture me, directing building work along the River Kwai; it wasn't meant to be a compliment.

Something scrabbled at the front room door. A gooey substance leaked from under it and spread across the tiles.

As we were dragging the last armfuls out, the clipboard man came back.

"I didn't see this," he announced. "You went inside before I got here, right?" He peered up at the front room window, pushing back his thinning hair. "Looks like a nasty one to me. 'Bout this size, sir, you say?"

"'Bout that."

"They metamorphosise. Some of 'em do. Start off one thing, then tomorrow you got summat else, and next day... Very nasty when they do that, sir. Never know what's coming, that's the trouble. Then some of 'em just keel over an' die, ker-plut. Don't like the air, I'm told.

Wouldn't believe some of the stuff I've seen just recently." He chuckled. "Been like bloody *Dr Who*, I'm tellin' you. I saw this one thing – nasty little bastard, pardon language, miss, sort of half machine, half – "

"Yeah," I told him. "Thanks for your help."

"Don't mention it, sir. All too happy to oblige. Got to pull together, got to – "

He was telling us the helpline number as we drove away.

*

Hannah was listless through the afternoon. I split the last of the Bush Mills with her, and then she phoned her Mum, and several other people, too. I tried to find a place to store her things. It wasn't easy. And did she really need the pop-up toaster? Or the radio alarm? The tubs of aloe vera, moisturisers, skin lotions and hair tonics? And why would anyone use three shampoos?

I couldn't settle either. I started looking through the bookshelves. H.G. Wells and all his steam-driven utopias... That got me thinking. Ray Bradbury, *The Illustrated Man*, a paperback so old it fell apart soon as I opened it. But I remembered all the dates inside, unlikely even when I'd read the thing, his Martian colonies and space flights in the '50s and the '60s – oh, such optimism then.

I put the book down and went back to Hannah.

"Seen that film?" I said. *"Two-double-oh-one?"*

She sat, hunched over her glass, as if to warm herself on it, as if the room were cold.

"You what?" she said.

"Two-double-oh-one. A Space Odyssey. Ever seen it? When it first came out?"

"It's called *Two Thousand and One*. And course I've bloody seen it."

I sat down next to her. I took her hand.

"Remember it?" I said. "The space station? BBC 12? The zero-gravity toilet? Yeah? Remember that?"

She nodded slightly.

I said, "You see it when it first came out?"

"S'pose so." She wouldn't face me properly.

"So when was that, then? '67? '68?"

"Something like that. I don't know, do I?"

52

"'The Ultimate Trip'. I'd say, '67, then. And the year – 2001 – the year seemed ages off, you know? Back then? And, like, it was all pretty convincing, really, wasn't it? At least, up to the freaky stuff...?"

Silence.

"BBC 12?" I said.

"Zero-gravity toilet? Instructions for the use of? Yes?"

"OK. So it looked real. So what?"

"So we thought that's how we'd all end up. Yeah? And I worked out I'd live long enough, I'd get a trip to the moon too, one day. That's what they used to say in comics. 'One day, you'll be able to go to the moon'. And what year is it now?"

"You know."

"Yeah. And where's the future? All of that? The wheel in space? Eh? Come on."

"Christ," she said. "It's just a fucking film for Christ sake. Jesus – "

"No. It's not a film. You think a moment. It's a year..."

*

It seems to me we missed our way somewhere. As a society, as individuals... We got it wrong.

The classic theory is the Freudian one, of course. That's what you'll hear discussed in pubs, that's what you'll see on cheapjack, made-for-idiots TV. We're told that we've repressed the future, and that anything repressed comes back redoubled, twice as nasty, twice as strong.

I don't believe it, personally.

Call me paranoid. But I think it's intentional. I think it's war.

The future's everything. The future's every possibility you ever thought about, or anybody thought about, just out there, waiting; it's the past that's limited, the past that's fixed, unbending, thin.

And we're the link between the two. We travel up out of the past and every second that we live, we're endlessly colliding with the future. Wiping it out. We're like a bulldozer, destroying all before us, all except that little sliver of what *really* happens, what we call the *real* world, *our* world.

And I think there are people up there, waiting to exist. Not 'real' people. Not yet. They're waiting to be born, waiting to breathe and laugh and fuck, to take their places in reality. Except reality's going a different way. We hit them and they'll wink out, buried in the Dow Jones index and the mortgage rate and Third World debt, in AIDS and cancer and the dismal little lives most of us lead. We will replace them – we will replace the *possibility* of them – forever.

I think they're trying to change our lives, to bring our history closer to theirs.

I think they're seeding us.

If they can plant us with their aliens, their worn-out space-suits and their crazy drugs, well, maybe then, against all odds, the world will change. And maybe, maybe, we'll turn into *them*. And maybe, maybe, something like the world they know will come about, and our descendants will wear silver suits and waltz to Strauss on Saturn's moons.

Maybe.

Yet nothing so romantic's happening in my life. We've got problems over Hannah's flat, and what to do, and though she's due for compensation nobody will tell her when, or how much, or any of the other things she needs to know.

They think the creature's breeding. Laying eggs. Whatever these things do. And there's a bunch of people, MoD, who want to get a look at it. And so it's not been moved. And Hannah's been here for the last two weeks. And I'm still sleeping on the couch, developing a permanent cricked back as a result. I'm serious. I've even started walking with a stoop.

Yet this time, anyway, we've had no major rows. We tiptoe round each other like the floor's covered in glass. We make a point of saying 'please' and 'thank you', and we each ask if the other cares to watch TV, or listen to some music, or would like a cup of coffee now, perhaps?

On rare occasions when it's got to me, I've bitten back my anger in a second, forced a smile up on my face, and smoothed things over like I never could before. And she's done much the same, I know.

But that's the secret of the future. Everything's there. Whether you want it or you don't, it comes down anyway, and even marriage can come back to haunt you, twisted, fractured and turned upside down, and sometimes – here's the oddest thing – a million times improved on what it was in life.

Homeground

It's five miles to the bottom of the garden now. A month back, it was two. Before that... Less. Much less.

They say it's all quiescent these days, anyway. We're off the danger list.

That's the official line.

And if you swallow that, says Mary, then you'll swallow anything.

I made the trip last week. She watched me go. I glanced back when I reached the lawn and waved to her; already she looked tiny, distant, and her arm came up like fending off a blow. The change had caught her badly, left her shaken and uncertain of herself. I'd always said she thought too much. It was a virtue, but she suffered for it, too.

It hurt to leave her, even for a few hours.

I'm shallow by comparison. I like a job to do, a task to carry out... I'd got my camera, flask, a pack of sandwiches; and if I'd stopped to think about it, I can guarantee I'd never have set off. No way.

And yet it wasn't all that bad at first. Everything twisted, bent up, like some piece of trick photography... Faint winds rose on a knife-back ridge I vaguely placed as one of the old flowerbeds, lifting little curlicues of dust. Remains of vegetation flapped at me like empty sleeves. There was a sense of growth and sickness intermingled here, a burgeoning that brought its own decay. Misshapen beetles shuffled underfoot, brittle as glass.

And then the sky began to change.

It happened in a mile. The sun became oblate, squashed flat, spreading its thin light in an arc across the sky. The shadows softened and a grey, pearl glow fell over everything. Soil crumbled where I trod. Great furrows cut the ground. Eddies of wind burst in my face, and rain stung at my skin in sudden squalls that vanished even as they came.

Soon after that, I saw the ship.

I felt – this isn't easy to explain – I felt that I was peering down a great dark well, and on the floor of it the ship gleamed like a coin. There was a pull that drew me on, a kind of gravity, and when I ceased to walk, it tugged me still, dragging me gently down towards the epicentre.

Yet there was no well here, no slope, the plain was level, flat, as if my sense of balance and my eyesight were at odds with one another, and I held my arms out, beating at the air for steadiness.

The ship looked just about as far away as Africa.

Above it, in a vast, dark chimney, clouds stacked up like smoke, and lightning cracked, and I remembered something I'd seen years ago in Sunday School, a picture of the tower of cloud that led the Israelites out of captivity...

But this led nowhere. Rather, everything bled down towards it, stretched and drawn, propelled towards the new reality...

An insect fluttered through the air. It spun, whirled, dropped onto my sleeve and crumbled like a flake of ash.

I lifted up the camera, busying myself with shutter speeds and apertures, drowning my fears in technicalities.

Already, though, I knew I'd reached my journey's end. I couldn't go another yard, not one more step across that vast plain, which just months before had been an ordinary, common field, dotted with cow pats, mole hills, grassy tufts... That now looked cruel and lifeless as the surface of the Moon.

*

She'd got the vodka bottle out when I came home. I didn't blame her, really. She looked tired, these days. The strain showed on her face. Her features had grown angular and sharp; her eyes had sunk, her cheeks caved in. Her nose was like an arrowhead.

It didn't hide her beauty, though. And just right now, it seemed to

56

match her mood.

I told her what I'd seen, and she said, "Tell it to the bloody Council, then," and took a swift, aggressive swig.

"I don't think you can blame them over this, you know."

"Can't I? Just watch."

It was a good, imported vodka, something to be savoured; but she gulped it down like medicine.

"I've got files," she said. "I've got a file on everything. They offed the bloody gyppos fast enough. And they weren't doing any harm to anyone."

"Well... Not to us."

"Oh no. But they just made the place untidy, didn't they? Bad for business, that. Bad for Mr Pinkney and his cronies. Bad for Fartface at the Dog and Duck. And that's what counts."

People and places change their names when Mary drinks. The Dog and Duck is actually the Royal Oak Hotel, the poshest place in town, with four stars and a restaurant we'd probably require a second mortgage just to enter; though we used to grace the bar, back in the early days. Hence our acquaintance with the manager, a certain Mr. Dempsey-Stringer, better known to Mary by the name of 'Fartface'.

"They'll do alright," she said.

"Conspiracies, conspiracies." I poured myself a drink. My muscles ached. I'd just walked fifteen miles, regardless what the map might say. I saw her gearing for a fight, but I just wasn't in the mood. "No-one's in charge of this," I said. "No-one's responsible. It's not some bit of government shenanigans. It's not a quick back-hander or a dodgy grant... It's from – oh, Christ knows where. Some place that even Pinkney can't get votes..."

"Oh yes." She was sarcastic. "I know that. The Act of God hypothesis. Like the recession. Unemployment. *Not our business, guv'nor. Act of God.* I know that one, alright."

"Please, let's not talk politics."

"*You,*" she said, "still think that a conspiracy means half a dozen blokes in trench coats, sitting round a table whispering. Don't you?"

"I can't see Pinkney in a trench coat. More your moleskin collar type, I'd say – "

But she wouldn't be derailed. Her face was flushed, not just from drinking either. "The real conspiracies are all invisible," she lectured me. "They're about attitudes, shared preconceptions, sense of good and bad. People belong and they don't even realise it – "

"We've been through this before."

"You know what our democracy's about then, eh? The great British democracy? It's there to make you vote against your own best fucking interests, that's what. And if you don't think that's some kind of a conspiracy, God knows what is. Look at the arms trade! Or this bloody nuclear sludge – this reprocessing lark. They're just – "

"It isn't nuclear sludge," I said. "At least, I hope it's not."

She talked some more, gesturing angrily, the way she used to do at meetings, once upon a time. I waited till she'd got it out. Then I said, gently, "Nobody can hear, you know."

"I know," she said. "I fucking know..."

We sat together, drinking for a while. Then she reached out and she touched my wrist, running her hand across it absently, the way you'd stroke a favourite pet dog. "I'd never make a politician anyway," she said. "Can't hold the booze..."

We listened to the hall clock, ticking off the minutes, while the light died slowly round us and the night began.

"It's all so shoddy," she complained. "I wouldn't even mind if they were competent – real Machiavellis and Big Brothers... If they'd got some kind of a *plan* or something. I dunno. But it's just anything that gets them by, anything to tide them over, short term... And bugger next year, bugger the year after. That's how Pinkney and his crew are, anyway. Like Westminster in miniature. Selfish, petty-minded, blinkered..."

She was talking quietly, her hand still on my arm. I put my fingers over hers, feeling her quiver, as if startled by the touch.

"They're so bloody inept," she said. "That – thing out in the field... Oh, says Pinkney, wonderful! Money! We'll make a few quid out of this! ...I reckon if you held a gun up to his head, he'd try and sell you extra bullets, just in case the first one missed. That's what he's like..."

"Methinks you don't approve the man."

I filled my glass again, then thought, the hell with it, and filled hers, too. She needed some relief, some way to ease the pressure. Even from a bottle.

"Course," she said, "the gun's not up to Pinkney's head. It's up to ours. I bet he's laughing his acrylic socks off over that, I really do."

And so we both got drunk. It meant tomorrow would be difficult. But then, tomorrow would be difficult in any case...

*

I've heard her called a radical, and an attention-seeker, even a subversive, once or twice.

She's not. But she's a dragon fighter, and for the last few years her dragon's been the local Council, and its leader, Richard Pinkney.

She'd appreciate the image, too. She thinks they're coiled up round a pot of gold, and keeping it from everyone.

We met as students in the 80s. She wasn't in the least political back then. She called herself a 'wishy-washy liberal', and used to laugh at all the earnest, middle class young men who'd flung themselves at Marxism like peasants in some Cuban hill village. Poor things, she'd say; it was the shock of leaving home, and missing Mummy's cooking, and the central heating, and the Sunday roast... And trying to make it on a grant.

Those guys have all got cushy jobs, these days. Media and government, the bulk of them. They passed her on their way to the establishment, while she was moving in the opposite direction.

They're a conspiracy, of course.

And me, I'd hardly even think of politics if Mary wasn't here. I wouldn't question things, I wouldn't rock the boat. She may call me her Legal Eagle, but Perry Mason I am not. Conveyancing's not very glamorous, but it pays the mortgage off, and that's what counts in my book, anyway.

We moved to Stickley Grange about ten years ago. I guess we're classic newcomers. We dreamed about a rural idyll and we got it, for a while. I'd drive back after work and feel I was on holiday. I'd wind the window down on freezing days to smell the country air. Even the stink of fertilizer. Well, I thought it was authentic, rural – *real*.

A dream. And just like all good dreams, you finally wake up and see the flaws, the bits of it that don't make sense... The worms eating the apple from the inside out.

Ten years ago, it was a lively town. White Mount and Galley St were full of shops; today, they're boarded up, and full of crap.

59

You wonder, sometimes, about all these blokes you see in town all day, lounging on benches, waiting for the pubs to open up. And then you realise: they've got nowhere else to go. You watch the news and there's another firm gone bust, another thirty or a hundred men laid off... *et cetera.*

The small-town unemployed don't riot, though. They don't stage marches. Nothing in their lives makes good TV.

You never hear of them.

And it goes on. The local college closed three years ago. You want an education? Fine. You've got an hour's ride – assuming you can find a bus. And if you need a hospital, if you're about to die – forget it. And goodbye.

At times like this, no-one wants economics, struggle, five year plans.

They want messiahs.

They want Richard Pinkney trumpeting his tidings of great joy, his snake oil cure, his all-in-one solution to their woes.

The *leisure trade.*

That's what he calls it.

Tourism.

And that's OK, so far. If Stickley's not the cutest place on Earth, it's certainly no dump. We've always had a thin trickle of tourists through the years. Tourism's good, tourism's great. But not when it's your only industry. Not when you're trying to float a whole community on it. Not when you've nothing else.

It's seasonal. There's competition (why bother coming *here* when you can go to Tenerife instead?). The slightest lurch in the economy, and tourism's the first thing out the window. Oh, there'll be some jobs, alright: hotel work, retail, catering – the worst paid, least secure positions you can find. And then a few good posts. Places for managers, consultants, specialists... They won't go to the locals, though. You won't get those by saying you drove Farmer Giles's tractor for the last ten years. No way.

The tourist trade's just icing on the cake, that's all. Except there's no cake any more.

I sound like Mary sometimes. But she puts the point much better, naturally.

She's done it umpteen times.

She'll tell you all the good things about tourism, as well. And who they'll benefit.

Like Richard Pinkney, for a start.

He owns the Royal Oak. He owns the Bluebird Tea Rooms, and he's other little ventures up his sleeve, as yet to make their roles in his great putative new empire clear.

When challenged, he'll admit it all.

Sly dog.

"I have invested in this town," he says. "I have invested here, in Stickley Grange, because it has a future. Because I am committed to its people, and their forthcoming prosperity..."

"*Whose* prosperity?" asks Mary, but he doesn't care.

He's got a salesman's tongue. He knows what people want to hear. His background's fuddled in the welter of his own publicity, somewhere in London and the North; though Mary says she wouldn't be a bit surprised if it involved used cars.

She stood against him in election, two years back. She didn't do too badly, either, considering it's true-blue country here; but then, she didn't win. And that's what counts.

Mary, as the papers say, "continues to be active in the world of local politics."

Last year, for instance, when the gypsies came.

They'd stopped off on the common land, out in the Vale. As former city types, I don't suppose we understood the conflicts between travellers and settled folk, and weren't about to play along. Even the gossip was a pain. If things went missing, straight away, it was the bloody didicoys. If anyone fell ill – well, everybody knew they carried germs. Wasn't that right?

To Mary, it was just plain prejudice. She wouldn't stand for it. She set up meetings, started people talking, trying to find a compromise... Some way both sides could come out the winner.

And she won no friends for that, I'm telling you. So, last year, Romanies. And this year: aliens.

It's notable the way positions have reversed between the Council and ourselves, regarding the two issues, and I daresay cynics might suggest we're acting in our own self-interest now.

But I just think we're worried that the world's about to end. That's all.

It seemed so innocent at first. A prodigy. A miracle. A wonder from the skies.

Not any more.

*

One of the things we'd always liked about the house was privacy. It wasn't overlooked. Behind us, we'd got Jolly's Field, and then the trees. I used to love watching their splayed bare tops poke through the mist on winter mornings, or the first budding in spring...

Acres of space.

The perfect landing site.

We didn't even notice when it happened. No big bang, no whoosh, no boom, no H.G. Wells kerfuffle.

It was silent. Overnight. And no-one seemed to know except the people at the air base, twenty miles away.

By morning, Jolly's Field looked like an army camp.

Trucks everywhere. Uniforms. Machinery. Weird civil service types in mud-caked shoes...

At noon, the TV crew arrived.

There were two of them, for local news: a girl reporter and a camera/sound man in a baseball cap. The military wouldn't let them on the site, and they wanted pictures from our garden or our upstairs room, if that would be OK, please, please?

So they wound up filming Mary, too.

She went out on the news that night. Official comment wasn't worth the air time, so I heard – and who better to use?

"Well, Mary. How d'you feel, now you've got Martians for your neighbours?"

But she smiled; she wasn't going to fall for that. "Assuming," she began, "only *assuming* we've a spaceship here – I think that we should welcome them, and offer them the sort of hospitality that *we'd* expect, in their position."

We watched the show. She cringed. "My God," she said. "Don't I look awful? I can't stand it! And I sound like Minnie Mouse – "

That's Mary, though. She didn't let it stop her when it came to national TV, next night.

62

We got a bit more info then. A spokesman for the MOD came on and chunnered about 'aircraft of an unknown origin' and told us almost nothing that we'd really want to know.

Mary was much more interesting. And more photogenic, too, whatever she might think.

"Imagine it," she said. "You've just come fifty million miles or so. It's a historic visit. Welcome to the planet Earth. And straight away, you're looking down some squaddy's gun barrel. *Now* how do you feel?"

Across the desk the MOD man started spouting about 'public safety', 'national interest' and the like. So Mary just demolished him in seconds flat. Oh, but she was wonderful then! It was her finest hour and if it's backfired on us since, it's not her fault, believe you me.

All she'd wanted was a cautious welcome.

Not the circus it's become.

*

Too many books, too many films, too many comic strips... We've got such preconceptions. And yet what really happened, once the thrill wore off, the first excitement passed, was... Nothing.

We couldn't even see the ship from where we were, barring a thin white arc of roof; the army'd put up canvas screens all round, just like a field latrine. It lay there, less than half a mile away, but we got all our best views on TV.

You might call it a flying saucer. Ovoid, more than round, perhaps. And it was white. Pure white. Not scorched and blackened like the lumps of tin that come back after *our* trips into space. It looked like somebody'd just scooped a snow dune up and dropped it, right there in the English countryside.

Impeccable.

There were no windows, portholes, hatchways, no clear sections or divisions in the thing. And chances were, it wasn't even fixed in any rigid form; the close-ups showed a web of bumps and flutings on the surface that would ripple intermittently and reconfigure in a different form. Nobody, so far, had worked out why.

A pile of scientific gubbins poured onto the site. Set back, they'd got the men with the bazookas, though you wondered just what kind of damage they could do, with toys like that...

63

The third day, and the aliens emerged.

You've heard the stories. One brief contact, one quick look, then back inside, with no more interest in our world, our guns – or us.

The aliens aren't human. They're not even humanoid. No bug-eyed monsters and no Spielberg elves. People who've seen them – and I'm not one, even now – describe them as vibrations in the air, strange shifts of light, accompanied by faint, electrical sensations on the skin. Goose bumps, in fact.

Also: they make you sneeze.

And nobody knows where they're from, or who they are, or what they want.

The aliens don't talk. The aliens don't *choose* to talk. The aliens don't give a damn about us, one way or the other, and if they'd found the field was full of cows, then they'd have treated them exactly the same way, no better and no worse.

The papers called it *The Polite Invasion*. And I suppose it's true, the loss of manners tended to take place on our side, rather than the other way around.

We remonstrated with a pair of special constables sent to evacuate us. We quibbled with a Captain Johns, here on the self-same mission. Mary swore. I quoted law at all of them, making it up when memory gave out.

We weren't evacuated. But we got our very own armed guard to keep us out of mischief. We'd see them at the bottom of the garden, just across the fence, and sometimes take them tea and stop off for a chat. It wasn't what you'd call the tightest of security. There was a bloke named Bill who'd tell us time and time again about his meeting with the aliens, and every version got a little more extravagant, more grandiose... We'd *ooh* and *aah* and laugh in all the proper places, and he liked us doing that. We made a decent audience, at any rate.

"So there I am, not ten yards back, and I can see 'em – great big fuzzy kind of buggers – hurts your eyes just lookin' at 'em, see? Like wearing someone else's specs. And they're, oh, six or seven yards off, an' I get this tinglin' in me arm, it's like a bloody feather duster goin' up and down, up and down... Me nose begins to itch. An' then – "

The only person that we hadn't heard from all this time was our dear friend, Mr Pinkney.

No wonder, either. First sign of trouble and he'd scuttled off to London, supposedly to talk to 'experts' on the matter. But he came back in a great blaze of publicity, once everything looked safe again, and even called a public meeting in the big hall at the Royal Oak (*kindly loaned by... etc.*).

This was what Mary would refer to later as "The Second Coming of Richard Pinkney".

The meeting was for seven; we turned up at twenty to. The place was packed. Old Fartface sat behind the bar, clutching a single malt as if his life depended on it.

"They're all wimps," he said, striking a manful pose. "All bloody wimps – whole bloody lot of 'em. Army, politicians – and that bloody PM, too. See it just by lookin' at him. No leader of men. Not fit to lead a flock of sheep, I say. Sense of direction – that's what people need these days, 'stead of all this namby-pamby shilly-shally stuff..."

He'd got an audience around him. Not just regulars. I recognised them. Members of the threatened middle class, I thought, already dropping into Mary's terminology; small businessmen, captains of industry – such as it was. The ones who might have welcomed the recession, with its cheaper labour and its hamstrung unions, at least until they'd seen their own interests start sliding down the tubes along with everybody else's.

I'll admit, my sympathies were mixed. Only they weren't with Fartface. I knew that.

"Not bloody good enough," he said. "Too much pontificatin'. Fancy bloody speeches. You need guts to put 'em into action, too." He waved his glass round, dangerously, narrowing his eyes. He'd got guts, alright – he wanted you to notice that. "They're immigrants, and that's a fact," he said. "And we've got laws. Or we'd be swamped by bloody foreigners. I don't care whether they're from Mars or Timbuctoo. The law says – "

I cast a glance at Mary.

"Save it for the meeting," I said then.

"Oh, I'm going to. Besides, it isn't Dempsey-Stringer that amazes me. It's all those other buggers standing round, nodding their heads, as if he's talking sense, for God's sake. That's the scary part."

I downed a vodka. Mary stuck to orange juice. She didn't want the

65

booze fuzzing her head; not this time round.

"If I had my way," Dempsey-Stringer's fervent tones came knifing through the air, "if I had my way, I'd say, *right then, Johnny Kaffir. Back on the boat for you.* And these Martian chappies, I can tell you, if I – "

We left him foaming there and headed for the hall.

People were crowding round the walls; standing room only now. Somewhere a child wailed. All night long, the stir of conversation hardly stopped, not even when the main acts stepped up to the mike to speak.

I'll skip the preamble – the vicar of St Luke's, and Pearsley from the chicken factory. Our first star turn was a Lieutenant So-and-So, who offered us a string of charming little rabbit smiles from underneath his neat moustache. "No reason for alarm," he said. "As far as we can possibly make out, no reason for alarm..."

At least he told us things, though. Gave us something we could more or less call facts.

He was the first to talk about the time discrepancy around the ship. Oh yes, he said, the scientific chaps were fascinated by all that! The smile flicked back up on his face a moment, and he rubbed his hands together in delight, as if explaining to a child. It seemed that time flowed differently as you approached the ship; a second's lag, that's all, hardly enough to measure with a stop watch... And no *danger*, certainly. Oh no. His troops were crack men, trained for anything. The British Army's record, he reminded us, was still the finest in the world...

Councillor Pinkney led off the applause. His round, red face was shining in the light, his tweeds and his cravat so perfect English Country Squire, he could have been an actor on the BBC. He, too, praised the military, though I'd have sworn it was a ploy: Pinkney's praise pre-figured murder, frequently enough, and Mary always talked about 'the smile that kills'. I thought he'd turn on the poor officer, demand the aliens be driven from our midst, towed out of town, or any way removed from his, Pinkney's, precious little kingdom.

Instead he smiled, resting his knuckles on the tabletop, and watched us like a priest with an unusually eager congregation.

Yes, he said, he understood our great concern, and he'd made sure that Westminster now understood it, too; he greased us with his tales of the discussions that he'd had on our behalf, until you almost thought he wanted you to stand and cheer. Yet it was tone that always won for him, not words. His speech was smooth, unhesitant, so full of confidence it crept beneath you, carried you along just like a boat across a calm blue lake; and if you wanted, you could sit back while he steered you anywhere he cared to go.

Or you could crouch down with your awls and chisels, longing for the chance to rip the bottom out, quick as you could.

Beside me, I felt Mary twitch impatiently, waiting for question time.

And that was Pinkney's smartest trick, his most annoying quality. You'd gear up for a fight, get ready to be outraged, brand him as the parish Stalin, and lo! He'd prove himself the soul of reason, slip through all your carefully-rehearsed objections, till you'd wind up actually agreeing with the man – and hating yourself for it, too.

Pinkney was flexible. A pragmatist. No policies, no credo. Anything that did the job, and did it well for Pinkney: that was all.

He thanked the army for their work. He praised them, mentioned their heroic role in peace-keeping, and then, without a pause, he told us just how glad he was to welcome our new visitors – how honoured that they'd picked on Stickley Grange for their first landing spot.

There were murmurs over that. He let them die, then carried on, soothing and pleasant as before. He speculated on the boost to Britain's status in the world, the arguable benefits for science and technology; he fully sympathized, he told us, with our fears, but so far, they seemed groundless. These people were a thousand times more civilized than we. Surely their intentions must be peaceful? Perhaps, indeed, they'd come here to assist, to aid us in our difficulties?

"Let's welcome them, then, as ambassadors, as honoured guests. No silly scare stories, no nonsense from the space comics our children read. In Stickley Grange, everyone's welcome..."

I heard Mary mutter something about gypsies, but she didn't say it loud. I think she was too stunned.

Then later, over drinks, she said: "He's up to something."

She was right, as well.

*

It was a Saturday – bright, beautiful and warm; a great brown dragonfly was doing pirouettes over the lawn, and I was sitting in a deckchair with the daily paper and a mug of Irish coffee when a car pulled up outside.

Two minutes passed.

And I'd got visitors.

They were a family group: a man of fifty-odd, dressed like a little boy in shorts and bright, striped T-shirt, then his wife, a little girl, and finally a sullen-looking teenager of far from certain sex. They came around the garage and I heard dad make some brief, disparaging remark about the rockery. They crossed the lawn. The man gave me a nod. He didn't seem to think it strange that I was there, or – more to the point – that he was there, as well.

I searched my brains. Someone I knew? A client, possibly? Or someone from the pub? They ambled up the path as if I didn't even count. There were some further comments on my gardening, a lot of tut-tuts and shaking of the head.

"*Excuse* me," I called out.

And realised, all at once, why they were there.

I don't suppose they'd been the first. Only the first we'd seen, that's all. What did amaze me was their clear assumption they'd a right to tramp across the garden (and make such obtuse and irritating criticisms of it) without even a by-your-leave!

I told them so. I yelled at them. I had to almost bar their way before they'd stop.

Confusion fought with outrage on the man's fat face.

"But this is history," he wailed. "I want the kids to witness it. I want – "

"Well, they can bloody witness it from somewhere else," I said.

"Bloke wants a fiver down the other place. A fiver each. It's robbery. Though we could come to some arrangement, you and me... eh?"

He was reaching in his back pocket, but he never got his money out. I told him just what sort of an arrangement we could come to, and I told him straight.

As they moped off, I heard his wife say something about 'words like that in front of children' – but I didn't care.

I sat down, picked my coffee up – it was cold by now – and then I thought: a fiver at the other place?

*

It didn't take me long to find. A quick drive up the road, past the hedges and the trees, then down the lane to Jolly's Field.

Bob Farnham had his tractor neatly parked across the entranceway.

Most days, I'd see him herding cows behind the house. But now he'd got a leather pouch slung round his neck, the kind that bus conductors used to wear; and there were crude, hand-painted signs up: VISITORS FROM MARS and SEE THE ALIENS (he'd spelt it 'ALEINS').

"Army bods don't much like it much," he said. "Still, I told 'em, gotta be some compensation, ain't there, if I can't pasture me cows? I shifts the tractor for 'em, when they wants, and so they lets me carry on." He winked at me. "You want a look?" he said. "It's free to pals..."

*

"*Pinkney*," said Mary, and she spat it like a swear word. "That man's incredible. He always gets exactly what he wants, you know? Like bloody Superman."

"Friends in high places," I said, pouring a drink.

"Low places, more like. He even makes me wonder if he set it up. Though God knows how..."

"A big sign in the back yard: *spacemen welcome...*"

"More like: *get here for the tourist season*. That's it. I mean, everyone'll want to see the thing. Everyone. Even if they're only passing through."

"That's good enough. A look round town, a pint down at the Royal Oak, meal in the Bluebird..."

"Build up Pinkney's lovely little tourist culture."

"Well," I shrugged, "good luck to him. At least there'll be some money going round. Just for a while."

I glanced out at the garden. "We could even make a bit ourselves, you know, if we were interested..."

She shot a look at me that would have felled a rhino.

"Tourism!" she groaned. "Quick bloody bucks. It won't be here forever. *Then* what do they do? We could have had some proper jobs, some industry, maybe. Something to *last*. And now..." She threw her

69

hands up. "What's the fucking use? It's not my fault. I tried. And anyway, it's that lot I feel sorry for." She nodded to the field. "Pretty undignified, I'd say, being the first intergalactic Disneyland. You know?"

*

That's how the summer went. The army cleared off, leaving just a token force. The tourists moved in. Grockles – that's what we called them. I fixed a big lock on the front gate, but it didn't keep them out.

And, for a while, things happened just as Pinkney had predicted. The streets grew crowded. We heard foreign voices – Germans, Japanese, Americans – and the banks were forced to shift their staff to the exchange counters to cope. New jobs came up, as well. Bad terms, maybe, but no-one was complaining yet. A job's a job; and there were people there who hadn't worked in years.

The town became transformed.

You could buy Martian Teas, and Mars Burgers, and Venus Cake, and drink a pint of Solar Ale; or get the kids a spacesuit each, an *X-Files* book, a whistling key-ring, and a bold, obligatory car sticker: *WE HAVE SEEN THE STICKLEY STARSHIP!*. Every shop had postcards of the thing – that, and pictures of the *Enterprise*, the *Tardis*, and a dozen scenes from *Star Wars*, all of them, apparently, outselling any real-life shots...

The aliens laid low. I couldn't blame them, either.

Bob Farnham rented out his field to one of Pinkney's firms, apparently at an extraordinary rate. They put a tollbooth up. A mobile shop sold souvenirs. The smell of hot dogs filled the air...

A low wood fence replaced the army's canvas screens. It kept spectators back, though they could rent out opera glasses at a quid or two a time to get a closer look... Such safety measures, and the small presence of soldiers and technicians lingering nearby, made tourists feel intrepid, brave, the way safari parks had once done, years before.

I watched from the bottom of the garden. It all seemed such an anti-climax now, this first real close encounter. No new gospel, no great revelation from the stars; and equally, as far as anybody knew, no government conspiracies, no plots... Apart from Pinkney's, anyway. The thing looked like a fairground exhibit; which then again, in certain ways, it was.

"They came too late," I said to Mary. "If they'd have got here in the 50s they'd have really stirred things up. It's old hat these days, though – and Spielberg did it better. Much more style..."

So August passed. Some days it rained – heavy, brutal downpours – and the tourists vanished for a few hours, off to cinemas or pubs or other towns; but next day, they'd be back.

The first complaints came in September. And even then, I don't think anybody would have minded much if they'd been charged a little less to view the thing. But people started saying it was too far off, they couldn't see it properly – it could be anything out there, it could be made of fibreglass, who said it was a flying saucer, anyway?

I knew what they were getting at. I'd noticed it myself, an odd distortion in the thing, like looking through a pane of twisted glass... The ship seemed further off, somehow, although I knew, given the landmarks, that it couldn't be.

Faint, radial lines appeared along the ground around it, furrowing and ridging, like the earth was somehow being re-aligned, re-ordered round a brand new hub.

The aliens weren't *doing* anything. But *being* there was quite enough.

Even today, the arguments still rage as to the cause, and half of them are so abstruse I can't even begin to follow them. Besides, for me, it's not a matter of theoretical debate. It's real. It's right outside my door.

So just try this.

Imagine a thin sheet of latex, stretched out, flat and taut. That's our space-time, the universe we're living in.

Then place on it a small, intensely heavy object. Like a ball of lead.

The latex shifts. It forms a dimple to accommodate the pressure. And the dimple stretches, distending like a pocket, deeper and deeper round the weight. The latex alters, changes and makes room...

Perhaps it's not a good analogy. Only that sheet of latex is our world, it's our continuum, it's all we know. The ship's from somewhere else. It's an anomaly. It's not from Mars or Venus, or from any of the nearer stars, but, so current thinking goes, from somewhere much, much further off, in more than simple distance. The longer it stays on, the more distortion will result. You can walk around it, same as always

71

– if you're, say, a mile or so away – but if you walk towards it, then the world begins to pull and shear. Soon you're in Brobdingnag, in Never-Never Land.

And it starts right here, right in our own back yard.

They say it's stable now. Only it's not. I know that much.

Our orchard's turned into a distant jungle, filled with broken trees as fat as old sequoias, brittle as the finest glass; our garden path's a highway, and the lawn, a broad, mutant prairie, glittering with winter frost.

Two days ago, I found a garden trowel; the stresses had attenuated it until the blade flared out just like a paper fan.

A small bird fluttered helplessly. It had been nesting in the zone. Its wings no longer had the proper shape to fly.

These and other prodigies are commonplace to us. The zone is growing, no matter what they say. After an hour here, in the back room, my watch will be a minute or two out against the big clock in the hall, a little longer with the timechecks on the radio...

Yesterday, we got a letter.

Richard Pinkney's made an offer for the house.

It's low. Ridiculously low. Accepting it would be like going right back to the days we were first married, back to the city, back to digs. But what else can we do?

"He knew it," Mary said. "He knew that this would happen. God knows how."

She's anxious, she wants somebody to blame. She's found him, too.

*

The town's still buzzing. Even in the wintertime. People have work. Jobs. Money. It's the best there's been in years. And when the spaceship's gone, the rest goes, too. They've got to cash in now. Or else.

So there are big plans for the coming season. A whole new fleet of mini-buses, all done up with rocket-tubes and lightning flashes, and then a big, bright logo: *Stickley Space Safari*. They look wonderful. Just wonderful.

I know, when I was young, I would have begged and begged my Dad to take us to see Stickley Grange. I know I would.

*

We lay awake this morning. Six a.m. A faint grey light was creeping

72

through the curtains. And then Mary said, "I'm going to talk to them."

I said, "They're opportunists. They're just using things, that's all."

"Not them," she said. "The aliens."

I listened to the big clock ticking in the hall. I watched her getting dressed. I asked her how she thought she'd talk to them, and what she'd say, and what the hell made her imagine that they'd just clear off because she asked them to, just *yes miss, no miss, three bags full?*

I couldn't hold her back.

She thinks if people talk, if they'll just sit round and discuss things, then they'll come to a solution. She believes it, deep, deep down. She still believes it, though she's never made it work.

Not yet.

I said, "I'm going with you," and she said, "I need you here," and loaded up the backpack with some food and water and a pile of Pinkney's colour tourist brochures. Then she left as soon as it got light.

Nine hours ago.

I'm waiting for her now.

I sit and stare out at the garden. I watch TV, but with the sound down, so I can hear her if she calls. I know I should have gone with her. I'm trying not to think what might go wrong. Too many things...

I peer into the bathroom mirror sometimes. I'll spend ages there. It horrifies and fascinates me, both at once; and yet I'm calm about it, too, almost detached, as if it's happening to someone else... As if I'm miles away, and safe, and normal still.

I've never mentioned it to Mary. But I think she's guessed. Or seen the changes in herself, her own mutation starting to begin.

I'm taller. Not by much. Enough to make me stoop a little now to see my whole face in the mirror. Nothing more.

My nose is longer. Head a wee bit deeper, front to back. Chin narrower. I know that, if I stay, my bones will go on growing, they'll turn brittle, break, and fall apart...

Mary's got gifts. Mary's got skills. If anyone can do it, she's the one.

It's just the waiting hurts. That's what I tell myself. The helplessness. The ignorance. Compared to this, her job's a doddle, really, isn't it? A cinch, a breeze, a dream.

She'll do it easily.

You know?

Up There

I'd never had much head for heights, and in that place I would suffer terribly: the city had been built over an abyss in the mountains, hundreds of feet deep, a net of cables, chains and massive iron struts that arched into the void like a gigantic spider's web; while at its heart, the body of the insect glittered, its spires and turrets twinkling with electric light.

I reached the entry road just before dawn, and made my way up slowly, stopping many times for breath. The air was thin. A wind arose. I felt the pavement shiver under me, and then, with gathering momentum, the whole edifice began to shake, and sway, and lurch – I dropped down on my knees, convinced my last moments had come, and any second I'd be flung off into space, just like the useless piece of flotsam that I was. I hugged the ground. I counted up my sins. The wind howled, shuddering. What foolishness had brought me here? What hubris, what insanity?

Yet with the sunrise, I grew calmer. Soft, white light fell on the world; my doubts about the city's permanence were quickly put aside. Parts of the structure were quite clearly old. The crumbling ornament on civic buildings, the modern bolsters set to prop up ancient brick... All these attested to a life of centuries, a structure solid, durable, ornate as a cathedral. Hardly likely to collapse just now, I told myself. Not during my visit, at least. Oh no, no, no...

Of course, the locals moved like monkeys, perfect poise on even the most rickety old walkway. Beside them I galumphed and tottered, reaching out for handholds every chance I got. Small children took me for a clown. Even adults laughed. Once, clinging to the railings of a flyover, half-paralysed with fear, I had to beg assistance from a bent old woman in her seventies, who strutted like a dancer, took me by the elbow and propelled me back to steady ground. Gasping for breath – and trying to hide my funk – I questioned her about the city's origins, its nature and its curious construction. She recited, as if teaching me a creed:

"Air alone among the elements is virtuous." (She pulled my eyelid down to check my colour, dabbed my forehead with her sleeve, shook her head and smiled at my discomfiture.) "For air is of the spirit, just as fire is of the heart, and water of the blood, and earth the lowest and most gross of all, for earth is of the flesh, and bones, and excrement."

I asked if there were others in the city like myself – landmen.

"A few," she said. "They never stay here long."

I told her I was not surprised. I still felt queasy-drunk with vertigo; the shifting of the city in the wind was constantly discernable, a motion I could never fully block from consciousness. Even a minor jolt would set my nerve-ends tingling. At night, it felt like rocking in a hammock. I dreamed of falling. Awake, I suffered dizziness and nausea, symptoms which abated only slightly as the time wore on.

Nevertheless, I stayed nearly a month. I was determined to see everything, if only for the stories I could tell at home. I roamed everywhere I dared, even once down to the city's underside, where giant chutes deposited great torrents of untreated sewage in the river far below. I saw the city's shadow, star-like, stencilled on the land. I saw the market-place, where panniers of vegetables and hulking sides of meat were winched across on pulleys from the mainland. Yet it was not, in all, a busy district. Less interest was paid to food and drink here than in any other place I'd visited, nor were there bars or cafés to escape to when I needed rest or sustenance.

It was, in fact, exactly as the old woman had said. The earthy aspects of our nature here were frowned upon, regarded as a necessary evil, nothing more. (I heard that in a nearby town were restaurants and brothels to which more worldly citizens might now and then, and secretly, repair.) Even the city in its web appeared to strain away from solid earth, much as a healthy man might flinch back from disease. Wealthier residents hired 'buyers' to attend the market and pick food for them. They ate enough to stay alive, no more. Fasting was virtuous. The fat – as in so many wealthy cultures – were seen as greedy and corrupt, yet also, in a specially contemptuous way, as weak.

I hired a guide, who took me to the city's saints. We climbed a fragile gantry up into the high reaches. Here, around a courtyard, were arranged a series of tall pillars, such as the stylites must have used in Medieval times. Atop a half a dozen of them, high against the blue sky, I made out small, thin figures, wrapped in rags of white. They never moved. I might have taken them for egrets, had my guide not then explained that these, themselves, were the very saints that we had come to see; men so holy, they subsisted almost totally on air. Such men might fast for months, he said, taking perhaps a little water, or in the early stages of devotion, a few small crumbs of stale bread, offered by disciples down below. When they died – often at great age, I was told – they tumbled to the courtyard without leaving so much as a mark upon the stone. Many were so light they floated down like feathers, while a blessed few simply dissolved into the air (a claim I strongly doubted, though I nodded, and dropped coins into the offertory bowl, as was required).

Leaving the city I was conscious of my grosser form, the heaviness of flesh, the stiffness of my limbs, the general earthiness of self. The nagging of my appetites was loathsome to me; I drank little and ate less. I walked for long, punishing hours through semi-arid country, where the valleys sprouted small, unhealthy-looking farms. I swayed now like a sailor, caught up in the rhythms of the high city, dizzied by them yet unable or unwilling to renounce their hold.

In the next town, as described, I found brothels, bars and eating houses, whole palaces devoted to amusement and delight... I shunned them all. I locked myself inside my room. Only the gnawing in my guts eventually drove me out.

I chose a simple meal: a bowl of plain green tea, a slice of toast. I blanked the waiter's looks, the mean-faced twitching of his brow. He brought my order and for minutes I just stared at it, unable to conceive how I might physically cram such quantities inside myself. I sipped the tea, like dabbling at the shores of an immense warm ocean. I nibbled at the toast. After each bite, each sip, I paused to rest and to regain my sense of self; to elevate my mind over the body's petty needs.

Nevertheless, almost without my realising, both tea and toast were quickly gone, and I was looking round for more. I chose the plainest cake on the display, and scoffed it in a bite. I paid my bill, fled back to the hotel; my face was red with shame.

Yet with what hunger I awoke next day! I marched out, plunged into the first café I found, and promptly, without any qualm, ordered a feast – pancakes, eggs, ham, bread and apricots; fruit juice and tea; I bought a pack of cigarettes, although I hadn't smoked in years. Out on the street again I was attracted by a sweetmeat seller's stall. Later, I called in at a bar. The food seemed to solidify me, anchor me. I felt the pull of gravity once more. After the second drink, I lolled there in my booth, conscious of my body like an old and rumpled suit. After the third, the beauty of the women of the town came home to me; not their looks, which to be honest were quite unremarkable, but their carriage, the way they walked, a walk not here dictated by the swaying of the pavement under them. Or perhaps, more simply, it was just their femininity, that sense of being *other* that compelled me, drew me to them.

I lit a cigarette with trembling hands and sucked the smoke.

This, then, was how I came back to the world of earth, and flesh, and appetite.

Without regret.

The Leopard Girl

It was the same place, the old shack with the tin roof and the potted plants outside the door; but it looked smaller this year, now that he was growing up. Inside, there wasn't room for him and Dad. The old man came home broody, sullen, and Michael found excuses to go out, to lose himself around the town or by the sea. He saw the boys again. They sat on pavements, smoked their cigarettes, and even now, thirteen or fourteen years of age, complained about the town the same way that their fathers did. He listened, wishing he could join in too, but feeling something glamorous about the place, for all of that: a sense of mystery, of secrets waiting to be given up... He felt it more this year than ever. He could hear it, even in the boys' disgruntled drawl, their bored talk and their gossip. He could hear it but he couldn't reach it. He was too young still, too new to be considered one of them. They called him 'Mikey' and they sent him to run errands for them, but he'd no real hold on their attention, or their time.

He watched women in the High Street, the girls in pleated skirts, the grocer's wife lifting the veg racks in her massive, muscley arms. On Sundays, men wore suits. The women wrapped their hair in sober scarves. The town band played old show tunes in the hut behind the print works, and the thin sound seemed to follow him along the streets, a remnant from a dim, forgotten time.

It was a small community. He knew the faces even if he didn't know their names or what they did.

The Life To Come

Tradition mattered here. It kept them safe, it kept them from the changes that might otherwise have overwhelmed them. He understood that now. It was as if the place existed under sufferance, perched on an abyss where the slightest jolt might topple it, and shatter all they'd managed to preserve.

*

Some days, strange winds blew from the hinterland.

The sky changed colour and the air in town grew sharp and edgy; once, he touched an iron rail and felt it tingle through his hand, as if the whole fence had become electrified. Then people shut their shops, went home from work. They closed their businesses. That was the nature of the time: you never trusted anyone on days the dream winds blew. People had moods. They saw strange things. The rooftops rattled and the newspapers blew down the street like tumbleweeds. The trees were full of noise...

Much later, he'd imagine that the leopard girl had come on such a wind, blown from the empty lands where no-one went, the dream places, out far beyond the hills.

He made up stories, thinking of her, getting hard inside his pants but never moving, too conscious of his father in the other bed, the old man's breathing, loud in sleep.

*

The town rose steeply from the bay.

Sand drifted in the lower streets. It filled his shoes with fine white powder he could never fully empty out, no matter how he tried. The buildings on the front had balconies with old signs hanging from them: *GRAFTON, BELLE VUE, PARKING.* Further on, the lanes were narrower and busier, the little whitewashed houses packed with people. On the hill, the mansions stood. These were the places where his father worked, trimming the hedges, doing repairs, cleaning the guttering. Each day, Michael brought his father's lunch, a little bread, a slice of cold meat or some cheese, whatever was available. At first, he'd been resentful of the chore; later, he saw the way it lent a structure to his day, gave him an air of independence. He'd pass the boys and nod to them, never too friendly, never looking like he needed them. He didn't tell them he was carrying his father's lunch. They didn't ask. Nothing he did, it seemed, could possibly concern them or arouse their curiosity; and he was too grown-up now to imagine he'd bamboozle them with games.

His father came back late, most nights. He smelt of booze and cigarettes, and stumbled in the dark, trying to get undressed. He wouldn't put the light on. He'd got a drunkard's courtesy, those times, moving so slowly every step would take an age.

Inevitably, Michael woke. He lay there with his eyes shut, feigning sleep. Sometimes his father muttered to himself. It was uncertain, broken-up, like hearing one half of a phone call.

Michael guessed it was his mother on the far end of the line, though what she told his father in those blurred, one-sided talks, he never could make out.

*

The sand looked grey, this time of year. Only a few old fishermen still went down to the beach to tend their boats, drawn up behind the groynes, out of the wind.

One day he found a strange thing, lying in a puddle on the sand, caught in a whirl of gulls. He shooed the birds away. They circled near and shrieked at him indignantly. The object might have been a small dog or a lamb, perhaps, but so mutated that he couldn't tell. Black knots of weed entangled it. A fattish, blue-grey tail with a translucent fin stuck out behind. 'It fell into the water and grew a tail to save itself,' he thought. A year ago, he might have buried it. Now he poked it with his shoe, watching the little, half-transparent creatures, shrimps and lice, that wriggled in its open belly.

Only when he left, the birds came down again. Their clamour filled his ears. It was as if a storm had fallen on the sands, frantic with greed, effacing everything: the feeding frenzy of the gods.

*

He had been travelling for four years, ever since his mother died.

His father couldn't settle. It was always just a few months here, a few months there... They moved between the coastal towns, sometimes inland, though never far. This was the winter town. Michael dreamed about it in the summer, when the beaches would be full of girls. He'd never seen it that way, but he'd heard the boys tell stories, talk of what they'd done, or claimed they'd done.

Also, he heard about the leopard girl.

81

Chink Loomis said he'd seen her. He'd been out one morning early, in the sand dunes near Little River. Said she lived down there, somewhere, away from people, where the townsfolk wouldn't see. She'd got no house, only a nest made out of grass, he said. That's what she lived in.

"And she's *nuddy*, right?" His chin stuck forward, and his eyes were bright with glee. "She hasn't got a stitch. You can see *everything*."

Chink was a tall, thin boy, who looked like he'd been stretched out past his proper height. He had a big red scar on one hand that went part way up his forearm, where doctors had removed a growth when he was young. The flesh looked rubbery and puckered, and he scratched at it as if it troubled him sometimes.

Chink was the oldest, and he worked down at the bakery, three days a week.

Michael listened, but he stood outside the group. He tried to judge when it was right to smile or laugh. He tried anticipating their reactions, joining them, acting like one of them. He caught the way they lounged, leaning on walls or squatting on the steps. He dug his thumbs into his pants pockets, the way he saw they did. When he began to get their actions right, to blend with them, he started to relax.

He saw Chink's cleverness was all in surfaces, the look of things, the what and where... All facts and figures. It still impressed him, only not the way it had. He hung back now, keeping his judgement, uncertain how much to believe.

*

The tin-roofed shack lay on the edge of town, a half hour's walk from Little River. He visited the river when he could. He even saw her, once, weeks afterwards, not in the dunes but in the rough country behind. She was a long way off. He didn't notice her until she moved. Then something seemed to streak across the hillside, very fast, below the skyline. Once it stopped, it seemed to vanish.

Michael put his hand up to his eyes. He didn't think about the leopard girl at first. He just kept staring, trying to work out what he'd seen. Only when she moved again, he caught a vague impression of her shape – not animal, four-legged, as he'd first supposed; but upright, moving with the rapid caution of a fox on open land.

She disappeared into the spinney close to Cotter's Field. He thought of going after her ('You can see everything...'), but couldn't budge. It felt like somebody was pressing on his chest, trying to force the air out of his lungs. His heart was racing. His hands shook and he held them to his sternum, trying to ease the pressure there.

He waited for a long, long time, watching till his eyes began to ache.

She didn't reappear.

*

He kicked a ball around with one of Chink's friends, Harry Moe. Michael stood in goal. Moe pranced and feinted, mimicking the crowd's applause, then turned and whacked the ball at him, trying to catch him off his guard.

It was Christmas Eve. White wedges had been painted on the windowpanes to look like snow, although it never snowed here any more. Michael wore a loose shirt and a vest. The air was mild. A pale haze hung across the world, so that the sunlight came down pallid and diffuse, the far hills disappeared like ghosts after the dawn.

Abandoning their game, they stopped for milkshakes at the Bluebird Cafe. Someone was grumbling about livestock: "...all they found was skin and bones, man..."

Michael turned round slowly. Three men, farmers, sat with mugs of tea, but none of them was talking now. Then Moe unscrewed the salt cellar, giggling as the stuff spilled, and the owner chased them out.

"I'll charge you for it, too, you bloody tearaways – "

Moe made V-signs with both hands, but only when the man was out of sight. "Fart-bum," he yelled. "Old fart-bum – "

*

Michael's father gave him a big red and purple kite for Christmas, diamond-shaped, the tail weighed down with twists of rag.

"To fly," he offered, awkwardly, as if it needed explanation. "Down on the beach... You and your friends..."

They ate cold lamb in sandwiches. Later his father went out to the pub, explaining that he 'had to see someone'. So Michael went out, too.

He found Chink and the fat boy on the prom. Chink lay back full length on a bench, eyes shut, his hands behind his head. The fat boy draped himself over a bollard, frowning as if deep in thought.

83

"Jane Millikan," he said at last.

Chink nodded to himself. "Good handful. Yeah. *Two* good handfuls. Why not?"

"Mary Compaine?"

"If I was desperate, you know?"

"Paula Binns?"

"God sake, man..."

"Gina Nesbitt?"

"You're sick, you are, that's what. You're bloody sick – "

They were both laughing. Gina Nesbitt, Michael knew, lived in the road up by the school. She must have been at least sixty years old.

The litany went on for several minutes. Names, and verdicts. But they never talked about the leopard girl, or not with Michael, anyway. She was too strange, too different from them... To look was one thing, but any more... He tried to think about it and got a weird sensation, like something catching in his throat.

Sometimes he thought he saw her in the town. A movement at the corner of his eye, reflection in a window... But always, when he turned, she'd gone.

He knew she must be near. He didn't understand, but he could feel her, somehow, like a special scent, the way you feel the seasons change, or sense the rain before the clouds have even gathered in the sky.

*

He found her one night, rooting in the dustbins by the shack next door. He thought it was a dog at first. He went to shoo it off, but when she moved the moonlight caught her dappled pelt, turning it silver, and he knew.

She seemed to flick out of existence for a moment. He could hear her breath. Then he saw her once more, deep down in the shadows, motionless. Each time she stopped she seemed to vanish, and he stared into the darkness, half-imagining her shape.

He couldn't bring himself to say hello.

He made soft, soothing noises, as if calling to a cat: *tch_ tch*... He took a step towards her, holding out his hand, until a low growl like a truck engine suddenly froze him in his tracks. Was it a person or an animal in front of him? He didn't know. He caught her odour, faint and warm, tangy with urine, and yet much too mild to be unpleasant.

Abruptly, then, she broke her cover, and she ran.

She made no sound. She moved so quickly he could hardly tell which way she'd gone. Far off, he heard the *shush* of breakers on the shore, like the echo of some ancient factory machine, like spindles turning, shuttles rushing back and forth.

He stumbled over rubbish from the upturned bins. Beneath his foot he found a doll, one arm gone, its nylon hair all shiny white under the moon.

Was this what she'd been looking for?

*

"We ought to talk," his father said. "You know... The way we used to. We ought to do things, you and me..." His face was dark from working out of doors so much. It never paled, even in wintertime.

The man made gestures, fumbling for his words.

"I don't know what you're thinking any more," he muttered, helplessly.

Then he went out again, and Michael was alone.

*

A yellow sky rose like a wall above the hills. He begged for offal and old bones down at the butcher's shop, to feed a dog he didn't have. That night, after his father left, he laid them out, a careful trail across the wild land down behind the shacks.

He waited.

It took two nights. Then, the second morning when he looked, the lures were gone.

He went back to the butcher's once again.

"Some appetite," the man said. "Big dog, is he?"

"Very big." He said the first breed he could think of, then, his favourite, the best.

"A standard poodle," he explained. "Called Rex."

*

"Dad," he said. "I had a dream last night..."

His father shook his head. "Nobody dreams these days. Only the land dreams now." But he insisted, and at last his father told him, "Well then... Perhaps it was the echo of a dream."

He knew his father still didn't believe him, though. He dug his

85

hands into his pockets, hunching up his shoulders till his collar brushed against his ears.

"I did," he said, under his breath. "I did, I did, I did..."

*

Chink held the book out teasingly. The boys all gathered round. They peered and grinned. The fat boy bucked his hips, pretending to have a hard-on like a wooden spar.

Once Michael would have huddled up with them, craning to see, but now he only glanced and hurried by, as if he'd got a mission to perform.

People were talking about animals: dead animals, dead sheep, dead birds... And lambing season coming up, as well, they said.

They'd had this kind of trouble other years. The older ones remembered it. They knew what needed doing. But instead they sat around, waiting for someone else to act: the mayor, the police, or else some outside agency...

While they did that, he knew that she was safe.

He laid the trail again.

*

She was his height, but looked smaller, for she crouched habitually. She was aware of him. She knew that he was there, back in the dark behind the window. She came cautiously, mistrustfully: but not afraid.

He hoped she recognised him now.

He'd left the marrow bone out in the yard. Beside it was the little plastic doll.

He watched her hesitate a moment, then seem to slide herself into the light, eyes huge and luminous.

Her fur was dappled, like a lynx's or a lion cub's, more than a leopard's. On her belly, it was pale. He glimpsed a tufting, a thickening of hair between her legs. His breath caught. He saw her breasts were slight and girlish, naked bar a gentle, near-white down. Her arms were long and slender, and the muscles moved within them, visibly, like pistons in a sheath of fur.

His belly hollowed, watching her.

Seeing her grace.

She stepped into the yard as if she bore no weight at all, a dancer, unconstrained by human rules. Her feet – her paws – were large. Dirt

86

smeared her toes. She moved towards him, elegant, implacable.

He noticed a clear patterning of marks, a trio of dark dabs across one shoulder, like a *fleur-de-lys* tattoo.

She reached down quickly, snatched the bone up, then the doll, and clutched them to her belly; her movements were like liquid, almost too swift to be seen. Her head was massive. Cat-like. Pointed ears twitched, flicked, responding to some sound he couldn't hear. Her jaws were long and powerful, thrust forward in a muzzle like a beast's. She gripped the bone and stared straight back at him; her black lips curled, revealing teeth of such enormity and sharpness he felt a sudden chill, knowing that these were weapons meant to kill, to murder in a second, if she chose.

And then his terror passed.

A snarl? No, not a snarl. A smile. A smile of thank you; shy, and cautious, and intelligent.

*

The boys would act as beaters.

Michael stood aside, wanting to be somewhere else, but knowing he'd be thought a coward if he didn't join. He held a saucepan and a heavy, short stick. Some boys had home-made weapons – Chink bore an assegai almost as big as he was, a broomstick with a knife tied to it; but all that was just for show. The executioners were farmers. They hid beside the river, waiting for the boys to drive their quarry down, onto their guns.

All night, Michael had lain awake. He'd made his plans. He'd thought about them till his head buzzed and they'd seemed as real as if they were already done and over with: he'd leave the others, circle round, run through the woods and warn her; he'd give away the gunmen's hide, somehow, or else – most nobly, and most damningly – he'd interpose himself, a human shield, between the killers and their prey.

Even as the sun came up, he'd still believed these options would be open to him, still felt he was free to choose.

Now though, beneath the eyes of Chink and his companions, and the nearby adults, he'd no course other than to join the hunt, beating his pan half-heartedly, or yelling when he thought someone was watching him.

They started out from different points, in fields and copses, all across the landscape, drawing slowly closer to each other as they walked.

It took all afternoon.

The sun was small and white, giving a little gentle heat. Michael fell back. He detoured, climbed a bluff to get a better view of what was happening; hopeful, but frightened, too. All round, the clatter of old kitchenware, the ululation of the beaters, set up resonances in the atmosphere. Small creatures fled. The birds took flight as if tugged violently into the sky. The air itself appeared to shiver and vibrate.

Ahead, he saw the line of trees that marked the Little River, and their journey's end.

The town no longer held him then. He wanted to be gone from it, away from Chink and Harry Moe, from all the girls in pleated skirts, the gossip that he only part-way understood. He wanted to deny he'd ever envied that – deny what he was part of now.

And yet, he knew, to any onlooker, he'd seem like one of them: another hostile resident, another willing soldier of the hunt.

And that was how the girl would see him, too.

The beaters closed on one another. Michael ran behind their lines. The briars snagged his ankles, bloodying his socks. He fled down to the beach. The wind tore at his hair. The ocean raged, and drove great waves against the shore, clawing and battering.

And that was where he found her. Or where she found him.

She slipped so quickly from the shadows of the cliff the world around her seemed to freeze. Time stopped. She knew that she was hunted and her hiding place was gone. Her great jaws moved, the blackened lips split open on a row of massive teeth. He held his hands up. "Please –" She ran at him. His feet slid in the sand, his legs gave way. And then she leapt.

He felt the wind of her flight, the taloned feet that missed him by just inches; and when he looked again, she was already far along the beach, running at a speed it was impossible to guess; while overhead, the seagulls screamed.

*

At evening, small groups of people moved across the land, uncertain now, devoid of purpose.

Their noose had come apart. They wandered, one way and another, sometimes with a sudden, last-ditch burst of pot-clanging and yelling, as if attempting to summon back their old enthusiasm. Once, a few shots had been fired; but it was only someone venting his frustration shooting blackbirds.

She had eluded them.

For all of Michael's plans, she hadn't needed him. She had escaped alone, by luck, or cunning, or some other means he couldn't guess.

She'd gone, he knew. She'd never come back now.

He wished he hadn't been so scared, wished he'd had the presence to explain, point out he'd had no choice, he hadn't really sided with her enemies... Excuses flickered through his head, but they were feeble, useless things. He couldn't answer his own accusations. He couldn't even hope to answer hers.

*

"What's this about a dog?" his father said. He wanted to sound angry, but it only came out puzzled and unsure. He fumbled with his jacket collar, turned it up, then down again. "It made me look a bloody fool. *How's your dog?* he says to me. *How's your bloody dog?*"

Michael didn't answer. He stared out of the window, at the new year's growth already brightening the bushes and the trees. Soon, the foliage would be so thick it might hide anything, anything at all...

His father, at a loss, pretended to be hunting something in his pockets, as he often did when he was trying to stall for time. Then, giving up, he said, "Is it a dog you want, then? Is that it?"

*

The bus driver had helped them stow their cases in the hold. The bus was almost empty. Michael and his father sat apart, both gazing at the scenery. Now there were flowers by the roadside, bright red poppies, yellow daffodils, brought by the fresh spring rains. A single cloud hung in the sky, slowly dissolving in the morning sun.

He'd hoped to feel the dream winds once again before he left, only they hadn't come.

He closed his eyes, the sunlight warm and red against his lids.

He could imagine, very clearly now, the texture of her fur, smooth as a cat's, clotted with dirt and burs; he'd reach out with his hand and gently brush her clean. The fur would have direction, like a current, like the sea. He brushed it all one way. His fingers traced the patterns of it. The dapples. The *fleur-de-lys*. Then, underneath, he felt the muscles sliding on each other, smooth, like well-oiled cables, so powerful he knew that, had she truly turned on him that day, nothing on Earth would have preserved him from her wrath.

The muscles tensed and moved. She reached out and she put her arms around him, tenderly; and held him there, forever.

*

His father asked again from time to time just what he wanted. A dog? A normal home, in one place, like his friends? His father seemed to think himself responsible for Michael's listlessness, adding to the air of guilt he carried round with him. But Michael couldn't tell him it was something else, something his father had no bearing on; he couldn't even find the words he needed to explain.

He took the kite with him, but then, before he got around to flying it, the struts detached themselves, the sail bagged like an empty shirt. When he noticed that, he hid it from his father, hoping to spare the old man's feelings.

He never saw the leopard girl again.

Home in the Light

He asks me out. It's pitiful.

"Please please please *please* – "

I can't even say no straight off, he's that pathetic. I just um and ah, and shrug a bit, and hope he gets the message anyway, before I've really got to spell it out.

He doesn't though.

No, does he heck.

Next night he's back. He stares at me. Just sits, and stares. It's like I'm Demi Moore or somebody. Up close, his skin's all smooth and sleek, like polythene, it gleams under the light. He's got no proper pores or something, I don't know. That's what I heard.

I feel my neck hairs prickle, just from being near. I tell him, "Look," I say. "I'm flattered, right? Honest I am. But it just makes me sick, you know? The whole idea. It makes me ill. Alright?"

I pull a face and rub my stomach, demonstrating, but he doesn't care. He's thrilled I've even talked to him. His eyes light up, this gimpy little smile begins to quiver on his lips, his fingers come together in a prayer.

"Tonight?" he begs. "Tomorrow night?"

"Not *any* night. Got that?"

I light a fag, blow smoke straight in his face.

But still, he reaches out, as gentle as a bird, and strokes my arm.

"Please then," he says. "During the day...?"

91

That's him. That's how he is. He never understands a thing, unless it suits him to. And sometimes, well – not even then.

*

We call him 'E.T.' or 'the Alien'. He hasn't got a name. He's tall and thin, dressed in a long grey coat down to his ankles, always buttoned up.

It hides him well. You'd reckon he was human, most days, if you didn't look too closely, or too long.

Or see him walk.

He'll sway past, reeling like a flagpole in a heavy wind. Or sit, and cross his legs too high, too low, some place a leg just doesn't have a knee. A proper leg, at any rate.

He hates it if you notice though. Hates looking out of place. If he thinks you've seen, he'll curl up, cringe, go almost purple with embarrassment.

He never takes his coat off.

Never.

Some people say he sleeps in it, curled head to toe like an old rubber tyre: a perfect, boneless curve... But how do they know, anyway? There's no-one says they've seen, no-one who'll admit. They just know, they say, that's all. They *know*.

*

I watch him down the pub one night. Can't help myself. I'm fascinated, somehow, seeing how he sits, this little glass of spring water held pincer-like in thumb and forefinger, delicate as jewellery.

I count the fingernails. The knuckle joints. They'll pass, alright. They'll pass.

But only just.

It's how he uses them, like foreign cutlery, or tools he's read about in some quick, botched apprenticeship, a long way from the Grant's Arms and from all of us.

His fingers, hands... Oh yes. *Hands of the Alien.*

They mark him for an amateur, a semi-competent – a fool.

He's shy. Won't even talk without a brief, preliminary cough, a "Please – " or an "Excuse me – ", like some foreign student, anxious not to give offence.

He lectures us on alcohol. Our relish for toxicity amazes him.

"But this is poison," he protests. "It damages the liver and the brain – impairs the motor functions – it leads to faulty judgement, false self-confidence – "

He sounds so serious, we laugh like drains.

"My new-found friends," he cries. "This is a very risky thing you do – "

So someone goes up to the bar, buys him a pint, and claps him on the back.

"There goes, mate. Get it down your neck, and cut the chit-chat, will you?"

It's his first social success.

It goes straight to his head, more forcefully than alcohol could ever do.

His life begins to change, from that night on.

*

"Bloody Alien."

I'm telling Jean and Barry, out there in the Close. They think it's all hilarious. They think it's wonderful.

I turn around, appeal to Ahmed, busy cleaning rust spots off his car.

"He won't leave me alone," I say.

"Good taste," says Ahmed, and he winks. He's got a wire brush in his hand. I feel like I could tell him what to do with it.

"He follows me around – "

Then Barry hums the tune from *Close Encounters*, and Jean starts giggling, and she digs me in the ribs.

"Close encounters eh?" she says, in case I haven't got the joke. "I mean, like – *close encounters*, eh?"

I wonder why I talk to people, sometimes, why I bother. Honestly I do.

*

He's moved into a squat, two blocks away. Got somebody to change the lock, and someone else to fix the gas and the electric. He's just not practical that way. He'll witter on for hours about the speed of light, quasars, pulsars, all that stuff, but when it's down to nuts and bolts, fuses and plugs, he's useless, like it's all beneath him, somehow, just too trivial to touch.

93

"Your world," he tells me, "*our* world – yes?"

"Maybe," I say.

Don't hold your breath.

He's writing off for jobs. He wants to be *responsible*, he says, he wants to *pay his way*... He signs his name as Cary Grant, because on telly, Cary Grant is always rich, and suave, and always gets the girl.

He thinks a name's a role or a profession, something to aspire to, and I try to disillusion him. He's not convinced.

"You can't send this," I say. "You need experience, qualifications... You've got to have a C.V., right?"

I rub my brow. He copies: first a little frown, pursed lips; his hand comes up and strokes across his forehead.

"God sake," I say.

He murmurs, diligently, "God sake..."

"Look. Make out you've been abroad, OK? Like you've been teaching somewhere. Saudi. Yemen. No-one's going to check."

He tuts just like a village schoolmaster.

"That's lying, though," he says.

I ask him how else he thinks anyone gets work these days – and who the hell's this Cary Grant when he's at home, in any case?

The name's a different matter, though.

He never tells me how.

And there's a pattern I've begun to see, a method in the way he works.

It's like the whole time, he's just looking round for someone to take care of him, someone to help... To give him clothing, food and furniture – whatever else he thinks he wants.

And people do. They do. They all feel sorry for him. He's so vague, so lost-looking, so tall and bumbling, like a stretched-out child.

I start to think he *likes* the way they run round after him. I think he *likes* the fuss, and the attention – all the do-gooders, the church people, the socialists, the anarchists, the little networks of community... He likes the kind of power it gives him over them.

If someone loses patience, then that's fine by him. He'll drop them, move to someone new.

Like me, for one.

He tells me, if he's got a girlfriend, it'll make him more acceptable,

94

then, won't it? And he'll fit in better, won't he? And everyone will like him more...?

I can't believe he thinks I'm moved by this, I really can't.

I shut my eyes and all I see is kinky stuff, prosthetics, weird drugs, body fluids, sex organs like something off a crab or cuttlefish... And I think, *No, no, no, no, no.*

I sneer at him. I'm cruel. I laugh at all his efforts at seduction, his clumsiness, his absolute stupidity. I tell myself it's kinder, giving him the truth like this, though deep, deep down, I know it's not.

It's only easier, that's all.

For me.

*

He gets depressed.

He sits with us, but doesn't talk much any more; he's realised no-one cares about cosmology – black holes and superstrings – the kind of stuff that interests him. We want a bit of gossip, local stories... Things he can't provide.

He starts to loath his individuality. He loathes whatever marks him out. He gets his hair cut short, thinking it's fashionable; he glues a bottle-top onto his coat front like a badge.

These things don't help.

He drinks.

Not much, at first, though the effects on him are strange. He doesn't stagger and he doesn't slur his words, he gets abstracted and distant, staring over people's heads at vague, uncertain spaces in the air... He'll saunter down the middle of the road, then stop, stock still, like he's forgotten where he is. Cars honk and swerve. He doesn't hear, he doesn't see. We try to warn him about muggers, cops. "It's dangerous, you know?" He thanks us, nods, then does it all again, the next night, and the next.

Till there's a time when he's so bad that even I can't leave him, and I drag him by the arm. I take him home. I make him coffee, roll myself a spliff.

I light up. Just the two of us, alone.

The only time.

That's when he talks about his home.

I'm floaty, spaced by then; I feel the blood flow in my arm, the

weight of it, I watch the patterns of the candle flame against the wall...
And I suppose I'm lost in stuff like that – sensations – and miss the first
part. He's been talking for a while before I finally tune in and listen.

By then I wish I could go back and make him start again, but I
don't dare to interrupt. It feels like, if I even breathe too loud, he'll get
self-conscious, stop. His voice is thin and tenuous, a thread the
slightest wind could break.

He's talking about light.

Seasons of light.

Days when the light's so high and sharp, so clear, it seems to fill
you with its energy; days when the distant mountains look so close that
you could almost reach out and take hold of them, or when a leaf
becomes so solid and so real, the veins in it seem sturdy as the struts
on some great iron bridge... Such days are wild and vigorous, he says:
the days when empires are conceived, careers carved out, courtships
begun; when life takes on a rapid, fierce dynamic, as if a year's activity
were squeezed into a few brief weeks.

And there are quiet seasons, too. Long days of introspection and
philosophy; cool shadows stencilling their patterns on the land,
transforming it to new and unfamiliar shapes...

I take another lungful of the smoke, and feel it lift me up, like a
balloon inside the head.

But then there's something he calls 'stain light', 'storm light' – he
can't quite pick a word for it. A light that you can feel, that drills down,
deep into your skull, bites you, torments you (and I can see a picture of
a man surrounded by mosquitoes, insects made of flame, buzzing and
whining; insects that you can't just flick away). In stain light, storm
light, you know ahead of time all your decisions will be bad, and then
you make them anyway. You misread signs. Somebody speaks, you
hear things in their words they never meant... A headache throbs behind
your eyes, a pressure, filling you; a quarrelsomeness, helplessness, lack
of control...

His voice is low, hypnotic, heavy with nostalgia. He isn't watching
me, he's staring into space, at something only he can see. One arm's
bent up behind his back, one hand clutching his shoulder so it looks
like someone else's hand. His face seems flattened, geometrical –
almost designed.

"You wake up in the morning, look out of the window, and you know exactly what kind of a day it's going to be," he says. "Things make more sense there. They're more... orderly..."

I want to ask him why he left. I keep on thinking of it but the question seems to tangle in my head, till I can't put it into words.

He seems to hear it anyway.

He talks about a process he calls 'folding', some way you can fold the substance of his world, push through from one day to another, transform the sequence of the hours. Pursue the seasons that once worked for you, live them again, but doing new things, launching new and grander plans.

In his world, so he says, successful people live their whole lives on a brief, bare handful of auspicious days, recycling them continually; they meet themselves a thousand times, exchanging information, passing tips down from the future, reworking and recycling past ambitions... With repetition, paths from one day to another grow well-worn, and easier to take.

To visit these high-flyers, you have to visit their auspicious days, the kind of days you know already give them more advantages than you could ever have.

Because, for most people, life's less clear cut. They fold with just a loose idea of where they might come out. They fold and hope.

Each bad day means the paths to bad days grow more frequent, and more easily traversed. Stain light and bad luck cluster like the Furies in some weird Greek play.

I think that, trying to outrun his bad days, he somehow folded so far that he missed, not just his target, but his whole world, everything, and wound up here, with us, instead.

*

That night's the end of it for him and me.

He shuts up like a clam. Won't talk to me, won't look at me. Like he's betrayed himself, he's said too much. He won't come near.

I almost miss him. That's the stupid thing. I almost do.

I hear about him, hanging round with some big drugs crowd now, all crack and heroin, the sleazy stuff I never touch. Perhaps he's trying to blot things out. Or bring back that special quality of light he dreams about, that feeling of a universe more orderly than ours.

97

If so, the drugs are failures, wasted time.

He's more and more on edge. He can't adjust. Now there's a panic in his actions that just wasn't there before. He paints his flat, inside and out, bright blue: blue walls, blue ceilings, windows, carpets, furniture... He keeps his telly running, day and night. The neighbours hammer on the wall. He won't come out. He disappears for weeks. He doesn't talk...

I see him, one time, imitate Old Ken, the drunk from three doors down; and God, he's good, alright: frowning and scowling, barking, shouting, face all twisted, furious – and then, like someone threw a switch, he stops, dead calm, and walks away.

There's worse to come.

He can't *belong*. He can't *fit in*. He starts to copy people, duplicating every move, miraculously, perfectly. You watch him in the pub, resting his chin against his hand, lifting an eyebrow, scratching at his crotch; and then, after a while, you spot the model on the far side of the room, maybe, someone anticipating every gesture by the barest fraction of a second.

And there's people take offence. You bet there are. Plenty of times, somebody's got to bail him out, step in and make excuses, stop him getting thumped.

Like all my friends, I've gradually abandoned him. He's got too weird, too difficult.

And now I've problems of my own as well.

The building's coming down. They've sold the land, they're going to put up office blocks. Six years I've lived here. Now I'm out. No deals, no bargaining. That's it.

I see him one last time before I go. He's up there on the roof, the place he lives, six stories high. He's pacing back and forth along the parapet. The height just doesn't bother him. A crowd's begun to gather down below, excited, curious – expecting blood.

I'm worried the police'll come. I'm worried, after all this time, he'll fall into the hands of the authorities. They'll lock him up. They'll question him, experiment on him, God knows. He's not my friend. He's not. Only I don't want that. I don't want that.

I climb the stairs. I'm out of breath before I reach the roof. I can't go near the edge, I just don't dare. I yell at him. He won't acknowledge me at first; but then, he turns, and looks. Black clouds are massing up behind him, sliding over us just like a lid.

I beg him to come down. I beg him to.

But he won't stir.

The last thing that I say to him is this: "Go home. Go back. This place is killing you. You can't stay here."

His lips move slightly, and his voice brings just the faintest echo of the words, like ghost tracks on an old cassette.

And then the rain starts up. It dribbles off his nose, it slips across his skin like glycerine; it soaks into his hair. It drives me back towards the stairwell, where it's dry.

I turn, just once, and look at him, this fragment from another world... And I just wonder... Could I? *Could* I? And would it all have turned out different if I had?

The Anti-Fan

It was the *Sunday Times* that did it.

"Downey's new routines," their guest reviewer wrote, "are like the works of Kafka, filtered through the brain of Beckett, retold by a Nintendo-age Max Miller... Seldom have the pangs of youthful angst been so incisive, or uproarious."

The act was changing all the time, of course; it always had. And yet from that point on, it seemed to take a new and darker turn. The crowd pleasers – the willy gags and tampon jokes, the digs at fitness freaks and people with unfunny T-shirt slogans – all these were nudged into the encores, or dropped entirely, replaced by long, discursive monologues in which he no longer took characters (as he'd been noted for) but *was* the character; his own life pinned out, raw and bleeding, like a specimen in some grotesque anatomy display.

Because the portrait wasn't flattering. It was as if deliberately he'd set out to destroy the very image he'd worked so hard to create, the it-boy, fashion-addict and compulsive clubber who'd turned heads all over London... Now, it seemed that he did almost nothing, but in endless, bone-wearying detail. He woke up, opened his eyes ("like prising up the lid on Pharaoh's tomb"); a hundred little things went wrong for him, a hundred little inconveniences snagging at his nerves. He put both feet into the same pants leg. He missed a step, coming downstairs, and nearly fell, but *didn't quite*. He burnt the toast. He found the marge was full of gritty black specks, because he'd burnt the toast the day before as well, and there was marge mixed with the marmalade inside the marmalade jar. "Don't you just hate that? Don't you *loathe* it? All that lovely golden marmalade, all smeared with grease and bits of toast crumbs, and you think, *what messy bastard's done all this? Couldn't they even clean it up? What gits, what animals* – And then you realise. *I'm* the only one uses the marmalade. *I'm* the only one has breakfast here. Because, you see – I live alone. And no-one comes to see me any more. No-one spends the night. The last time – honestly, the last time I had sex, I was so young, I had to get my dad's permission first. It's true..."

He still looked like an angel, though. No-one who knew him ever quite believed the stories of his loneliness, his empty life – he was too *busy* for an empty life, for God's sake, and the girls came flocking round his dressing room just like they'd flocked round rock stars in the days gone by. Don't say he never took advantage there. Besides – wasn't there something just a little odd about this new act, anyway? The handsome, smart, athletic boy who yearns to be the classroom nerd? Like Walter Mitty in reverse? Just what was that about, in any case?

He grew his hair long, left it matted and uncombed, developed an ungainly, shambling walk, and even off-stage, sometimes, could be seen to limp. He mimed disaster, hid his own inherent grace. But most remarkable of all, perhaps, the audience – whom many had predicted would desert in droves – they lapped it up. They loved him, all over again. Would-be sophisticates, who'd once dismissed him as a boring pretty boy, grew suddenly intrigued. Existing fans found something deeper and more binding in his work than they could ever have imagined; they saw their own flaws, magnified, the failings of their friends blown up to giant size... And forked out for his gigs accordingly.

He had detractors. Still, who hadn't? Folk who'd been with him back in the early days, who said he'd never been the best of that crowd, just the pushiest, most desperate to get on. He never saw them any more. His former friends and rivals, both alike, had vanished from his life. It wasn't planned. It wasn't snobbery, like some said. Just that he moved in different circles now, he worked so hard, there wasn't time to keep in touch.

And so it shocked him, to discover the resentment he aroused. Right on the threshold of success, so nearly making it... To learn that he was hated, too. It wasn't fair. It wasn't just. And worse: it hurt him. It really, really did.

He'd gone out to the pub one night, just to a local, nowhere *media*; Downey and a few mates, nice guys, part of his latest entourage. He'd wanted to relax. Unwind. A quiet, easy night, abruptly shattered by the voice that bawled at him across the barroom:

"Downey! Paying for your own drinks now, are you?"

He froze. He wouldn't answer, wouldn't look up, wouldn't even show he'd heard.

"Hey – Downey!"

It was a long, long time since he'd been heckled on the stage. His gigs cost twenty quid a throw these days. It kept the riff-raff out.

His friends, smart guys, were talking politics and history. The Cold War, Klaus Fuchs, how the Russians got the Bomb. And Downey, still half listening, could feel the germ of an idea start in his mind, already testing it, trying it this way, that, to see if it would run: *So there's Klaus Fuchs, Philip K. Dick and Jackson Pollock, they're all sitting in a bar, and...*

"Downey! Lend us a tenner, will you mate? You bloody owe me, you do."

His friends hugged round, protecting him, as if he were a prize someone might try to steal from them. "Relax," he said. "It's just some arsehole..." By now he'd singled out the culprit, a plump-faced young man in a beret and goatee, like a disgruntled beatnik. Downey's age, or thereabouts. Someone he knew? Someone he'd known? But then he'd known so many... Was there something just a bit familiar here, something he recognised...?

He told his friends, "Come on. I don't need this. Let's piss off out of it."

They stood; but as he reached the door, the voice came once more, sharp as a razor slash: "Don't tell him any jokes, will you? 'Cos if you do – he'll fucking *nick* them off you, won't he? Won't you, Downey, mate?"

Till that moment, Downey'd kept his cool. But now he whirled, a fury blazing in his face.

"You – "

The young man merely smiled, drew on his cigarette, then, still holding Downey's gaze, blew smoke at him.

A stranger.

Downey was sure of it. He'd never seen the man before in all his life. And the words he'd meant to say died in his throat.

Helpful, avaricious hands ushered him out, into the safety of the street. Clinging fingers brushed his hair and straightened his lapels. They fussed over the look of his cravat. There was another pub close by, a better pub, they said. "You'll love it there, Mike, it's a great place..."

"Mike." They used his first name all the time. Mike, Mike, Mike. As if by saying it they drew him closer, became old and trusted friends.

There was a girl with them – Jeanette? Janine? – who slipped her arm through his and snuggled up to comfort him, then wrote her number on his shirtsleeve with a felt tip pen. "Call Saturday," she said. "My boyfriend's going away..."

The evening, though, was ruined, and he went home early and alone. He woke at ten the next day, a dryness in his throat, a stiffness in his limbs, and something nagging in his memory, like the echo of an ugly dream.

He forced himself from bed, put both feet in the same pants leg, swore, rubbed at his eyes, took several Paracetomol, and went downstairs to burn the toast.

*

He did a chat show on TV, determined to talk straight for once. No script, no jokes, no silliness. He'd be himself now, let the public see him as he really was. He owed them that, he thought; or owed himself.

Asked for the best part of success, he pondered for a while, then answered truthfully, "Having your own tour bus."

He caught the faintest tremor of a laugh, a sound just like a small wave breaking on a sunny day.

Dismayed, he sipped his Evian.

Asked for the worst part, he said, "It's like... like, everybody wants a *piece* of you, you know? Like everyone wants something that you've got..."

104

The interviewer hovered, raised his brows expectantly.

"Or something that you haven't," Downey said, straight-faced.

The studio erupted.

It was hopeless. Even when he wanted to be honest, they *still* thought he was joking. He gave up. From then on, he did gags and silly voices, talked about his girlfriend problems, and the audience – they roared. They begged for more. He did old sketches, tried out new ones. Applause went on interminably, forcing him to higher flights of fancy, spasms of hilarity... He didn't even try. He could have read his laundry list and he'd have had them in the aisles.

Two years ago, he would have begged for such acclaim.

Now, it felt like someone draining blood out of his neck.

*

The critics were less kind. It was the surest sign of his success. He was too big for them, too popular; it didn't matter how they'd championed him once, when he was theirs, their own discovery, their pet; they'd never manage to forgive him going public, as it were. "Mike Downey's self-obsessive whine," wrote one, and every gig he played sold out. "Dreary Downey," wrote another, and his fans perched on their seatbacks, straining for each nuance, every hint and shade that he could offer them. His tone grew more and more confiding, more intimate. ("I've got to talk to you. I've got to, 'cos my girlfriend doesn't understand...")

"Being famous," he once said, "it's like the front seat on the big dipper, you know? Like, you pay to get in, and it's dead exciting – up you go, it's wonderful, wave to your friends – then *whooo*, over the top, and suddenly you're screaming, *Get me out! Get me out!*"

He'd poured his insecurities into his act, and now he poured them back again, into his life.

He told his manager, "I'm losing it. It's all slipping away..."

His manager ran one hand through his greying hair, and wondered how he'd ever got caught up with these artistic types. He'd trained to be a meat technologist, a decent, serious profession; everything since had been a detour, a louche if lucrative distraction from reality.

"You're paranoid," he said. "Forget it," and he listed Downey's recent triumphs, TV show and sell-out tour, with bookings pouring in already for the next.

105

But Downey quibbled like a barrister. "I saw some empty seats."

"That's 'cos they rush the stage. They *love* you, Mike. They want to sleep with you, for Christ sake – all of 'em. Even the lads." He chuckled, lit a panatela. "Might even fancy you a bit myself, you play your cards right..."

But Downey wasn't listening.

"I don't think I can do it any more, that's all. I mean... it looks alright. I know that. It's professional and everything, but... it's like going through the motions. It's not in me any more..."

The manager gave his most sympathetic frown – he was good at that – then blew a smoke ring, and smiled, as if a lightbulb had just gone on in his head.

"Well, my friend. I'd say that what you need is just a wee bit of a break, uh-hm? A working holiday? Change of direction? There's something I've been meaning to discuss with you..."

*

He went to Paris, checked into a small hotel off Place Pigalle. The district had a charm all of its own, a mix of sleaze and bourgeois cosiness, where shopkeepers displayed their wares, comfy-looking matrons brought their kids to school; while just around the corner, sex clubs throbbed and drooled, and touts called out to him, offering 'suckee-fuckee', 'boy-girl', and other items in the international pidgin of the sex trade. Only a foreigner – no, only an Englishman, he thought – would have been shocked by the proximity of two such different and yet complementary worlds.

At night, across from his hotel, a massive black woman would stand, jigging to music only she could hear. Her fringed skirt scarcely draped her crotch. She'd approached him twice during his first days here, but now ignored him. He nodded sometimes as he passed. She eyed him with a bland contempt.

He would have liked to talk, strike up a conversation. Take her for a drink, perhaps... At sixteen he'd read Henry Miller. Seeing her wide, black shoulders and her massive, idol's face, he knew there was a story there, a novel infinitely better than the one he'd planned to write. Except his French came from the same time as the Miller books. Oh, he could order drinks and ask directions, tell people, "My name is, and I live in," but he couldn't talk to prostitutes. It was a lesson sadly missing from his schoolboy language class.

Each day began with croissants and a lukewarm *café au lait*, after which he'd dutifully return to his hotel room, open his laptop, and then work till dinner time.

This, according to the press release, would be his 'first' novel, inviting prospects of unending follow-ups. His manager was right. It was the proper thing to do. A novel leant him gravitas and dignity, a novel would establish him, in ways being a stand-up never could.

And so he typed. At first, the prose moved confidently, rattling along, then less well; then it stuttered. He spent more and more time staring at the screen, reading the newspaper, or lighting up *Disques Bleus* in an attempt to jog his mind. The plot was all laid out. It shouldn't have been hard. The hero was a stand-up comic, hounded by his fans, who'd fled to Paris and become embroiled in espionage; these chapters alternated with his memories of school days, and the bully who'd tormented him for years – the bully who, grown up, would make his re-appearance as the villain's henchman in the Paris plot...

He'd practically extemporised the whole thing back in London, lunching with his publisher. Ideas had flowed from him, impossible to staunch; the publisher had made just one proviso. "Keep it funny, will you?" and he'd eyed up Downey with a shrewdness that had made him flinch. "Let's keep the Graham Greenes for later, eh?"

And he'd promised. He'd promised and he'd meant it, too. But now...

"7 a.m.," he typed. "McIlvey woke, opened his eyes (like prising up the lid on Pharaoh's tomb) and faced the hotel wallpaper. Roses, roses, roses... `A rose is a rose is a rose,' he thought, turned over, and went back to sleep."

That was the trouble: back to sleep. What next? To sleep, to wake again? He kept on hitting points like that, nice situations that refused to move him forward, full stops he couldn't jump. The overall storyline – well, that was easy. But these little, incidental moments – it wasn't like writing a sketch. Oh no. He couldn't handle them at all.

One evening, in a bar, he heard his name called, quite distinctly, "Downey!" and he turned, imagining some young fans must have spotted him, some students, here on holiday, perhaps. But he saw no-one. Nobody at all.

He sipped his wine. *Un rouge. Un balon rouge, monsieur, s'il vous plait.* The notebook lay in front of him, a few stray words, scattered down the page like pebbles on a tabletop, as if, by leaving spaces in between, he could pretend he'd written much more than he had.

He lit a cigarette. He liked the smell of other people's smoke more than his own; he was a passive smoker, and enjoyed it. At home he hardly ever smoked. But Paris... Paris was a town for smokers. Sometimes he woke up coughing in the night. His chest hurt. All he had to do was finish off his book. Finish the book, go home, and never smoke again –

"Downey!"

His head shot up. He peered about. Something unpleasant in the voice; not a fan's voice, more like a schoolteacher's, or...

"Downey, you little *shit.*"

He glared around the bar. No-one had spoken. No-one had even glanced at him. He checked behind: met only blank wall.

Someone had just called him a shit!

Someone in here, someone –

His temples ached. His vision fogged, a pulse beat in his forehead, and he sucked the cigarette to calm himself. He gulped his wine. A moment later, he wrote this:

"He worked for fame, and when it came, he ran from it, like a commuter leaping from an express train, or a housewife, wilfully dismantling the dishwasher, then leaving home."

They were the last words he would ever write in Paris.

*

He wasn't fleeing fame. Anything but. Yet the idea of running... It stuck with him, it fascinated him, a toy he couldn't work out how to use.

He walked to Père Lachaise, thinking of Morrison, imagining the singer hadn't died, he'd faked his death and fled. A second novel, *Mr Mojo Risin*, slid seductively into his mind. An easier book, possibly, promising release from the first. Morrison in Africa, like Rimbaud. Morrison the gun-runner. Morrison the golf pro. The gynaecologist. The stand-up comic...

It began to rain. The pavements shone like polished leather. The city held no glamour here, no tourist-traps or monuments. The crowds pushed by him. Passers-by looked harried and unwell. Many were arab, some were black. Perhaps he ought to move here, get to know the

'real' Paris. A bit of local colour, local life... The shops sold spiced
Tunisian food. He stopped to peer into a window, weighing up the
option of a couple of samosas (and the prospect of a gut ache later on),
when something in the glass caught his attention. Reflected there, a
roundish face, a dark goatee –

He spun. The man was gone.

He walked on. Once more his head began to throb, a dull beat
pulsing through his skull; his appetite was gone. And yet a million
people wore goatees – especially the French! His eyes were tricking
him. His mind was tricking him. And oh, alright, he'd stolen jokes –
who hadn't? But it wasn't really stealing, not a bit. You saw some act,
some no-hope dying on his feet, and maybe there was one line, one gag,
one little thing that caught your fancy, and you... well. Adapted it.
Made it your own. It wasn't stealing, it was... Christ! He hadn't even
recognised the man! This was stupid! To be chased, pursued by... He
tried to calm himself. It wasn't the same man. Couldn't be. Who else
knew he was here? Who even cared? In England, certainly, in England,
he was loved, if in the fleeting way of youthful heroes. He was known
a little in Australia, too. But in the States, he was a whisper; in Canada,
a muffled sneeze. In France – a tourist, nothing more.

Afterwards, they said he'd had a fever, had it for days most likely,
fighting it, holding it off, the way he did when he was ill on tour, to
keep working at whatever cost.

It hit him when he reached the cemetery.

It hit him, and it hit him hard.

First weakness, like his bones had turned to water. Then the
pressure in his head. The world around him seemed to fold and twist,
the graves and obelisks stretched out, a sea of spikes, an endless bed
of nails under a hard, grey sky. Perspective changed. Size changed. If
he should fall, he'd cover the whole place, he felt, his feet would loll
over the edge, hands pierced and pinioned, body grown so huge he
couldn't tell where he left off and where the world began...

He stumbled, sucking air.

"Oh, jolly good. It's Oscar Wilde, come back to view the premises,
eh wot?"

The young man's sharp, Woosterish tones were sour with sarcasm.
He wore the beret and goatee, and picked his way over the graves as

over stepping stones. The light seemed to recede around him, simply to drain out of the air. Downey watched him from a long, dark tunnel, blackness closing, inch by inch. He fought for breath. For consciousness. He struggled for the kind of quip he'd launched at hecklers in the early days, but his tongue refused to work. "Buh-buh-buh – "

"*Bollocks*, is it, Mike? Best you can do, eh? *Bollocks*?"

The voice was soft, close, hideously intimate. He reached out, fell, but there was no pain, just a jolt, like landing on a mattress. Several chunks of gravel dug into his cheek. Events moved with an aching slowness, endlessly delayed, until he almost wanted to cry out, "Go on! Get on with it!" but couldn't find his voice. Nor, no matter how he tried, could he stand up again.

"Well then, Downey, me old mate, me old mucker – "

He'd seen too many films to question what would happen next. He braced himself, mouthed, "Not my face," he tried to plead, to beg, to fold himself so that his face, guts and genitals would be protected from the worst. He huddled, foetus-like. He had a sense of others round him, half-familiar figures, hating him, despising him, their voices gabbling in the dark...

And he was gone before the first blow fell.

*

Downey returned to England two days later, tottering and pale. His condition had been given as 'exhaustion', later as 'recovering from a virus'. There were whispers: 'exhaustion' meant cocaine, 'virus' meant AIDS. The gardens of his Greenwich home were stalked by paparazzi. His manager persuaded him to step out on the balcony, dressed in a blue silk robe, and wave, and smile.

"Good boy." The manager poured out another scotch. "Want one?"

Downey closed the curtains. "My scotch. I think I can decide whether I want a drink or not."

"Fair 'nuff, lad. Give 'em a good grin, did you? Keep 'em happy?"

Downey fidgeted. He went back to the window, pulled the curtains just a slit, peeped out.

"Something up, old son?"

"No. Yes..." He turned, digging his hands into the pockets of his robe. "I'll have that drink now, please. Thank you."

110

The manager applied himself to the cocktail cabinet (disguised as a TV set, something Downey had once found amusing, though no longer). And while the man's gaze was averted, Downey asked, too quickly, and his voice too high, "Did you see someone – bloke with a goatee? Bit plump? Goatee?"

*

The book was not the one he'd planned. He carefully disguised himself, made his hero a retired rock star, a sort of English Morrison, in Paris to write poems and the story of his life. But the man with the goatee, the bars, the cemetery, the two days on an IV drip – all that was real, and he wrote it quickly, hardly sleeping, as if by putting it on disc he'd leave it all behind him, wipe it from his life. Well, hadn't Nabokov said somewhere that, once he'd written about someone, that person finished being real for him, replaced by his own fiction?

It seemed to work for Downey, too, at first.

His publishers were rather less pleased. 'Clever', 'literary', 'postmodernist' – they complimented him, but in tones he could be fairly sure that Martin Amis never heard.

He sat there, stoically, swallowing the meagre praise, thinking at least the book was done, and with it, one part of his life was safely over, sealed off like the reactor in *The China Syndrome*. He was free now. He could start again. He had his hair cut short, shaved almost to his skull, pleased with the roundness it brought back into his face. He joined a gym, attending regularly, later buying weights to work out with at home. He told his manager he wanted to prepare another tour.

"I'm ready for it now, I think. The big one, eh?"

The 'big one' was a code they used: it meant the States.

"Great stuff. Great stuff. Few warm-ups here, first, eh? Tie in with the book, OK?"

"I'm ready. Yes I am." He shadow-boxed, right-left, left-left, right, then paused a moment, and in quieter tones, said, "I think I should learn self-defence, don't you? Kung fu, or judo... I mean, in my position. You hear about things, don't you? I mean, just in case..."

*

The book came out. There was a launch at Waterstone's on Piccadilly, after which a small group gleefully adjourned to more exclusive premises, where the toilets echoed with the sounds of sniffing, and the atmosphere itself was luscious as the perfumes of a Turkish harem. Back to health and strength, star of the show, Mike Downey circulated happily, until he found himself with a comedian of an older generation, a man whose role as family entertainer had been shattered by the tabloid stories of his drug use and his sexual tastes; who'd made a comeback as a serious actor, winning, if not popular acclaim, then critical respect. Here in the flesh, he towered over Downey. His hair was streaked with silver, and his famed spaghetti build seemed more substantial, more dignified than on TV, wrapped up in an expensive pin-striped suit.

"You know about them, then?" The vowels were rounded, plump, with just a fashionable hint of cockney.

"Oh, well," said Downey, who'd sampled the full range of chemicals available, and was feeling mildly combative, meeting someone much more famous than himself. "I know everything, you see. I really do."

"Your book. That piece you read." The older man jutted a finger. "It's real, isn't it? The man with the goatee? And there are others, I'd expect. Or will be. Do you dream about them yet?"

"Fiction. Fiction. That's why they put it on the cover. F-I-C-T – "

Downey looked around the room for someone else to talk to, somewhere to escape.

"Get used to them." The older man gave a sadistic smile, pointing his finger like a gun. "We call them anti-fans. Even quite... minor persons can become afflicted. Still – not to worry, eh? Chin up."

Downey tried to side step. The man reached out a long, spidery arm and caged him.

"I can always tell, you know. Your piece about the price of fame. Always good to look around the audience at times like that, see who knows, who thinks it's just a joke. Would you happen to have a cigarette on you, by any chance? Oh, good. *Disque Bleu?* Oh dear. Still, beggars can't be choosers, eh? I've given up a thousand times, but old habits... As the bishop said." He flashed a lighter, held it out to Downey.

"I... don't really smoke." But he took a cigarette and put it in his mouth, allowed the other man to light it for him.

"No," sighed his companion, "you don't find many people who'll discuss it openly. Nearly openly, in your case. Myself, I see it as a basic function of Newtonian physics, hm? For every action, an equal and opposite reaction. Anti-fans. Dreadful, dreadful things. Like miner's lung, or asbestosis. Occupational disease. But as I said before..."

Someone called to Downey. He turned a moment, waving to a woman publicist he'd flirted with a little earlier. He tried to signal, 'Get me out of this,' but when he turned back, the older man was gone, gliding away among the guests, his long head visible above the crowd, nodding to right and left, blowing a kiss and making pouting mouths.

The girl was on his arm. "What happened to you? Where d'you go?" She pressed her lips against his cheek, briefly (but not too briefly; he noticed that). He wondered if he'd have to pay for her affection, if each kiss would spawn some other carping, goateed hate-monger, waiting for him somewhere, further down the line.

He gave a practised, laddish smile, looked in her eyes (large, bright blue; too wide, like headlights) and ran his tongue-tip delicately over her top lip, corner to corner and then back again.

He said, "You won't believe it. That old bastard made a pass at me."

"No!"

"He did."

From the crowd he caught a moment's dissonance, a crude, sarcastic laugh, but it sank back in the swell of sound, a bum note in a symphony. He slipped his arm around the girl's slim waist and led her off towards the bar, his gesture of defiance, though to what, or whom, he'd no idea.

Michael Downey toured America.

New York was cool, LA was hot, and in between, the tour was a success. Enough for him to think of buying property out there, becoming, in the best tradition, transatlantic. Channel 4 commissioned a third series; he negotiated with the BBC over a prime time slot hosting an 'edgy' new game show, *Risky Business*. His second book came out, the funny one his publishers required, a coming of age novel complete with ghastly details of the hero's family and friends, early sex and brief conversion to a mystical far-eastern sect with offices in Neasden.

This, too, was a success.

He keeps the same London address, the Greenwich house, though these days he's much less inclined to go to pubs and clubs, and when he does, his friends have noticed a degree of caution – nervousness would be too strong a word – and a habit of announcing, suddenly, "I don't like this place. Let's go somewhere else." They put it down to fame, a child-like sense the world revolves around him, but they never question it. His friends are fewer now. He doesn't seem to mind. And once a week, when he's in London, he attends a small, exclusive self-help group, members of which are household names, and suffer an affliction they remain unwilling or unable to divulge to us, the common members of the human race, their 'public', as they call us. Gossips claim the group must be for alcoholics, drug addicts, or worse: a ring of traffickers in kinky sex, paedophiles or black magicians. They are, however, wrong.

Downey now employs a minder, a beefy, dedicated man named Pickering. He has a scar across his belly as if someone's tried to chop out his appendix with a meat cleaver, and for a pint or two he'll tell you what he did to earn it, what happened to the men responsible, and why their wives divorced them shortly afterwards. His other trick is eating glass. Yet Pickering has proved at heart an amiable soul who thinks the world of Mike and would happily walk into hell for him if need be. This, however, is a job he's so far not been asked to do.

At first he was instructed to look out for men with goatees, and on no account to let such people near (difficult, in light of the prevailing fashions). Since then, others have been added to the list. There is a small, pixie-ish girl with dyed blond hair, an old man who pretends to be a marketing executive, and sisters, twins, who like to dress up in Victorian clothes (though sometimes favouring more recent modes: glam rock, hippie, goth).

Downey's new series will air in autumn. Advance opinion says that it's his best to date, both funny and incisive, and he tours the States again in the new year, playing to bigger venues, bigger crowds.

Pickering's workload will not ease. In fact, just recently, another *bête noir* has been pointed out to him. The man is middle-aged, wears a shiny suit, string tie, and speaks with an accent of the American south, possibly Georgia or the Carolinas.

Quite what he blames poor Downey for is still unclear.

Rif

It was a cheap hotel, the kind where there's a shower and a toilet and they're both the same place: hole in the floor, spout in the ceiling... shit everywhere.

I didn't wash a lot that week.

Mostly, I hung round with the guys upstairs. They were older than me, cooler by a mile, and from the moment I set eyes on them I knew they were the people I'd left home to meet. It wasn't just their hair, their beards, that look of cultivated savagery they wore; to me, they were like figures out of Kerouac or Brautigan, embodiments of an ideal I'd dreamed about yet seldom seen. I was a schoolboy hippie, seventeen years old. They were the real thing. I wanted nothing more than to be one of them, and only wished my hair was longer, wished I had an earring or an Indian shirt, my own supply of traveller's tales, or even a discreet (though possibly obscene) tattoo.

On their part, I'd have liked to say they took to me as eagerly as I to them, but this just wasn't so. I was accepted well enough, it's true – though with the same slack tolerance they put up with the plumbing and the broken furniture, as if I'd somehow come with the hotel. They called me 'English' or 'the Kid'. I shared my cigarettes, I followed them around. I acted nonchalant, laid back, yet I was watching all the while, trying to memorize their gestures, mannerisms, storing up their anecdotes for future use (by which time, naturally, I'd place myself at centre stage). A lot of what they said, I realise now, was pretty routine stuff – the lists of bars and beaches, cheap places to stay – but even these small drops of wisdom seemed like pearls, to file away and catalogue in case of need. If nothing else, then I could pass them on to other travellers, knowledge being one more source of status which at present, I too obviously lacked.

Among us, Pedro stood out instantly, as he'd have done in any group. Half-Cuban, half-American, with skin burned almost black, he'd stride into the streets in only shorts and sandals, blind to local mores. Small children trailed him, giggling; prim young Arabs scowled at this barbarian suddenly thrust into their midst. But no-one ever challenged him outright. He'd got the muscles of a wrestler and the temper of a bull. I never saw him still. Even when he sat and talked, his body seemed to dance in place, his hands wove patterns in the air, or tugged and stroked the charms around his neck – drilled stones, beads, a piece of bone, a silver key – the significance of which, if I was ever told, I've long ago forgotten.

Ade was his foil, his counterweight. Pedro fascinated me, but Ade I trusted, practically on sight. With his long, thin face, his quiet manner and his little, Christ-like beard, he seemed to radiate an almost saintly calm. Ade came from Portland, Oregon – 'originally', he'd add, implying decades of adventure, wandering; he was twenty-two years old.

And there was Col, the Aussie surfer, six foot three, so cautious with his health he'd check the fly-blown kitchens where we ate and then, inevitably, slink back to his room for packet soup brewed on a primus stove. He'd been in India, a fact that even Ade and Pedro were impressed by; though it seemed the main thing that he'd learned was to be careful with the food. Besides the stove, his rucksack had been stuffed with rolls and rolls of good, soft, European toilet paper.

These people were my friends, the way that strangers become briefly intimate while travelling. They were also a convenient source of local hash, a pleasure which, at that age, I was powerless to resist.

*

Day and night, we'd sit up on the roof and smoke. The great maze of the old town spread itself below us, though we seldom went there any more, except to buy supplies: food, drink, and cigarettes. At such times I was careful to keep quiet. I knew nothing would betray me as a novice faster than my current catchphrase, 'Isn't it amazing?', which nonetheless still echoed through my head at least a hundred times a day. But only if the other guys expressed surprise, then I'd allow myself a gentle little flicker of a smile. My best bet, I soon realised, lay in doing nothing, and I turned out to be good at it. Once, in the market-place, a snake charmer had thrust a cobra in my face and I'd strolled blithely by without even a flinch. This proved to be the height of cool. Everyone saw. Ade clapped me on the back, Pedro called me 'Snake Boy'; Col just grinned. I grinned right back, though more to hide my bafflement than anything. I'd had my glasses off, polishing them on my shirt, and missed the snake almost entirely – just a quick blur in the corner of my eye. By the time I'd worked out what had happened, there was no way in the world I'd have admitted it. 'Snake Boy' or 'Kid'? No choice, not in my book.

And so we lazed, and smoked, and then, as tends to happen, we started to grow bored and restless, ready to move on.

We'd got a little money then, between the four of us. And Pedro had a plan.

"You go up in the Rif, right? They fuckin' *farm* the stuff up there, man. You want a good deal, hell – you go to *source*, right? Go to the organ grinder, not the fuckin' monkey!"

Ade was nodding, slow endorsement, talk and gestures pared down to a minimum; the litmus test of Pedro's schemes. And if Ade said it was right, then...

"I tell you, these guys sell it cheap, man. *Real* cheap." Pedro's eyes were huge and black, gleaming with energy. "Then all we gotta do, we get it into Spain. And people do that all the time, y'know? Like, all the fuckin' time." He looked at Ade. "How far across the strait, man?"

"Oh... three, four miles, I guess."

"Three miles! That's nothin', hey? A guy can *row* that far!"

He danced, a wild, Red Indian dance, hopping from foot to foot, his body cutting shapes against the sky. He flung his head back and he howled.

"Hot *daaaawg!*"

I saw faces turn, a dozen rooftops off.

"Listen, listen." He leaned close, stage-whispering. "You guys got dollars? Cash or traveller cheques? 'Cos, like, way I hear it, the people here, they'll do just about *anything* for dollars, man. I mean *anything*. 'Cos their economy's so fucked. And I reckon, we walk in, tell 'em we got dollars, they'll damn near *give* the stuff away, you know?"

"Hard currency," said Ade.

"That's it. That's the word. You look around you, man. These guys are desperate, you know? They *need* us here. No lie..."

It took us three days to get organised. Not bad, I think, considering the state we were all in.

*

The bus was old. It smelt of sweat and dust. The gentle murmur of Mogrehbi filled my ears. The other passengers were small, and fitted easily into the tiny seats, while we sat with our knees up, wriggling from arse-ache, back-ache, leg-ache... It was going to be a long, long trip.

We drove through tin shack suburbs, pre-dawn, and then out into a country that seemed scoured with light: the rounded hills, the red, raw earth, and here and there a distant, cultivated field, slung like a rug across a valley floor. We stopped whenever passengers appeared. We waited at a hill town while the local dwarves and cripples climbed aboard, trawling for alms. I did my usual trick, pretending not to see, but there were things there I'd remember always: the legless man perched on his little cart, grey rags tied round his fists; the boy with limbs like pretzels, bullying and fighting off his rivals in the dust outside...

I wouldn't give, but Pedro gave, and shamed me.

"Poor fucks," he said. "Know how they get that way? Guys ain't *born* like that. Oh, no sirree. Family's got kids, more than the land'll feed – fuck it, they think. We'll get the youngest, break his arms and legs – can make a living as a beggar, see?" He shrugged. "That's fuckin' Islam for you, man. That's how it is."

"That's poverty," said Ade.

"Same fuckin' thing."

It was noon before we reached our destination. I'd expected farmlands, fields and fields of weed, the green tops waving high over my head, and thick, sweet perfume on the air. But this was just another one-street town, a red-dirt road and little, faceless houses... Pedro asked around. He flashed some dirhams, and in seconds, we'd got half

118

a dozen street kids clamouring to take us to the right address.

"You sure this is the place?"

The boys were. We weren't. To us, it looked like every other house in town, crumbling, modest, far from new.

Then Pedro shrugged, and stepped into the gloom.

It felt as if we'd broken up a card game or some other deeply masculine pursuit. Whatever party'd been in progress instantly dissolved. Small, knife-faced figures scuttled past us, out into the street. A fat man in a white djellabah presently appeared, his smile a yellow gash, his arms spread wide; he welcomed us with all the courtesy of some great desert sheik. In seconds, so it seemed, the house was ours. Soon we were lounging in a cool, tiled room, on cushions thick as mattresses, imbibing hot mint tea and passing round some of the fiercest hash I'd ever had in my short life. Two drags and it was like the whole scene vanished down the wrong end of a telescope, while at the same time, tiny sounds – the clinking of a spoon, a foot tapping the floor – would boom and jangle right inside my ear. I'd glance up, startled by a cough, the faint click of a finger-ring on glass, then feel foolish and try not to laugh.

Pedro negotiated. He and the fat man sat together, side by side, nodding, smiling, swapping compliments... Perfect rapport. The boss guy passed the spliff, and Pedro toked it like a connoisseur, expanding his great barrel chest, filling his lungs, breathing out slowly, slowly, till the vapour hung around him like a cloud over a mountaintop.

"Is good?"

"Good?" He coughed. A hot, black light shone in his eyes. "Oh yeah. It's good, alright..."

"Good! Good good good!" The big man clapped his hands, a sound like gunshots, and I almost jumped out of my skin.

The dope kept coming. A henchman sat off to the side, busily skinning up, joint after joint. He didn't speak. He didn't join the fun. After a while, I noticed something odd about his face: a long pink scar that ripped up through the stubble of his cheek from lip to ear, a vivid, crescent-shape, like no kind of an injury I'd ever seen before. And he kept working, spliff on spliff, and never said a word. Real hospitality. I felt myself begin to drift, to melt, to sink into the floor...

And then it changed.

I didn't catch on straight away. That shift in mood, that edge that came into the boss-guy's voice... I'd tuned out, missed it, like the cobra in the marketplace.

What frightened me was Pedro.

Pedro.

The way he lunged back in the seat, and his hands came up as if to block a blow –

I gawped, said, "Wha – ?"

And everything went straight to hell.

The boss was on his feet, yelling and yelling, and it made no sense, no sense at all. "You want I fuck you? Yes? You want I fuck you?" His hand went to his belt. The henchman, Scarface, leapt up too. "No, no," said Pedro, quickly. "You got it wrong, man – "

"*You* got it wrong, my friend. You got it *very* wrong."

What had happened? What had I missed? I put the joint into my mouth for comfort, realised it was probably the worst thing I could do, and dropped it. I could barely breathe. The pressure in the room was suddenly unbearable. It crushed me, pummelled me. Yet even then, it wasn't really fear I felt. No, this was physical – a spasm in my gut that shot up through the centre of my being, almost pulled me inside out. I gasped. I gagged. And all at once, I didn't give a damn for looking cool. I lurched up from my seat. I took a step. The floor had turned to rubber. I could hardly stand. Scarface scowled, but no-one stopped me. That's the miracle. A dozen paces, I was back outside. The light smashed in my face. The one street stretched away to left and right, the red road and the blue sky... I was alone now. Wrecked, stoned and scared.

I wasn't alone long.

*

"My friend!"

"Hey, English! Mr Englishman!"

"One dirham! One dirham, please!"

"You give me, please!"

They hemmed me in, dark eyes and broken teeth. I towered over them, but it was their town, and they worried me. I didn't dare stand still. I walked, but there was nowhere left to go. A hand tugged at my sleeve. A gang of children pressed around me. I ducked one way, then the other, trying not to run. My only friends were back there in that little room with Pedro and the hash dealer, and every step I took took me away from them.

"Fuck off!" I yelled. "Fuck off!"

I fought back tears. I pushed into the crowd. I felt – I thought I felt – hands on my bag, hands in my pockets, and I spun round rapidly, convinced that I was being robbed. I dodged across the road like that, turning and turning, struggling to look everywhere at once, surrounded, helpless –

There was a doorway. Someone in a long grey robe, a raised hand, beckoning. "Want haircut, yes? Haircut?" Zombie-like, I moved towards him, or the doorway came to me, a crooked rectangle that swept me up and swallowed me. Inside was like another world. The noise and hassle fell away, cool shadows folding round me, soothing, gentle... I saw a barber's chair, a chipped and spotty mirror on the wall, a row of coloured bottles. Surroundings so familiar, so English, I blinked in disbelief.

"Want tea, yes? Tea?"

"Please. Yes."

The barber had a thin, Mongolian-type face, a grizzled beard, flat nose. His voice was soft and calm. He smiled to reassure me, looked out at the street. "Bad boys," he said. "No problem here. No problem."

No, no problem: none at all. His shop was like an isle of calm. He called a street boy to bring tea. We talked. He knew why I was there. He knew about my friends. It seemed that he knew everything. "Is OK, yes? No problem." I felt my heart slow down, the blood come back into my face. I even managed to explain – confess – that it had all been just a bit too much for me outside.

He smiled, sipped his tea. "People here – they have not much. They see the Englishman, they think, money, yes?" He laughed. I let him cut my hair, something I didn't really want, but after all his help, it seemed ill-mannered to refuse. "No-one hurt you." Snip-snip-snip. "No-one hurt you, no-one hurt me. Is true." Snip-snip. My lovely long hair, which I'd been growing for a year, falling in tufts all round. "Only way I can be hurt is, if my God allows." He let me think about that. "Yeah," I said. "That's good. Good attitude..." And then he slipped a little lump of hash into my hand. "Is present, yes? From me, for you. You understand?"

I waited with him in the cool. There were no other customers. We drank more tea. And then, at last, the guys appeared. Pedro, Ade and Col. "You see?" the barber grinned. "See, see?" He hurried me outside. "You go now, yes? Go with your friends." I left the shop and turned to wave. He stood there in the door, his smile a dentist's nightmare, and I smiled right back. Everything was different now; the dope was wearing off, and Pedro, despite all the odds, had done the deal. "Kinda hard work," he said, wryly, "but we got to see each other's point of view."

"Eventually," said Ade, and tapped his pockets with a certain pride.

*

We were a gang again. The locals couldn't touch us now, we strode like kings along the main drag, bigger, stronger, richer than the lot of them. We were in festive mood. Plenty of jokes about my hair. We waited for the bus, played lazy football, kicking a rock around, and when the bus arrived, we settled in the cramped-up seats, each of us smug and satisfied. So I'd been scalped, and I was hot and tired, but I was happy, nonetheless. I'd had my own adventure, got my own dope – free, what's more. I watched the landscape steadily unreel, like closing credits on a film, and shut my eyes, and dreamed...

*

My head snapped back. My neck hurt and my throat felt dry. The bus had stopped. But there was no town here, no house, no passengers waiting to board. Nothing but heat and dust and desert hills.

A car stood by the roadside, an old, dishevelled thing. They must have broken down, I thought. We must have stopped to help. Well, that was nice of us. And even when I saw the two cops talking to the bus driver, I still didn't worry; just a friendly chat, that's all...

And then I woke up properly.

Both cops wore shades. The first was thin and stringy, with a cheap Moroccan cig between his teeth; the second, round-faced, short. They looked about as charming as a pair of conger eels.

And in they came. Straight at us. Straight along the aisle, pointing to Ade and Col, Pedro and me. Jerking a thumb towards the door.

They didn't give us time to think.

The shouting chivvied us. That, and the driver's mate flinging our bags down from the roof. Pedro called out, "Hey – "

The thin cop's hand went to his gun.

And Pedro shut up.

We stood there in the heat. Our bags lay in the dirt around. The bus revved up. It shook like an old horse, then pulled away, leaving a fog of dust. I watched, expecting any moment it would stop, reverse, come back for us. A joke. A prank, that's all... Except it didn't stop. It kept on, and soon even the dust-cloud vanished, swallowed by the distance and the haze.

No-one spoke.

The road was airless. Faded hills. No bus. No passengers. No witnesses.

I started feeling sick.

Now both cops drew their guns. They barked their orders, gestured angrily. They made us empty out our bags, our pockets, each in turn. They kicked our clothes across the road, trampled our T-shirts and our shorts. They made us kneel, unfold our stinking socks and underwear. They laughed at our peculiar garments, souvenirs and fancy western toiletries. They knew what they were looking for. They quickly found it. Even the lump the barber'd given me. The second cop just dipped my pocket, flipped it out, and grinned.

A lucky guess? Coincidence?

I thought I'd faint. Somehow that worried me much more than anything, the thought of looking weak, unmanly, and I squeezed my fists together, trying to stay upright, trying to stay calm.

They got us all. Apart from Col.

Poor, cautious Col.

We'd known he'd hide his stash – that's how he was – but even I began to wonder what he'd done with it. Just left it on the bus, or magicked it away somewhere? The cops weren't buying that. They tore his bags apart, they pulled his pockets inside out, slapped at his sleeves, his trouser legs.

It pissed them off. It pissed them off no end.

He wouldn't, couldn't talk. It wasn't bravery – I think he was too scared, as if anything he said would only make things worse. They had him strip, right by the roadside. Shoes off. Socks off. Shirt, pants, underwear... The second cop was at him, runtish, ugly, half Col's size: a little man holding a gun.

Col's body, naked, shone with sweat. His hands were up above his head. His bottom lip shook. His whole body trembled. He tried to speak but now the words just wouldn't come. And the second cop was circling him, round and round, screaming, screaming, "You fuck! You fuck fuck!"

He kicked Col's feet apart. He bent down, staring at Col's arse. He raised the gun. And probed.

And he began to laugh.

His mate went over, bent down too. And laughed.

It wasn't vicious laughter; it was rich, and warm, like two old pals sharing a joke.

They motioned Col to turn around so we could share it, too.

We didn't laugh.

There, taped between the surfer's bollocks and his arsehole, was a great fat block of beautiful green draw, tacked in place with bright pink band-aids.

And this little squib of a policeman, poking with his gun-muzzle, holding Col's balls up with it so that we could all enjoy the show.

Col shook. His face was grey. His eye sockets were hollow and his cheeks sunk in. He balanced on his toes. Teeth set. A muscle flickered in his cheek. The cop jiggled his balls. Kept jiggling them. The gun wagged up and down, then side to side. The cops thought this hilarious. Col shivered. Then the thin guy, with a single movement, reached down and ripped the dope away. Col's face imploded. He staggered, caught himself. His eyes closed in relief.

They let him dress.

And started talking cash.

Spot fine. No bargaining. Spot fine, or jail.

The word 'jail' made them leer and show their teeth.

They wanted everything – cash, traveller's cheques – even credit cards if we'd have had them.

"Monnaie! Argent!"

We couldn't match the sum they asked.

It was the first time in my life I'd ever looked straight down the barrel of a gun.

Christ, I thought. *Midnight Express.*

I thought we'd had it.

Until Pedro spoke.

Faced with the guns, he'd hardly said a word. But now he drew himself up, tall and brown and muscular, and pointed to the car. That's all. Pointed, and sneered. And then he said, "Hey, guys. You look. There's four of us. There's two of you. So how the fuck you gonna fit all *six* of us inside that fucking little shit-heap of a car then, huh?"

A faint breeze blew, lifting the dust along the surface of the road, and far away, a lone bird – eagle or vulture – floated in an empty sky.

The cops were awkward suddenly. They blustered, swore, then muttered to each other. And the price began to drop. Dramatically.

We argued for a long, long time. But now we shouted back at them. And when one guy put his hand onto my arm, I shrugged him off, gun or no gun.

"These creeps," cried Pedro, "they're on the fuckin' *take*! This ain't no fuckin' legal shit! No way!"

"No take! No take!" The cop was furious. "Is law! Is *law*!"

We quibbled. Bargained.

And when we reached the bottom line, we paid.

They got the dope. They got the cash. And as they climbed back in the car, they got a parting shot from Pedro, an old Cuban curse: "You didn't have a mother. You had two fathers and a do-it-yourself kit."

They drove off, back the way we'd come. Not hard to guess who they were going to see.

*

Evening came quickly after that. The light grew soft, the air began to settle. We were stranded in the mountains. Soon, it would be cold. It would be very, very cold.

We walked. We kept on looking for a truck, some way to bum a lift, but no-one came. And only as the sun dipped down behind the hills we saw something – a spread of green, a few old buildings – a valley farm. We set off, hurrying. The night dropped like a shutter. We stumbled down a rocky track, a few small, yellow lights to guide us in.

"Hello? Hello? Anyone home?"

There was a family there. A huge, extended family. We asked to stay. They nodded eagerly, and named a price. We tried to bargain down, but we were tired, lost, and miles from anywhere. The price just didn't drop.

125

An old man, gap-toothed, searched round mockingly, mouthing a single word, over and over: "Hil-ton? Hil-ton? Hil-ton?"

We drank mint tea. The hash pipe came around. We hesitated, then thought, what the hell? and smoked it anyway. Dinner was served. It was thin stuff, I suppose – couscous and vegetable stew – but it astonished me how hungry I'd become. I ate and ate. And afterwards, one of the young men sang a slow, sad, haunting song that seemed to wind its way into my head and linger there, repeating itself, on and on...

Through all of this, Col never said a word, not one. He ate and smoked mechanically, like somebody in shock. Ade, too, was very much subdued. But there was one point, later in the night, I followed Pedro out onto the porch, and we sat, passing a spliff between us, and he cleared his throat and spat into the dirt.

"This country's fucked up, man. Y'know? *Fuckin'* fucked up."

I hugged myself against the cold. Above, the sky was thick with stars.

"I tell you, man. Tomorrow, or the next day – first fuckin' chance I get – I'm outta here, y'know? First fuckin' boat to Spain. First fuckin' boat..."

I sucked the joint, watching the tip glow red under my nose. And in the quiet and the dark, it was like something struck me – one of those clear, stoned, sudden revelations that seem so intense, so obvious, you wonder why you never thought of it before, or why it feels so hard to put it into words.

I tried, though, anyway.

"See – look – I just thought. I mean, what if – "

"You gonna hog that joint all night?"

I took another toke, then passed it over.

"But, like – say we'd done it different, yeah? Like, not gone to the farmers, and..." But that part had been Pedro's plan. I struggled for diplomacy. "I mean, like, great idea, and, you know, should've worked, but, I was thinking, see. Suppose we'd just gone to the cops instead? And dealt with them? Seeing they're in on it. Like, must be possible. And then, then..."

He didn't answer me, and I began to wonder if I'd finally said something so naive, so stupid that it didn't even merit a reply. A cricket

126

thrummed out in the dark. I scratched my nose, felt in my pockets for a cigarette, although I knew already I'd none left. Then slowly, like a rock coming to life, he turned to me, he tipped his head back, and he grinned.

I loved that grin.

"*Snake Boy,*" he said.

It was my first taste of the business, and already I was planning my next move.

Oi

"Here. Stand here."

I faced the painting.

"Shout," he said.

My mouth opened.

"Go on, lad. Shout!"

I couldn't make a sound.

It was a gloomy little picture, as old oils often are: a gloomy gorge under a gloomy sky, a twisted-up old olive tree that sprawled against the clouds; I was amazed that anyone could use so many colours and still come up with something like a daub in mud.

That took a kind of talent, I supposed.

I said, "What shall I shout?"

"Shout what you always shout."

"I don't shout anything."

(Not true, of course, though it was what my mother would have liked. Shouting was vulgar and uncouth, she'd say; 'No-one wants to listen to small boys.')

My Uncle frowned.

"Don't shout?"

"Well..." I smiled.

"Say *oi*."

"Oi."

"Louder. Louder now."

"Oi!"

"Give it some gumption, lad! Full whack!"

"That *was* full – "

"Never mind. Again."

"Oi!"

"More! More!"

"Oi oi oi oi!"

"More!"

"It hurts my head..."

And then I heard it, just the faintest little echo from that dismal, painted scene: "Oioioioioi..."

I looked at him. His arms were folded, smug and proud.

"I told you so," he said.

*

I found him outside, hard at work.

"Is it a bonfire?"

But I knew already, from the way he stacked the wood, the way he'd pause, humming and muttering before he placed each piece, it wouldn't be a bonfire.

We were almost at the bottom of the garden, far from the house and Aunt Kate's sceptical perusal. She'd grown too used to Uncle's schemes by now to hope for any good from them; even the cost of buying wood had irked her – a few pounds at a house clearance, netting him the odd assortment of materials assembled here: split floorboards, old table legs, a chair sawn into pieces; and the door from someone's sideboard, carved with flowers and vine leaves, luscious and ornate. It caught my eye immediately. I picked it up. I held it so the light gleamed on its varnished front, catching the angles and the curves; I ran my fingers over it, the wood not cold in the November chill but somehow warm, as if alive.

"Can I keep this?"

"Keep it? And what d'you want to keep it for?"

"It's nice." ('Pretty' and 'beautiful' weren't boys' words, and I didn't use them).

"Vital equipment, that," he said. "Vital." But then he softened,

130

added, "You can see it any time you want to, though, eh? How's that?"

"Well... OK."

He stacked the wood in complex ways. He lashed together poles that towered over him (I noticed my Aunt's clothes prop in their midst). He nailed old beams to chairs and bits of tabletop, he made up frameworks and inclined them at peculiar angles, using wire and fishing twine and lengths of household tape to hold them firm.

Bit by bit, the pile acquired a shape, a spiralling, elaborate geometry: a tilted cone, a snail made out of scaffolding...

He stepped back, shifted to the left, then shut one eye and marked off the proportions with a finger held before his face.

He gazed up at the sky.

"See that? No wind. Not so much as a breath. It's perfect. Perfect!"

And he bent low, tugged the carved door from its niche, and gave it me.

"There! Don't need it after all, do I?"

I took it in both hands, and grinned.

*

The painting was still there. I couldn't pass it by. I stood up close and scrutinised that dreary little landscape like you'd scrutinise the face of someone you suspected of a crime.

The paint was knobbly. It wasn't smooth like pictures were in books. Here and there the canvas showed, but I could see that it was only cloth. What looked like rock from two or three feet back became a smear of red and yellow, blue and black, the brush strokes clear as tyre tracks.

I tried to make my gaze a solid thing, a beam to pierce that world the way my voice had done; to peer around the corners, see the far side of a rock, the land beyond the frame.

I reached out, touched it with my fingertip.

Nothing.

Just canvas, paint, and wood...

*

The leaves lay in great piles beside the path. I ran, kicking them high, delighted as they swirled up round my face. They got into my hair, caught on my jumper, and I batted them away. I marched, swinging my arms. The park was empty. No-one saw. When I grew tired, I stopped,

131

and stared up at the sky. My Uncle had been right: no breeze, no clouds, nothing to stir the atmosphere... So beautiful, so still.

When I got home, my Aunt brushed furiously at my clothes.

"What's this? You look like you've been rolling on the ground!"

I tried to reassure her that I'd never, never rolled on any ground, not here or anywhere, but when she asked me how I'd got so grubby, I grew shy, and said I didn't know.

Anything, rather than own up I'd been acting like a child.

*

"The weather's good. They'll settle soon... like sand in water. Pulled down by – well. By this, in fact."

He dropped his gaze, mock-modestly, and knocked the nearest strut, then knocked again, enjoying the hard, solid sound it made.

"You ever seen a moth circle a light bulb, boy? Eh? Hm?"

"Sometimes."

"That's it then. That's exactly it." He nodded, rubbed his hands. "It's all in the geometry. If you could see this from above... A lovely thing, I'd think, viewed from the air."

"I bet," I said.

Or just a heap of junk, I thought.

But I remembered how he'd given me the door panel, and I felt charitable; curious, as well, to hear him out.

He sat down on a stone, produced his pipe.

"I'd say, on Mars, for instance, time runs differently from here. Don't you think that?"

"It might."

"Oh, I'd say it does. It definitely does."

He took a penknife, scraped the pipe bowl, tapped it on the ground.

"And what time do you dream in, eh? What time is that? How do you measure time in dreams?"

"I dream – I dream for hours, sometimes. All night! But sometimes, I don't dream at all."

"You dream for seconds. Nothing more. And yet... not normal seconds though. No. Not... terrestrial seconds."

"I dreamt – one night, I dreamt, I dreamt – " I fought for ways to tell him what I'd dreamt. "It went on ages. Honestly it did."

"And where's your dream gone now, d'you think?"

132

"Up here?" I put a finger to my head, then hedged my bets: "Or nowhere."

"Neither."

"No?"

"I'd say a dream's a strange thing – not what you'd call an *earthly* thing at all, eh? A dream starts here, with you and me... That doesn't mean it stops here, or *belongs* here. No. A dream wants to go off... up there, somewhere." He gestured, vaguely: the roof, the treetops... Then the wide blue sky.

"That's what you're trying to do?" I saw it, suddenly, his scheme. "Find old dreams? Your old dreams? Or mine?"

"Oh, heavens, no. What gave you that idea?" He shook his head, lowered his gaze to hide his disappointment in me. Sunlight shone across his bare pate. "No, no, you see, the way I reason it, if *our* dreams go out there, then *theirs*... yes?"

His lips peeled back; a slow, tight grin.

"They dream their way to us. That's how we'll meet, you know. That's how we'll talk. None of your *Dan Dare* nonsense – flying saucers and all that. Not with the substance, but with dreams, that's what I say, the husks of dreams, still drifting through the void... Dreams dreamt on Mars and Mercury, on Venus, Neptune, Jupiter... On distant worlds. They come to us. They're all around, if we just look for them. They teach you that in school, don't they?"

"Well, um... not yet."

"Then I shall write to your headmaster, *tout de suite*. Frankly, your ignorance amazes me. A lad your age..." He squinted at the sky that seemed to stretch away forever, on and on.

"Mostly they stay up there. Drift round a century or two, then fade... Some never come to us at all. Lost, lost... A dream's not a substantial thing, you know. Not so prone to gravity as you or I. It has to be... lured down. Coaxed down...

"Think of it, boy. Think. How many years have they been coming here? What's the philosophy of dreams? The night thoughts of an alien mind? You tell me that now, eh?"

He was silent for a while, and when he spoke again, his voice was wistful, self-absorbed. "There was a fellow I once knew... A great man, I might say. Forbade himself even a sip to drink for days on end... And

133

every night, before he went to bed, he placed a glass of water in the next room. And dreamt of it! You see? Now what d'you think of that?"

"I think... He must have been extremely thirsty."

He must have been a bloody lunatic, I thought.

My Uncle's gaze roved upwards once again. "This is the season for it. Yes. Now we'll see Mars up in the sky. The medium so clear, the way so still. This is the time..."

*

He took the painting off the wall. I don't know why. It left a square of clean, unfaded wallpaper, a small pin jutting just below the top edge.

I told my Aunt.

"Has he?" She went back to her ironing. "Another of his notions, I daresay. Daft old codger..." But she smiled, affectionately, even when deriding him.

I asked my Uncle where the painting was.

"Which painting's that?"

"You know – the one – you made me shout at it. That one."

"I made you what?"

"Shout at it."

"Did I? Really?"

"Yes."

"Good God. I wonder why?"

*

"They'll come down here. Right in the heart. You might say it's hypnotic, like a flower to a bee. The look of it."

"Moth to a flame?"

"Yes. Yes indeed." He seemed impressed, forgetting that he'd used almost the same words to me yesterday. He drew himself up, lecturing: "Certain shapes, my boy – certain geometries affect the mind. It's well known. Look at a spiral, eh? The way it just goes on and on, no end to it. You want to simply... drop into the centre, yes? Don't you? And this – " he raised a hand, as if in reverence, towards his ramshackle contraption "– this, I'm sure, will seem the same to them. That's my belief. My hope."

He had the manner of a slightly tipsy vicar, opening the village fete; but he was proud of what he'd done. No doubt of that.

For three days he kept vigil there, wrapped in his wife's old mohair

134

scarf, fingerless mittens and an ancient and encrusted army greatcoat. For three whole days, I ferried mugs of tea to him. I took him biscuits, rock cakes and tobacco. And I remember just how noble and intent he seemed, that first day. He was a pilgrim then, eyes on the sky, constantly searching for the promised land.

By day two, though, his manner had grown vague, even distracted. Only when he saw me would he rally, lift his head and strike a bold, heroic pose. One time, I'm sure he was asleep. I'd got within a yard or two and still he sat there, huddled on his stone. I coughed. I shuffled back and forth. Then I retraced my steps, and called out, as if to my Aunt, "I'll just take him his tea, shall I?" That did the trick. A moment later he was rigid as a sentry, head back, face like a hawk. He took the mug and gripped my wrist, a fierce gleam in his eyes. "Look, look," he breathed. "They're circling. Can you see them? Can you, boy?"

I stared into the empty blue. I stared until my vision blurred and little silver spots went wriggling round in front of me.

"Yes. Yes, I can see them."

"Where? You point them out. Exactly, now."

"Well... Everywhere, really. All over..."

"Ah." He dropped his gaze. "All over. Yes..."

But he was troubled, I could tell.

He sipped his tea. "I was expecting... Two. Three at the most. Or four. But... all over..." He forced a smile. "That's good, though, isn't it? That must be good..."

*

I kept the sideboard door propped up beside my bed. It was my special treasure. And now one by one, the carved flowers changed. The wood began to pale, took on a delicate, roseate flush, turning to saffron; while the petals became swollen, fleshy, and their scent grew sweet and strong. After a time they'd drop without a sound, so light were they, and in an hour begin to curl and die. By evening they'd be little more than dust, to sweep away and drop into the litter bin with my old bus tickets and sweet wrappers, the fragrance all evaporated, gone.

Now half the board had cleansed itself this way. It made me sad; the timber underneath proved dark and pitted, as if something had been leeched from it, taken away to give this brief and fragile mimesis of life.

*

135

My Uncle came indoors now only to relieve himself or grab a sandwich to replace his evening meal. I wondered if he spent all night outside; he'd be there when I woke, there when I went to bed...

My Aunt brewed tea. What else was she to do?

"He'll catch his death, I swear he will. And you, too, if you don't wrap up. Make sure you're warm before you take it to him, hear?"

This was the third night. Still nothing in the trap, for all his talk, the sky still full of stars. He pointed to a single light that twinkled through the trees (Mars, say? In memory, it seems to cast a reddish glow). And then he gripped my shoulders, holding me as if – it was his coat put the idea into my head – as if I were a gun to fire at some far distant, half-seen target, somewhere he couldn't reach alone.

"Shout," he ordered. "Shout, on four. Loud as you can."

And we counted. And we both went "*Oi!*" together at the full stretch of our lungs. He held his hand for silence. We listened, listened, cupping our hands around our ears; but there was nothing, no wind in the trees or rustling in the grass, as if the whole world had stopped dead, frozen, and would never start again.

We waited.

There came the gurgle of a car engine from somewhere in the town, stirring to life.

I let my shoulders drop.

"I've got to go," I said.

But neither of us moved.

"I've really got to go..."

*

"Oi! Oi! *Ooooiiii!*"

His voice was strained and hoarse. I'd been asleep; it came to me out of the dark, a faint, lost sound, an animal abandoned in the night.

I vowed that when I slept I'd dream, so that at least he'd have a dream of mine to keep, an earthly dream, regardless that the ones he sought eluded him.

But it was many, many hours – or so it seemed – before I slept again...

*

Next day it rained.

The sky was low and grey, and though the chill was gone, a damp

136

breeze blew, poking its fingers down my neck and pawing at my face. The trees were stripped. The piles of leaves turned into slippery wet matting, treacherous, no longer fun. I strolled down town, watching the housewives struggle with their bags and their umbrellas, tottering lopsidedly; the marketplace became a field of parasols, dripping with rain.

I circled, came back through the garden gate, the water dribbling down my neck.

The dream trap lay in ruins.

Not just broken – scattered, flung all over everywhere, like debris from a hurricane; and then, for thirty seconds, I was certain it had worked. No normal English weather could have shattered it so thoroughly, so irreparably. Surely some cosmic power, some planetary force –

I saw my Uncle's face framed in the window of the potting shed.

And I knew immediately what must have happened.

I turned away.

He knocked the glass and called, but I pretended not to hear. Was it so painful to him, then, his failure? So terrible, he'd rather wipe out every trace, every reminder of his work, than face the loss?

*

The flowers ceased to fall. The panel, half-stripped, became ugly to me, and I left it with the other wood outside, to soak and swell under the winter rain.

My Uncle moped during the day, and once again, I wondered at the disappointments of the adult world, if they were so much worse than those of childhood; or if, as I'd begun to think, grown-ups just made more fuss about them, always raging and complaining at their lot.

We schoolchildren had no such privilege, pushed here and there by adult whims, our grievances unheeded, even if we gave them voice.

He cornered me that night. He caught me in the kitchen while my Aunt was gone, pushing his face up close to mine.

He had an earthy, sweaty smell after so long outdoors, not altogether likable.

"Tell me," he begged. "What did you dream?" His breath was hot against my cheek. "Please, quickly now – what did you dream?"

137

Everybody's Crazy in the West

"No." I wagged my finger in her face. "Not after last time. Oh no no."

"Jimbo."

"They're maniacs. They're head cases. They almost got me killed, for Christ sake! I can't, I won't, I – "

"*Almost*." Her voice was smooth and calm, like silk talking. "I think that's what we call the operative word in this case, yes? They *almost* got you killed. Hm?"

My agent, Lena Krautz, is a persuasive woman; it's her job. But there were days I wondered just who she was working for.

I pouted like a child.

"You're still alive," she said. "Do we agree on that?"

She steepled her long fingers, long almond nails lacquered in gold to match her rings.

I looked down at the floor.

"Pardon?" she said.

"Yes. Alright. Yes, yes."

"Good. Common ground at last." She settled in her chair, brushed back a strand of hair, and studied me. "We're talking money here," she said. "Second operative word: *money*. Remember that?"

"Not very well."

"No. Quite. We're talking alimony. Child support. And where did you say you were living now...?"

I squirmed under her gaze, and shrugged, as if the name had suddenly gone right out of my mind.

I'd been with Lena about seven years, from golden youth to leaden middle age; and to be fair, she'd stuck with me. She'd never told me to get lost, or find another agent, or go back to my teaching job, and that itself was some kind of a miracle, if probably a temporary one. My terminal ingratitude was less than she deserved.

She knew it, too.

She fixed me with a rigid stare.

"You want to hear about the favours I called in? The strings I pulled? Do you?"

"Uh..."

"No, no. Better still, I'll show you what I saved you from."

She slipped a sheet of paper off her desk and then – with sudden, tennis player's grace – she flung it at me. Very theatrical. I jerked back like she'd thrown a snake.

"Go on," she said. "Just take a look."

I didn't have my glasses on. The schedules were a blur of print, but I could make out all the main lists well enough: the teen pics, war movies and thriller films, a string of porno sleaze (*Sex Vixen, Sex Vixen in Chains/Lace/PVC*, etc); *The Clementines*, a 'light family comedy'; the third remake of *Baron Munchaussen*... And Lena carefully recited the entire long list from memory and gave her expert and considered views on each.

"Turkey. Turkey, turkey, turkey."

"Then... I don't see why...?"

"Because." Her smile was so precise it could have been mathematically defined. "Because I think you need a break, dear Jimbo. Because I think you're ready to get back to work again, and to repay a little of the time and effort I've invested in you through the years. So I have made some promises on your behalf. I've talked to people. And you know how much I hate to be let down."

I nodded. Something rumbled in my guts. Hunger, perhaps. Or fear.

"There will be one big movie this year. Only one. It isn't on the list. And I have begged, cajoled and fawned to get you in on it. Do you accept? Do you? Or do I call these people back and tell them, sorry, no dice? Well?"

I shut my eyes. I took a breath...

Snookered again.

*

There's something happens on the west coast, some kind of madness no-one's put a name to yet. I think it's all to do with living at the junction of tectonic plates; this is the point the whole civilized world gets sucked back down into the magma once again. You feel it in the rocks, the soil, in the geology. No wonder they're all crazy here.

I should have been prepared. Needless to say, it took me by surprise, as usual.

The airport was on fire. I kid you not: great sheets of flame blazing and raging on a nearby runway, so we taxi'd to a halt beside a Bosch vision of hell, the tourist cameras clicking all around. Excitement, chatter, wolf-whistles... I stumbled through the concourse, tripping over luggage, trying to find the exit signs. A man dressed like a four-star general grabbed my bags. I fought with him. We struggled back and forth, and only when he called my name the second time I stepped away, eyed up his uniform, his medals, cap badge... A Mickey Mouse button...?

"Like it?" He flashed his perfect L.A. teeth, twirled like a fashion model. I felt sick. "Your chauffeur, sir. And if I *may* just take your bag...?"

Outside, the scent of burning filled the air, the far off clatter of machine gun fire; there came a long, low boom like thunder, and the pavement shivered under me.

"Oh, fuck – "

"Big one there, sir. See the smoke? They'll have to finish in an hour or two. Light's almost gone..." He grinned again. It was an easy grin to hate, the way he'd pull his lips back off his teeth, as if to dazzle me with the expanse of toothpaste white. "Don't worry, sir. Only a movie, hey? Only a movie."

"Yeah. That's why I'm worrying."

*

So there I was. Just one more crap assignment. Not the screenplay, not the novel, not even the comics adaptation, this time round. Oh no. I get *The Making Of. The Making Of!* Forty thousand words of advertising

141

copy, strung between a stack of glossy pics, just on the off-chance some poor sucker out in Movieland still thinks that he can read. Which personally, I doubt.

Hack work. Hack work I'd had to go down on my knees and thank her for, my dear Saint Lena: saviour, tyrant, hand of God... Payer of bills.

I sighed.

And yet I knew the job. I knew exactly what they'd want: those pointless little incidents for movie buffs, a bit of tangy gossip – but no real star snits, no cost analysis, and do not even ask what all those muscle boys are doing, hanging round Ms X's trailer at a grand a night; and no disasters – not unless they all pan out OK, in which case it's 'heroic triumph in adversity'. With *lots* of little details about who wears what, and what they get for breakfast, movie gossip – all that shit.

I just had one small snag.

The set was closed. Strict secrecy. They wouldn't even let me in to see the beasts; drove out there once and ran into these guys like psycho footballers, waving their AKs, acting like they'd caught me doing something awful to their kids. I told them, hey, guys! Hey! We're on the same side! I've got a job to do as well, you know! Let's cut a deal here, hey?

You get a weird sensation, looking down the barrel of a gun. It isn't true, that thing you read, that you can see the bullet waiting for you; usually you're shaking far too much. You suddenly feel very small and weak and nowhere near as vital to the great scheme of the universe as you'd have liked to think you were.

But still, it's like my old gran said: if at first you don't succeed... then go ahead and cheat.

A movie set's all rush and muster and then hours of zilch. I took advantage of the zilch to name some names, to talk some talk, to spread a little jollity around... By Day 3 I'd got clearance of a sort. I'd been assigned a guide.

*

Back then the movies were the place where life left off and something new began. Later that changed. Life is to art as movies are to... what? James Bolton Klinkenberg, *The Culture and Philosophy of Cinema,* unpublished MS, p.22.

*

Ana Francesca Limoni was clearly not in Hollywood to shepherd writers round, especially writers who weren't even *screen*writers, for Christ sake. She didn't bother hiding her resentment, either, though luckily she turned it on her bosses, not on me, and once I'd shared a little something from my private stash, we seemed to get along alright.

"Jeez, but I could I dish the dirt on some of these guys. Things I can tell you, you would not be-*lieve*, y'know?" Her slightly heavy features lowered like thunderclouds. "You gonna write it for me, hey? You gonna?"

"In my memoirs maybe, yeah."

She smiled.

Hers was an old, perhaps an ancient story: do this for us, Ana. Work hard, earn peanuts, it's a foothold in the business, it's a start. Do that for us, Ana. OK, OK, we *know* that it's a shitty job and no-one else'll do it, except it gets you *in*, and if you're willing to exert yourself, and show that you can run round every day up to your neck in sewage and survive, then next time, when a better job comes up, and people know they can depend on you, then next time –

"Sure," she said. "They can depend on you to do the shit. So shit is what you get.

"Hey, sorry, y'know? I don't mean – " She touched me lightly on the arm. It felt like an electric charge. "This ain't so bad. This is a good job, next to some. You ought to – " She flustered, and her head went down. "Hey, how 'bout, you know, another toot? And then I'll show you round."

Ana wore a tight, striped dress that gave a good view of her butt. She had a plastic thumb-ring that was actually a torch. Long hair, dyed red. She wanted surgery.

"I want real wings, you know?" She looked at me as if, just for a moment, she genuinely thought that I could get them for her. "*Heaven Can Wait*," she said. "Like that. Warren's a changed man now. Like *totally*. Down in his *soul*."

"I bet."

She sniffed. She smiled. I think her face was handsome, more than pretty, but she'd the kind of bone structure that just gets better through the years. Unless it was the coke making her look that way. Some days, it's like you can't trust anything much any more.

*

The Life To Come

Unique among the arts, the cinema speaks of veracity. The camera does not lie. The contract between audience and image is a contract based on trust: "I was there, I witnessed it, I saw." Even in the work of Méliès, say, we have a record of authentic theatrical performance; only the proscenium arch – along with a few frames of film – have been judiciously removed. Other critics may have pointed to alternate possibilities, to propositions briefly followed then abandoned in the history of film-making; and yet in film we search for truth, for what cannot be faked. If we examine, therefore, the aesthetics of the modern cinema (and I count aesthetics as the most neglected of all academic disciplines), we find a semiotic system which resembles that of normal life, yet amplified: reality raised to the highest power, though in a form even the great Bazin himself could scarcely have conceived.
James Bolton Klinkenberg, *The Culture and Philosophy of Cinema*, unpublished MS, p.424.

*

"You smell them yet?"

The wind blew in my face, bringing the sweet aroma of L.A., the smog, the gas stations, cheap booze and sperm; the wisps of Ana's perfume, like a heavy, hothouse flower, wrapping us round...

I shook my head.

"You will. Don't worry now. You will."

We'd got permission from the studio at last. All morning, some young hoodlum on a motorbike had seemed to shadow us, camera in hand, and I was sure the Studio had sent him as a spy, to catch on video any infringements of its rules. The Studio was like a fascist state, demanding, paranoid, forever prying into people's lives. I mentioned him to Ana, but she shrugged him off. "Some jerk," she said. "Like every guy in town thinks they're a movie maker, yeah? So what the hell..."

As we approached the lot, I finally lost sight of him, and I was not displeased.

Armed guards checked our IDs. I was aware now of a certain... odour in the air. We left the car. A man named Steiner met us. "I am your babysitter here." He didn't smile. He had an accent, possibly South African. A thin white scar cut through his eyebrow, down his cheek, into his lip; it looked just like a seam. "You will do everything

I say, and you will do it without questioning. You understand?"

He could have stepped straight out of Hemingway. I wasn't going to argue with the guy.

We signed the legal forms, one swearing us to secrecy, the other to exonerate the Studio in case of accidents. They didn't cheer me much. Then Steiner led us through the gates, two sets, each closed and locked behind. The smell was stronger here. Ahead now, something hooted – deep and resonant, like one of those big alpenhorns, and something else replied, and then a third, a fourth – the unknown, trumpeting us in.

Steiner cocked his head. His scar made every smile a sneer. "I hope they scare the public, man. Because they sure as hell scare me."

The compound covered more than three square miles. Pines shaded it. Under the trees were screens, sound baffles more than twice my height, and fenced-in paddocks. Everything here stank. A smell of shit and piss, of stale sweat, a zoo smell, and yet multiplied a thousand times; rotten meat, old frying pans, stale farts; and something else, a taste, almost metallic, right down in my throat... I brushed away a fly that settled on my lip, looked up – and saw them.

At first, I thought the trees and fencing must have blocked my view, that's why I'd missed them, looking round. But no; I'd missed them just because they were so big. So motionless. And now, as one turned sullenly to stare, it felt as if a small apartment block had shifted place. Almost too big to comprehend.

"Don't move." Steiner was whispering. "Do not upset the boy."

There was a double fence between us and the beasts, the inner one electrified.

"It's a..." I said. "It's a..."

"Bronto."

"Yeah..."

The creature peered at us with cynical, grey eyes. It rolled its shoulders loutishly, and snaked its head into the air. Behind, its mate came shuffling up. The two beasts jostled, seemed to curse at one another in an ugly, reptile kind of way.

"Do not move fast. Do not alarm 'em. Clear?"

"But, they're," I fumbled for the words, "they're what d'you call it, herbivores, aren't they? Like, they look fierce, but..."

"Know any vegetarians, man? Hey?"

145

"Yeah. Some."

"They more or less aggressive than the meat eaters? Ja? Know Hitler was a vegetarian? A bean eater? Got any Jewish blood, my friend?"

"I don't see – "

"Ha. It's not the diet that's the problem here man, anyhow. I tell you that. It's not the *natural* diet."

We moved on. The paddocks were all screened for sight, but there was no way they could mask the smell. The beasts looked agitated, nervous. A half-grown Allosaurus kept down in a pit made constant forays at the walls, running and jumping, over and over, with the tireless repetition of a mechanism. Its jaws were vast, its head enormous. A rope of spit swung from its chin. You couldn't look at it without thinking of death.

"Ever see a polar bear down at the zoo? How crazy they get? Same behaviour. Same behaviour." Steiner nursed his gun, cradling it as if it were a child. "One of these boys makes a run though, dunno what we'll do. Can't kill 'em. Not allowed."

Each of the animals had been pre-sold to zoos, museums, corporations, even to governments to help finance the film. Several were worth millions each.

"The Allo there – I kill 'im, the Studio kills me. Either way, I'm dead."

I took this as a joke, and smiled.

"It's hormones, man. These boys – how old you think they are? The Stegos? The Brontos? How old?"

"Well, I dunno. I'm not an expert. I mean..."

"You give a guess, man, huh?"

"Ten – twenty years?"

"Uh-uh. Two. Two years. Two years, the oldest of 'em."

"Well. They grow up pretty quick."

"Na na na. You don't see it. They don't grow quick. Except the movie *needs* 'em quick. So they get growth hormone. Steroids, this, that – stuff I never heard the name of. *Ach.* Make 'em look good. Make 'em look big and fierce. Act fierce, too. The crew, man, they all terrified. One chance, these things – any one of 'em – they chew your fuckin' head off, man."

146

Ana said, "You should have talked to Malick. That guy'd fix you up."

"Oh sure, yeah, Malick, he is good. But, more time, more money – *ach*." He shook his head.

"Malick?" I said.

"Works for GenEx," Ana said. "Real smart-brain. Good rep." She batted at the flies around her face. "He made the talking pig for *Babe*."

*

A deep smog hung over the city, a faint, soft-focus haze that from a distance made a fairy tale out of it all. Then for a while it really was the magic kingdom everybody dreamed about; and there were people said that you could see the neon, captured in the air, a shining mother-of-pearl glow that lingered through the daylight hours and brought a beauty to the dullest condominium, the plainest stretch of road. But there were people who'd say anything. That didn't make it true.

"You want me to, um, drop you somewhere?" I was driving. One way to stay in control, at least.

"Oh – you know. Anywhere."

"I mean – you busy, then? You, ah, you doing anything right now?"

"What? You mean, apart from sitting here? With you?"

*

Ms A.F. Limoni gave me a short, dismissive shrug.

"Seen that," she said. "Kids' stuff."

"*Au contraire, mam'selle*. The movie is a masterpiece."

"Says you."

We'd smoked a joint back in the car. I'd needed something, just to get my thoughts off all those monsters. Those renegade, runaway monsters. The joint gave us an appetite. And an excuse. So here we were, sat in this little restaurant out on the coast, slurping spaghetti marinaire and trading film gossip. Except my gossip wasn't new, and hadn't been, not for a long, long time.

"You've got to think. It was all different then." I forked a mussel up into my mouth, pressing the soft flesh with my tongue. "They did the whole thing, everything by hand... like, frame by frame, right?"

"Yeah?" There was a challenge in her voice we both knew meant much more than just, "Explain yourself."

"So what they did, OK, they got this guy, O'Brien, Willis O'Brien, and they locked him in the studio for something like a *year* with all these models, and he shot the whole damn sequence one frame at a time. Stop motion. Think of that? Every single action that you see on screen was built up, bit by bit, thought out, every detail. Nothing left to chance. And that's why it's incredible."

"Alright." She gave a cynic's smile. "So this jerk, right, he spends a year on this. So maybe he should, you know, get a life or something, hey? You know?"

"You missed the point."

"Uh-huh?"

"I'm saying it was different then. They didn't have what we've got, all these... processes, techniques and stuff. To them it was a backroom industry. I mean, these guys were visionaries – pioneers, you know?"

I leaned towards her, carried by the fervour of my argument. "I've got this theory – this idea – I think things changed somewhere. Some time. I wrote a book... It's like, you watch a movie and there's *feedback*, yeah? Some kind of leakage from the other world, the movie world, and – "

She twirled pasta round her fork. I'd lost her interest, and I'd lose her too, now, if I wasn't careful. Yet I blundered on, regardless.

"It's all in the book. It's all explained. It took me ten years work, and one day when it's published I'll..."

"Oh," she said at last. "A book."

I looked down at my plate. "I'm saying, right, I'm saying..." I tapped my finger on the tabletop. "Those guys had discipline, you know? O'Brien had it. Discipline. While we're... We think a different way. That's all."

"Good thing," she said, "from what you're telling me."

"Like, when the dinosaur, when it just sort of stops, scratches its ear – that's beautiful. It's beautiful. You won't get that from what we saw today."

"You weren't impressed?"

"Oh, well." I stopped, sucked in a long string of spaghetti, mopped my chin. "Oh, sure, I was impressed. Who wouldn't be? It's just..."

"You weren't even impressed by me?" she said.

*

If a photograph resembles, of necessity, the object which it represents,

148

likewise the object must resemble its own image; then we might ask ourselves, which is the icon, which original? Which, then, is the true and worthy matter of our study here?
James Bolton Klinkenberg, *The Culture and Philosophy of Cinema*, unpublished MS, p.936.

*

She said she knew a quiet stretch of coast, a place where no-one ever went, and so we drove there. She called out directions. Now and then, she'd put her hand upon my arm or thigh. She rolled another joint and as we drove the sweet smell soothed me and my body settled, easy in the seat. The blazing California sun transformed the highway into one long train of mirages, a zebra-stripe of lakes that loomed and vanished endlessly in front of us.

"You watch a lot of old stuff, then?"

"That's what it means, being a Film Historian. That's what I do. Or used to do... Then I went freelance, and..."

"You're weird. Know that? You're very, very weird."

Her lips were hot and moist and all too brief against my cheek.

*

It looked exactly how she'd said it would: a white cove flanked by rocky fists of headlands, no-one in sight. We stripped our clothes and flung ourselves into the great Pacific rollers. The water stung us, fought us, played with us. Its violence delighted her. She leapt and screamed.

Later, I lay upon the sand, feeling the harsh rays of the sun, the pressures of the UV light... Her hands traced patterns on my chest as delicate as feathers, round and round, squeezing a nipple gently till I moaned. The light was red against my eyelids. The crash of waves filled up the world. Her lips brushed slowly over mine, then touched my throat, moved down. I felt her hair against my chest, my belly, then her hot, wet mouth enfolded me. I gasped. I breathed more quickly as she worked. My eyes came open; I stared up at a bright blue sky, then, turning slightly, saw the cliffs, the bushes at the beach's edge... A sudden, heliograph flash.

I sat up.

"What's wrong?" she said. "I didn't hurt you...?"

I put a hand to shield my eyes. And then I saw him, half-hidden by a scrawny tree, some kind of instrument catching the light... Behind, nearer the track, a Harley Davidson...

It was the guy we'd seen before. The studio spy.

I stood up.

"Hey! You! You fucking perv! You – "

"Jimmy...?" she touched my arm.

I shouted, shook my fist. Then, naked as I was, I went for him. He backed up, slow and calm, the camera in his hands. I broke into a run, knowing already I was too late. He'd reached his bike before I covered half the ground. He gunned the engine mockingly, swung round and offered me a jaunty wave.

"Son of a bitch – "

I stood there, helpless. I felt dirty and ashamed.

Behind me, Ana pulled her dress out from the heap of clothes.

"You should have stayed," she said. "I hadn't even gotten to the good part yet."

*

Disaster hit us, two days on. It's in the book. I didn't even gloss the facts, beyond a little cautious editing. I praised the crew, the actors, everyone, used words like 'level-headed' and 'courageous', when really it was chaos, and the acts of bravery (which truthfully there were) proved foolish, ill-judged, ineffectual; which doesn't detract one iota from their daring or their true, unselfish heroism. Except, perhaps, in movie terms.

The thing I didn't mention was the sheer stupidity of shooting that day in the first place.

The beast was uppity. We all saw that. They'd dragged it from the paddock, out onto this tacky-looking jungle set (the palms were all about half-grown, to make the thing look bigger, tougher than it was). I caught the fishy stink of it. The sweaty stench. And yet it wasn't that that scared me. It was when I saw the handlers. They knew, they knew beyond a doubt, we were in trouble. One quick glance, a nod, a trade of looks – it sent a cold knife slicing down my spine.

Crack! I heard a shockprod fire. The beast let out a snort. Its long, snake neck snapped upwards like a broken hawser, arched, then dropped again, dropped and dropped –

It froze. A string of drool hung, swaying like a pendulum from its chin; for maybe five, six seconds then, I told myself they'd calmed the

150

thing, that it was all OK. Someone was shouting, way back in the crowd. This fat guy crept up with a hand-held, lens almost kissing the dark, pebbled skin. The creature hardly moved. I saw its nostrils flare, open and close. It looked like stop-motion, like that was all they'd thought to move, in all those frames – the nostrils, nothing more. I tried to hold that shot, to keep it in my brain: the blunt head almost scraping on the ground, the great rhinoceros legs – the sun a rainbow on its flanks...

All hell broke loose.

The creature twisted, suddenly. Guy with the hand-held staggered back, I don't know where he fell, he vanished – gone, like that. The tail flicked out. Fast, fast. There was a tower behind – wood scaffold, camera mount – the tail just hit it like a wrecking ball. The whole thing shook, and then, with aching slowness, it began to tilt, to burst at all the joints and fall... Someone jumped free. But there were others, clinging on... I don't know what became of them.

The beast got bigger. Bigger. Coming at me. And that's all I saw. I felt completely calm. Detached. I couldn't take my eyes off it; and as it howled, I realised it was every bit as scared of us as we of it, that this whole scene was one gigantic error, and like all mistakes, it only needed someone to step in and put it right –

Then Ana pulled my arm. She had to almost drag me out of there. For that, when I look back, I can forgive her everything: she must have damn near saved my life.

*

We owe to Heisenberg the knowledge that the act of observation is itself participative; that anything observed is modified and recast by that act. And so the screen becomes a membrane, permeable in both directions; a gateway, if you will, between the Present and Eternity (and if such terms should smack of an unnecessary religiosity, then let me ask what else is Cinema, except the elevation of mere mortals into gods?). Through Cinema, we see the hyper-real; it follows therefore that the hyper-real also sees us. In this way, like it or not, our lives are changed. James Bolton Klinkenberg, *The Culture and Philosophy of Cinema*, unpublished MS, p.2,326.

*

I finally caught up with *Sex Vixen*. Some place like Nowhere, Texas, stuck out in this dim hick town with nothing but the movie house to keep me from the bars. So I thought, hell, why not? Because I knew about it then. I'd pieced it all together, one way and another. Sussed the plot.

It must have been nostalgia, I suppose. Nostalgia for what happened only two years back. A sign of getting old. I spent the first half hour just trying to work out where they'd put the cameras. Oh, one in the ceiling, sure. And then the others...? That damn *tracking shot?*

I reckon half the soundtrack's fake. At least. I have never, never called a person 'doll' in my whole life. I do not yell and scream in orgasm (for God's sake, anyway: it wasn't that good).

But on the beach scene – that's my real voice. Oh yes. I stand up (mid-shot), shake my fist, yell 'pervert', 'scumbag' and the rest, while every eye in the whole house is focused on my prick. I rave and rant. And all the time I've got this big, dumb-looking hard-on stuck in front of me, that goes down bit by bit, like a balloon with a slow leak... The audience just rocked with laughter. Loved it, every minute. I walked out. I bought a bottle and went back to the motel. After a while I started looking round, checking the night-stand and the window-frames, the telephone, looking for lenses, microphones, but there was nothing. Not in Texas, anyway. Not in the Lone Star State.

I poured a drink. Ana, I thought, you made the movies, anyway. I hope you got your wings.

One time I said I'd never have gone back. But there's this new project, and Lena's in negotiation. They'll let me do it *seriously* this time round. A book, like Lillian Ross. The thing's a re-make, one of the greats, so I'm well up on it: *San Francisco* – gambling, bordellos, double-dealing, then a big, big earthquake... They've got the boreholes dug, explosives set, everything ready now. The biggest movie of the year. The biggest since the last big show... And I'll be there, they say. I'll see it all.

I told them, fine. Just fine. So long as I can leave before the end.

Jinner and the Shambly House

"Insect heads. We brought back... insect heads..."

His pale hands seemed to float above the blankets, tracing a shape that only he could see, big as a rugby ball.

I said again, "Uncle?"

There was a sickroom smell, stale sheets, pyjamas, Dettol and Vick's Vapour Rub. He kept the curtains closed, long after breakfast time.

"We brought..."

"Uncle!"

His voice was like a sigh cut into words.

"...brought back..."

"I've brought a cup of tea," I said.

That's when he noticed me. He turned, he squirmed to lift himself up on the pillows, reached out – eagerly, I thought – and stopped. His hand hung, trembling; then fell just like a slaughtered duck.

"I couldn't. No. I couldn't keep it down. Can't drink, you see. Can't eat..."

He touched my arm.

"You've been a good lad. Good and kind. But it's too late for tea. Too late for anything, these days..." He whispered, low and ominous: "I've seen the house again. I have, I have..."

I heard his breath, the way it whistled in his nose.

I said, "I'll, um... I'll take it down again, shall I?"

153

"What's that?"

"The tea. I'll take it down?"

"No... no. Leave it. In case I find the strength..."

To hear him though, I thought he'd never find the strength again.

So active, so ebullient in normal life, I can't explain how it upset me, seeing him like this. He lay there like a stranger, leaving me helpless to communicate. I bluffed and stuttered, and then finally, I fell back on my training. Cheerful and polite, as if he were a guest at one of mother's coffee mornings, I enquired, "And do you, ah, do you see the house a lot?"

But in that meagre room, my words were hollow and embarrassing.

"It's there. It's there." Now he was barely audible. "Each time I shut my eyes... I got out once. I won't get out again."

He slumped into the pillows. I waited till his face went slack, his breathing became slow and regular. And then I left the tea beside him, tip-toed out and closed the door as softly as I could.

*

Next time I saw his tea-mug it was standing in the kitchen sink, and it was empty.

"Oh. He drank it then. That's good."

Aunt Kate just raised her eyebrows at me, comically. "And what d'you think he'd do? Use it to wash his feet?"

"The way he smells – " I said, only she clicked her tongue and shoo'd me off into the garden.

"You go and put some colour in your cheeks, young man. Can't have you going home all pasty-looking, can we?"

I hesitated, but she waved me on, and I was banished to a world of trees and flowers and sunshine, which I nonetheless tried ardently not to enjoy.

*

My Aunt might put a brave face on it, but I knew the truth. Edward was dying. All week now, he'd languished in that dismal room, stinking of medicine and dirt. At times he grew so weak his voice would fade almost to nothing, and he'd wheeze and groan like an asthmatic bluebottle, then fall back, helpless in his pain... Yet there were moments, too, he rallied, begging for tit-bits, drinks or biscuits, and on

154

one occasion, chocolate ginger sweets. These wishes I'd convey at once down to my Aunt, who met them with a cool, dismissive snort; nevertheless, I noticed he got everything he asked her for – bar the gingers. "Thinks I'm made of money, does he? Lord High Whatsisname. He thinks it grows on trees?" She jerked a thumb towards the ceiling with a savagery which, in the circumstances, struck me as uncalled for, just to say the least.

And yet the times he talked the most weren't these, his energetic times. They were the times he spoke about the house, and then his eyes would shut, his voice would sink into a low, hypnotic drone... The house haunted his dreams, he said. Always the same, lit by a light that shone on it and nothing else, a pale house in a world of gloom; and as he talked, I knew one thing: for him, the house was Death. He didn't have to spell it out. In every dream, it grew more real, he said. In every dream, he found himself a few steps closer to the door.

"And yet it wasn't by the door we entered. Not when I was young. Not then..."

"It's somewhere that you know? Somewhere you've been?"

"It's somewhere I went once, yes. And I regretted it... for all my life."

He breathed out, slowly, sounding like a puncture in a bicycle tyre.

"Those days... Ah. There were the three of us. Poor Jack and I, we were just followers. We meant no harm. But Jinner – Jinner! It was his idea. All his. If not for him, we'd never... Never. No."

Outside, the birds called, I heard the *weep, weep* of a magpie, and the noises of a summer world. His room felt small and airless by comparison.

"Jinner was older, bigger... Coarse, ill-educated, everything our parents frowned upon, and had they known of our acquaintanceship, they'd certainly have banned it in a trice. Being the age we were, of course, that only added to the lad's appeal.

"Yet we were wary of him, nonetheless. He'd meet us by the oak tree on the old coach road, slipping from the shadows like a troll up from its den, grinning his hideously gap-toothed grin... For our part – Jack's and mine – our first delight in him soon turned to something much less comfortable. I know I always felt a flutter in my chest as we approached his lair, a faint, barely acknowledged hope that this time, *this* time, he might not be waiting... And yet what a revelation to

155

discover Jack felt the same way! His brief, crestfallen 'Oh' as Jinner came in sight one day – it told me everything.

"Not that we spoke about such things. Perhaps we were scared of what we might reveal, some shameful aspect of ourselves, something unmanly, weak... In consequence, his hold on us persisted, unchallenged, unopposed.

"For Jinner proved a costly friend. The price was not material (although it could be that, too, if he'd a mind for it), but something in our souls. We feared his mockery. We feared his laughter, more than we feared the things he made us do. Jinner was Jinner; and, though he possessed no admirable trait, no quality for which he might be loved, we wanted his approval, just the same.

"When he appealed to us, he did so through our basest instincts – always strong in youth. This alone might have been cause to loathe him, once the fever he'd engendered had died down. But we were flattered by his rough attentions. Already a prodigious scrapper, swearer and (so rumours had it) drunk and thief, he promised things we scarcely even knew we wanted yet. He told us, if he felt like it, he'd let us watch the cow 'put to' the bull, and he described the act in luscious detail. Strange how his face went red, his breath grew thick, his words starting to fog as if he spoke them through a thick lint mask. Strange how excited we became. I hear him now, sometimes... He haunts me. That voice –

"'You seen an 'orse's dongle, 'ave yer, boy? 'Ave yer?'

"His speech was soft and slow, at odds with both his looks and with his words.

"We giggled, awkwardly.

"'Thick as yer arm, it be – jus' like a big black snake...' And he leaned closer, told us... things we didn't dare believe.

"He led us into mischief. Nothing so terrible at first; he got us to steal plums and apples from the orchards, pointing out that we were small enough to reach the topmost branches where the good fruit was. He'd stay below, keep watch, he said. There was a tune he'd whistle, telling us to run; another that meant, stay and hide; a third to signal the all-clear. But they were all the same – vague, off-key fluting; while other times he'd whistle for the simple pleasure of it, which confused us utterly.

156

"It never crossed my mind to quibble when he took the greater share of loot himself, as he invariably did. Nor, the one time I was caught – by a retired major, who, worse luck, knew Papa from the bowling club – did it occur to me to put the blame on Jinner. No. That wouldn't have been right. Instead, though I was soundly thrashed, my new friend's name never once passed my lips, my only faint excuse that I'd been 'hungry' – as if I were some starving Chinese peasant child. 'No-one goes hungry in this country,' snapped my father. Our relations, never good, diminished further with those words.

"I should have learned my lesson. But there came a day in spring, a listless and unsettled sort of day, when none of us could think of what to do. And that's when Jinner, out of nowhere, said, 'Let's go an' see the Shambly House.'

"The Shambly House was folklore among children then. High on a hill outside of town, a crumbling wreck concealed by trees... Not quite a haunted house, but still a place to shun, like nettle beds, or cemeteries at night, or ponds where poison toads were said to live.

"I looked at Jack. He looked down at his feet.

"'Well?' said Jinner, cuffing him lightly on the ear. 'You scaredy, eh? You scaredy cat?'

"I tried to save face for my friend. 'What about the river, then? We'll catch some tiddlers, or...?'

"But Jinner just grew more determined, and his perceptions, if not deep, were usually deadly.

"'You scaredy too, eh?'

"'No – course not. Just thought, I, just –'

"'Oh ah. Yer full o' bleedin' thoughts, you are. More thoughts than's bleedin' good for yer, y'ask me.'

"So I shut up. He set off, swinging a stick, knocking the cow parsley to shreds along the way; while Jack and I tagged on, not daring to say more.

*

"I'd seen the house before, of course, but always at a distance. As a child, the merest sight of it had sent me running, as if the air itself might carry a contagion. Now here I was, crouched in the bushes not a hundred yards away, both ankles itching painfully with nettle rash; and there was worse to come.

Beside me, Jinner shuffled, fidgeted, and grumbled to himself.

"'Any ol' bugger can do this. Any ol' bloody bugger can jus' sit an' stare.'

"There was a pause, as if his brain took time to formulate the words, letting them fall into position one by one; and then he said, 'We're goin' in. That's what we'm goin'a do.'

"We argued, shrank back, and yet – inevitably, so it seemed – we followed him.

"My mood... It's hard now to explain such things. But all at once, beaten and battered for so long by Jinner's will, it seemed the fight went out of me, and I resigned myself. Jack stumbled onwards, jittery and pale, mumbling his terrors like a litany. In contrast, I felt calm – astonishingly so. I had the strange sensation that I floated high above the ground, my true self happily detached and safe from harm. I watched my body as it trailed in Jinner's wake, propelled by his volition, not my own, and discovered I felt no concern, no fear... No, none at all.

"There is a case – it's well-known – of a traveller in Africa, saved from a lion. Recounting his experience, he spoke, not of the pain and terror, but of the balm that stole across him in the creature's claws, a soothing anaesthesia divorcing him from all anxiety, even as the brute tore at his flesh... Nature is merciful, sometimes.

"So, too, with Jinner and myself, that awful day.

"I have but one regret: that my passivity would not allow me to surrender to Jack's urge to flee. Together, we might finally have broken Jinner's spell; and Jack, with just a little loss of pride, might be alive today.

"For Jinner, I feel no great loss. He was a bully, marked for bad. Yet Jack... Poor Jack..."

My Uncle turned to me. His eyes sought mine, and I was shocked to see that they were full of tears – shocked, because, in those days, I believed that only women and small children were supposed to cry.

"Companions of one's boyhood are the finest, lad. The very best. They never come again..."

He fell silent for a time, and when he next spoke, he was slow and halting, as if the memories came from the deepest part of him; as if he hardly recognised his own tale any more.

"It was, to outward eyes, perhaps a fairly ordinary-looking house. Large, dilapidated... No clear signs of occupancy. Nonetheless...

"Something... I do believe that something happened to us as we slipped across that ruin of a lawn, bent double so to shield ourselves from any watchers at the dozen windows. For already, I was sure we'd been observed, even while we ran towards the source of fear.

"We crouched against the walls. Jinner found a window with a tiny gap under the sash; he dug his fingers in, struggled to lift. The window stuck. I turned around, looked back, and realised I no longer recognised the countryside we'd crossed. The trees jutted in wild, unlikely shapes, the sky was wrong, somehow; and then a wind came, roaring in the branches, and the sound grew, louder, louder, till I thought I'd scream unless it stopped; then Jinner said – his voice was very clear – 'That's done it!' and the window came up with a rush.

"I couldn't stand the noise. It seemed to me that if I stayed there, I would die. My quietude evaporated instantly. I scrambled after him, into the House... The labyrinth that would confound my life.

"In waking hours, only the faintest memories remain. I think of Jinner, ransacking a giant sideboard, wrenching the drawers free from their runners, scattering the cutlery and broken glass... Tearing the dust sheets from old armchairs, tumbling shelves of antique plates to crash and shatter on the floor. In certain rooms, black tide-marks had been leeched into the walls. There was a smell of mould and damp, a sound like – singing, could it be?

"I dreamed about it afterwards. Each dream was different. In some, we roamed from room to room, up stairs, down endless corridors with row on row of doors... Our footsteps echoed, thrumming back to us at intervals of minutes, hours... As we moved higher, so the decor grew more opulent, but always dusty and ill kept, as if unused for years. Great gilded mirrors, chandeliers of crystal teardrops, fogged with dust and spider's webs... We were alone, and yet I felt a presence in the place. Sometimes, a glimpse of shadows that were gone the moment I looked round; a brief reflection in a window showing four figures, not three; a sound of breathing, almost in my ear, yet when I turned – no-one in sight.

"'Jinner...' Jack's voice was thin. A single tear rolled down his cheek. 'Jinner – please, Jinner, stop, please – '

159

"But Jinner rounded on him, yelling, mocking him. I was more frightened by the noise than anything. I flapped my hands for hush.

"'They'll hear, they'll hear!'

"'Who'll hear? Who'll hear, you nancy dick?'

"And then he turned and stormed ahead, leaving us no choice but to follow.

"Soon the way grew more eccentric. There were corridors so narrow we could only slither through them sideways; stairs we climbed bent double, sometimes on all fours, always up, up... There is a dream in which I yell at Jinner, ask him what he's looking for, what he could ever hope to find there. Another where he races on ahead of me so fast I beg for him to stop, and somewhere up a rickety old slatted stair he vanishes, and when I look round Jack is gone as well... I'm so alone that I can hardly keep the tears out of my eyes, and wake in such despair, it's like I'm back there, all over again.

"Picture a great hall, big as a railway station, polished parquet floor, with potted palms and velvet curtains, and we float across it, light as seed-heads drifting in the wind; see our reflections sail beneath us, deep within the wood. Then from a narrow window I look out into a sky with stars that never twinkle but are fixed and firm as lanterns, and a blazing sun that nonetheless fails to illuminate the blackness of the void; while far below, an arc of blue swells up, on which the whole house seems to balance like a sea lion on a ball; a ball patterned in shapes I recognise out of the atlas that we use in school...

"Imagine," and his hand closed on my wrist with a surprising strength, "imagine, instead of rocketships, instead of sputniks, space programmes, those silly squibs – imagine *houses*, yes? Great houses that go up and up, room after room, stair after stair... If we could move across the universe as easily as from the kitchen to the hall, the attic to the parlour – think of a house with zones and climates all its own, a scullery as red as Mars, a bedroom high as Pluto, carpet of helium and counterpane of ice... A house like that could take us anywhere. And as we went up, then surely, surely, others might descend, and – who knows...?"

I prompted him. "The insect heads? That's where you found...?"

"Not just heads! Whole carcasses, clicking and twitching, rotting in the dying light! Insects the size of dogs, or ponies! Yes! A room of

160

them, a hall that stretched away, where swarms and swarms had entered and then perished, struck down here on the borders of the world... We brought back heads – only the heads..."

He shut his eyes. His breath came heavily.

"Please? Uncle?"

"How long did we stay?" His outburst had exhausted him, his voice was cracked and scoured with effort. "How long? Our families found nothing untoward, and yet in dreams it seems that we were gone for months, for years – an endless time. Time out of reckoning...

"Jinner we never saw again. He disappeared. Society, as is the way, found explanations. Tame, acceptable... A burglary had been committed. Jinner's absence naturally confirmed his guilt. Soon gossips had him running off to London, Bristol, joining the Navy or the Foreign Legion... People are keen to see the obvious. Never the... unobvious...

"We hid the heads we'd brought back, fearful they might somehow implicate us in the crime. Poor logic, and yet in its way, I daresay sound enough: eventually we buried them beneath the oak where Jinner used to wait, our final, ugly tribute to him. For in daylight they turned out to be disgusting things, like black steel helmets, with great honeycomb eyes, and clacking mandibles that you could lose a finger to. They moved and shuddered sometimes with a reflex action, as if some stray current of life still burned within. Yet *our* lives – our lives had been changed forever. Nothing could alter that.

"Jack... died. It took a year or more, but I'd no doubts about the cause. They said it was the sleepy sickness, but I knew, I knew... He languished. Dwindled. Couldn't be revived. He saw the House, I'm sure. He spoke to me of it, before he died. He spoke. Oh yes..."

*

That night I cried and cried. The gloom that fell upon me was impossible either to shift or to conceal, and my Aunt Kate's natural concern just made me weep the more. I couldn't talk to her. I couldn't understand her attitude. She seemed so careless of my Uncle's fate, his suffering... Why wasn't he in hospital? Where were the doctors? The medicines? The nurses at his bedside, day and night?

She slipped a piece of chocolate in my mouth, and sat me down.

"Now then." Her voice was stern. "Will you explain to me exactly what's been going on?"

I wailed. The chocolate dribbled down my chin.

"It's not more of Edward's silly stories, is it?"

But I couldn't talk. I told her I felt ill. She pressed a hand against my brow and warned me that, in that event, I should go straight to bed. And so I did – without even a quibble or complaint.

"Ah well," she sighed. "Least said, then soonest mended, I suppose..."

I heard her in the night. Unless it was a dream, that powerful, haranguing tone she sometimes used, my Uncle's feeble groans in counterpoint... Then for a time I feared that I, too, might see the pale house, rising up before me like a tomb; but if I did, by morning I remembered nothing, and in that respect at least, my sleep had been as blank and uninspired as death itself.

I was surprised – delighted! – to find Uncle Edward back there in his chair beside the breakfast table, not just dressed but washed and shaved, his bald head almost glowing in the morning light.

"My boy, my boy – "

His movements spoke of an extreme fragility, as if the slightest knock would shatter him like glass. He coughed persistently, but most of all when talking to my Aunt, even a simple 'Yes' or 'No' taking an effort that had her – unfairly, so I thought – tapping her foot and scowling at him. With me, she was as charming as could be, as if to emphasise his fall from grace ("Milk, dear? Bacon? Boiled egg?"). Just once, while she was at the stove, I smiled at him. He raised a harassed eyebrow in return, sign of a comradeship I little understood but relished all the same.

"Houses, not rocketships," he said.

"You." My Aunt was at him like a shot. "Get on and eat, you daft old man. You've done enough harm this week as it is."

And so he bowed his head, submissive, as he must have been to Jinner, all those years before.

*

The pale house did not claim my Uncle. I tried to talk to him about it, but he brushed me off with that evasiveness which came so easily to him, and to me was his most irritating trait. Where *was* the house, I asked? Was it still there? And how, above all else, could it look

162

normal, built the way he said? It must be visible for miles, I said, *hundreds* of miles, climbing up towards the planets, like a dark thread running through the sky? Or did some strange twist of geometry conceal it, possibly? And once more – *how*?

He talked of other things instead: a history of alchemy, the works of Jung, the best way to eat prickly pear, a fruit I'd never seen nor specially expected to.

I went into a sulk.

Neglected, spurned, my curiosity gave way, first to pique, then disappointment, then to doubt; and finally, forgetfulness.

The years went by.

I'd come to visit him for one more time, though to be truthful now, my interests had begun to lie elsewhere, in areas perhaps as scurrilous as those which Jinner'd introduced him to, back in his youth.

It was an English spring. All morning rain and sun had chased each other back and forth across the sky; black clouds piled over me, the first faint raindrops pricked my skin. I hurried from the station, racing the deluge, counting off the landmarks as I went: the shops, the chestnut tree, the chapel yard... Five minutes. Ten. I saw his house, perched high above the road, put on a final burst of speed – and as I did so, something happened. Something so natural, so normal, and yet so astonishing, it stopped me in my tracks.

A single ray of sunlight lanced down from the clouds, catching the house front so it seemed to leap out of the darkness like a cinema projection. Every detail shone, each windowsill, each carefully cut block of stone or tile upon the roof, even the little tufts of grass along the guttering. Behind, the sky was black, an abyss without even stars to brighten it.

I stood. I couldn't move. The memories came back, a sense of *déjà vu* so fierce that my whole body shook, and it struck me that the Shambly House was not some distant or fantastic edifice as I'd assumed, but *this*, *here*, the very place my Uncle lived in, and that after all, he never had managed to leave –

The clouds opened. The rain poured down. And only as the sunlight faded, like a curtain drawn across the world, I felt the life come back to me, the power to move returning to my limbs.

I ran. The rain fell in a solid wall. It soaked my pants, it got into my eyes and ears, it seeped into my shoes. I fled across the road, I hurtled up the drive, pounding the door.

"For goodness' sake, child!" My Aunt pulled me inside. "Just look at you! You're drenched!"

She made me stand next to the kitchen stove. I watched my trousers steam, my hair drip plink, plink, plink onto the floor; and as she handed me the towel, a strange thought came into my head, and I began to grin. For suddenly I knew – and knew beyond a doubt, the way you know in dreams – that I would never die, that like my Uncle I would slip into the pale house and then out again, neat as you please; and for a moment, in my tiny, adolescent way, it seemed I caught a glimpse of immortality, or held a fragment of the power of God.

And that, perhaps, is where my downfall actually began.

Boomtime

They got me in the boneyard late one night – four young thugs they were, pushing and shoving, calling me a wino and a dosser and a load of other names. It was a lark to them but I was scared, alright. You can't show weakness on the streets. You can't look soft. I told them, "Easy lads – it's consecrated ground, is this."

I tried to run. They hit me. Decked me, first time out. Then it was *bam bam bam* – boots in the head and ribs and bollocks, bolts of total fucking pain right up the spine and banging in the skull –

Put me in hospital a week that time.

I got out shaking, desperate for drink.

I couldn't walk so well. The knee was all fucked up. I staggered down the street, I jumped a bus, got thrown off near the park. Soon found some mates. Fast Eddie, Mac, Big Steve... They'd got this other geezer with them too, tall thin bloke, looked like a mental case to me. Not that I'm picky, mind. Got other things to think about, you know?

Fast Eddie takes a look at me. "Christ, John. What happened to your face?"

"Row with the missus, Eddie. Got a bottle on you? Jesus, but I need a drink."

Well, they'd got something alright. Else they'd be asking me, fuck sake! Weren't keen on coughing up, though. Not at first. Tight gets!

"Come on," I said. "Been banged up all week, DTs, the fuckin' lot. "

165

Then Big Steve slips a mitt inside his coat and shows me. And I stare.

"The fuck..."

I could have rubbed my eyes. I could have pinched myself. Good Scotch is one thing – Bells, Teachers, any supermarket brand – but this was something special, right enough. One look said that. Big fancy label, gold and scrollwork... Glen-something, it was called, and if I live to be a hundred, I don't think that I'll ever see the likes of it again.

"Don't worry, John. It's come by honest. You know us."

Big Steve gave me a grin, all spit and broken teeth. Didn't put me off though. I took a swig, just let the stuff go gliding down... And oh, sweet fucking Jesus! Mary, Mother of Our fucking Lord! Like liquid fire it was, not rough but smooth and warm like honey, and the taste, that hint of smoke under it all... I mean, not like I'm a connoisseur or anything, but even my old wino's palate got a whiff of it. Oh, Christ to fuck – this was a rich man's drink, alright!

"Steady, John. Don't hog it all."

Eddie'd got his paw out ready. "Greedy cunt," he mutters, seeing what I've put away. Except he's laughing, too, like.

"Just making up for lost time, lads." I felt the warmth start spreading out, like someone smearing melted butter on my belly, and then higher, higher... Soon the head felt better, and the ribs – even the knee felt not too bad.

"So what d'you do then? Rob a bank?"

"Jesus, John. You ask more questions than the bloody Bill, you do."

But Eddie gave a glance back, nodded to the thin bloke standing there.

Truth to tell, I'd not been giving him much mind till then. He'd just been watching us, that's all, and now he sort of meets my eye and there's this gimpy little smile comes on his face, all keen to please... Didn't look much like an alkie, which was one reason I'd tagged him for a nutter, first off. But if he was buying – what the hell?

We drank. Got well oiled. All the aches and pains just seemed to fade away like magic. And it was dandy for a while, just real, real grand.

Then something happened.

I can't explain it now. But all the time, we'd got this thin guy, peering at us, right? And fine, I know the saying about gift horses and that, but something in him got to me, you know? It put my back right up.

I'm not a racialist. Known good blokes come in every size and shape and colour. Bad ones, too. So it wasn't what he looked like pissed me off so much, although I will say this – it didn't fucking help, you know? It didn't help one bit.

Thin, he was, but not thin meaning skinny, more thin meaning *narrow*, like a long, tall building. And this shapeless bloody coat he wore, this kind of tube thing with his head poked out the end. Even his head was thin, like somebody'd just put it in a vice and squeezed. I mean, the profile wasn't bad, it wasn't Cary Grant, but it'd do, you know? Then from the front – no way. He wasn't right. He wasn't right at all. You get some queer cunts down the park, but this guy beat the lot, I'm telling you.

He wasn't drinking either. Which was weird. I mean, why hang out with the alkies if you don't fancy the booze? He wasn't anybody's social worker, that's for sure.

So I called Eddie over. Got him on one side. "Long cunt, Eddie. What's his game?"

"Him?" Eddie's well gone now, can hardly hold himself up straight. "Man From Mars," he says, and shakes his head. "Poor bugger can't get back..."

"Oh. Right. Sure. I mean, like – should've realised it, you know."

Ask a stupid question...

We'd got a crowd around us now. There are folk who'll smell an open bottle ten miles off, I swear. Horseface Lilly, Joe the Blag... Small world, and when there's drink on offer, everybody in it's suddenly your best, best pal. Long as it lasts.

Only it *did* last, that's the thing. That's what I couldn't figure out. Maybe the week in hospital had cleared my head, but I just smelt a rat about it all. Nobody else was bothered – they'd struck lucky, why bother? But it wasn't adding up to me. Once in a while, somebody'd yell out for another Glennie, and then, presto! – thirty seconds later, there's a brand new bottle going round, full to the brim, and good stuff, too. Soon we'd got empties everywhere. Big Steve fell over one.

167

Rolled round, clutching his arm. Gave us a laugh, that did. The rest kept drinking. A dozen of us, maybe more. I put away my share. But from the corner of my eye, I kept on watching him – that cunt. That Man From Mars.

I watched him till I saw what he was doing.

Or, more like, *didn't see.*

The cry went up, "Hey, *Glennieee!*" And one minute, he's standing there, all on his own, the next, he's reaching out, feeling around for some place high up in the air, except there *isn't any place.* There's nothing there. His hand just disappears. Winks out. And when he pulls it back, he's got a bottle in it.

Well, I've seen some artists in my time, but this guy – Jesus.

And it's like no-one else had seen it. That's the laugh. All too pissed up, I bet. The thin cunt passes round the bottle and someone lifts it to him like a toast, and he goes, "Why, that's quite alright, sir," in this squeaky little voice of his. Fair set my teeth on edge, I'm telling you.

I'd got a rep for fighting then. I don't mean I was good at it. I mean I'd get a few drinks down and then, sooner or later, catch someone trying to wisecrack me, or giving a sideways look, and I'd see red. It wasn't too predictable, even for me, but it was happening now, and big time, too.

This Man From Mars. I reckoned he was pulling one. Taking the piss. And all the others, they were in on it, the lot of 'em, all laughing up their sleeves. It made it worse I couldn't work out what the trick was.

So I slithered round. Dead subtle, like. And bit by bit, I got up closer –

"Hey, pal! How 'bout some smokes as well, eh?"

He smiled at me. Next thing, he's tossing me this pack of fags, like no fags I laid eyes on in my life before: black shiny box, and inside, every bloody smoke's a different colour, like a pack of kiddies' crayons. Everyone comes crowding round – ladies specially. Well, they were women's fags. That's how it looked to me. And what's the fucker doing, giving me women's fags, I want to know?

The bottle came along. I took a good long swig.

I made my mind up, then.

You don't think straight on drink. It's like it was just him and me, all of a sudden: me against the Man From Mars. I stood up slow and casual. I staggered over, wobbly on the pins. He smiled, real friendly-like. Looked like the vicar at the old folks' tea dance. But I got behind him, and I grabbed the bastard. Threw my whole weight at him. God, he didn't look like much, just like a streak of piss, I thought he'd drop, no sweat, except he didn't. Just kind of bent and swung, like he'd been planted there.

And something else, as well.

He didn't feel right. Under the coat, it felt like all his bones were jumbled up, all the joints re-fitted and the angles wrong, and everything in places where it shouldn't be... Then I was holding him and trying to get my foot around his leg to trip the cunt, but nothing doing. Christ. I *swear* the geezer wasn't human. Swear it. And God, I hated him! I could have killed him, given half a chance – making a fool of me like that! But Steve and Eddie – just protecting their investment, like – they knocked me to the ground. Gave me a good few kicks. Could have done for me, after the last good kicking that I got. Lucky I was tight. I got my wind back, slunk off down the shithouse, shut myself up in a cubicle and slept. Fuck all of 'em, I thought, fuck all of 'em...

*

It didn't stop me going back next day.

Tall thin guy, he was there again. Weird thing, he was the only one looked pleased to see me. Even knew my name. "Good morning, John," he says. Next minute I'd a bottle in my fist.

I tried ignoring him a while. Can't say I liked him any more than yesterday. Some of the lads were looking at me funny, too. The ones who could still see straight, anyway. I got some drinking in, enough to cure the shakes and get me feeling civilized again, then thought I'd strike off on my own. Well, I reckoned, what's to stop me coming back a wee bit later if I fancy it?

Didn't need to, as it happened. Ran into Davey Blunt, old prison mate, just out and flush already. Smart operator, Davey boy! Glad to see a friendly face as well, so we sank some in the boozer by the market, and a few more somewhere else... Old Davey didn't drink much, but I could drink for two in them days. Then back to his place with a carry-out. Grand life.

169

So it was next day when I found out what had happened in the park.

It's Eddie told me. Wish I'd seen it now. Some things, you can't imagine, not even when you try.

It seems like word had got around and every bloody wino in the district turned up that day. Not just your local crews. I'm talking *everyone*. Young punks and scallies, posh tarts, even a vicar with a taste for the communion wine. Blokes Eddie'd thought were dead, they'd been away so long (I told him, "Well, a drop of Scotch'll make a grand restorative, you know, Ed.").

It looked like feeding the five thousand all over again. The cops turned out, soon called for reinforcements. Choppers buzzing everywhere. The papers tagged it for a full-scale riot, a plot by left wing anarchists, or some such bollocks. Fat lot they knew!

There were arrests. Looks good on some cop's record sheet does that, rounding the winos up. But they never found the Man From Mars. Just disappeared, lost in the scuffle, I suppose. Can't say I missed him, though I missed his booze alright, especially first thing, waking sick and cold, the horrors clawing at my shoulder... I'd have taken drink from anybody then, I tell you, even if he'd popped up wearing horns and a long, pointy tail. No kidding there.

*

I had a run-in with the Law myself, soon afterwards.

D & D, it started off. No probs, like. Thought I'd pull a few good weeks in nick, clean up and get my strength back, then it's back out on the streets. No bother, see?

Two fucking years, I got.

It was a fit-up, naturally.

Turns out some tosser did the lav attendant down on Blakey Street a few nights back. Cops said it was me. Hadn't even heard about it till they started in. You can imagine how pathetic the old geezer looked, stood in the witness stand, nose done up in sticking plaster. Said he recognised me. Course he did. Been going there for years, haven't I? Wasn't me that done him over, though. But as the trial went on, I soon saw who was going to get the blame. They've got to have a villain, see. Got to have a culprit. Don't much matter who. I thought about it and I felt my stomach sink into a deep, deep hole.

Turned 30 in the nick, that time. Amazing, I suppose. I never thought I'd last that long.

There was a lot of gossip going round. Lot of talk about the riot in the park. It seems the numbers just got bigger every time, and there I was – the only bloody alkie in the place who'd missed it all! I talked about the Man From Mars, but these guys, they just tapped their heads, said I was screwy. "It's the booze, John. Makes the brain go soft." They reckoned it was just some rich bloke, giving drink away. Rich nutter, that was all. Till I thought, what the hell? How can a wino trust his eyesight, anyway? Best just forget it, let it go...

I got a letter from my Mum. My Dad was dead. I hadn't seen the guy in years, and now I never would. We'd been at daggers drawn most of my life, but even so, it made me sad. No chance to make the peace. No chance of saying hi. They gave me leave, just for the funeral. I reckon that's what did it, really. Seeing the family after so long. Mum all dressed in black. She looked like an old lady now, hunched-up and little... Choked me, that. You get used to not showing your feelings on the street or in the nick, but that day really cracked me up. Not on the outside, so you'd see. But inside, where it hurts.

*

I'll cut it short now, anyway. When I got out I went back to my Mum, I told her I was going straight, if I could manage it. I'd no illusions then. I knew I couldn't do it on my own. We talked about it for a long, long time, and there were some awkward moments. Then finally she told me if I'd try and beat the bottle, she'd have me back. I don't blame her for hesitating. If I was her, I'd just have thrown me out. Thank God she didn't. Jesus and Mary, was I grateful.

But that's not what I'm trying to tell about. That's just to tell you how I wound up with a family and a roof over my head again when I'd long ago given up hopes of either.

Things had changed a lot, the time I'd been away. Not just at home. The whole world seemed a different place. You don't much notice on the streets. Out there, it's where to find a bottle, or a place to kip – the Dow Jones Index isn't like your big concern, you know? Now I was looking for a job. Not easy for an ex-con. Or anybody else, for that matter. The industry was gone. Couldn't believe it, sometimes. Seemed like every day you'd hear about some firm gone bust, some factory closed down. Well, half the blokes around were on the dole, which in a way I was quite grateful for, it meant I didn't feel like such a down and out, like everybody'd stare if I was hanging round when other folks were all at work.

I steered clear of the parks. Steered clear of anywhere I'd meet old pals. Didn't leave the neighbourhood for weeks. I didn't take a drink, either. I read detective stories out the library – read the whole shelf full, end to end, then started it again. Something was nagging, though. Took me a while to pin it down.

No-one had money, but they all had *things*, you know? They all had *stuff*.

I'd see these young lads on the corner – flashy jackets, trainers, mobile phones – dressed up like a bunch of poofters, not a quid between 'em. Not a cent. Nowhere to go, all sort of listless, quarrelsome, like kids who've got too many toys and can't get *interested* any more.

Or take my Mum. She did a cleaning job, to make ends meet. Still wound up stumped for rent some weeks. But when I looked around the flat, I mean, my eyeballs fairly boggled. Colour telly, DVD, microwave, big fancy sewing machine... I'd ask her now and then where something came from – casual, like – and she'd tell me, "Oh, our Jimmy got us that."

Well, Jim's my younger brother. He lives around the corner with his girlfriend, Claire, and *they've* got nice stuff, too – karaoke, barbecue, computer games, all that.

I wasn't one to play big brother. But I told him, "All this knock-off gear then, Jim. You're into that, OK – it's on your own head. But get our Mum involved, that's something else."

He laughed at me. "It isn't knock off, John. Don't talk daft."

I asked him where he got it then. Oh, he tells me, various folk. "That telly there," he says. "Cost me a fiver. No-one sells a knock-off for a fiver, brand new – not unless they're desperate!"

"And no-one sells a straight one, either!" I put my arm around him. Still felt funny doing that, getting up close. I'd had to practice it. "Look, Jimmy, God knows, I've no rights, coming on like this. But I don't want you messing round with bent gear, eh? One pillock in the family's enough..."

"It *isn't* bent. I swear to God! You been out in the parks too long, that's your trouble. You ought to see how people live these days."

"Yeah. Well..."

"This stuff – it just comes up, you know? And people sell it. One week they'll have fridges. Next it's DVDs. Microwaves. Toy cars. Good stuff, an' all. These guys aren't fences, man. I never known the cops stick anything on anyone for it, you know?"

"Sounds weird to me."

"OK, OK. I mean, we got no dosh for Tenerife and that. But this lot, see – " he gestured round the room, "never been cheaper, this. Few nice little luxuries, keep your spirits up."

I shrugged. Well, maybe he was right. I'd felt like some kind of a savage, seeing how smart most people looked. But it was all a kind of patchwork smartness. Fancy shoes, and pants in rags. Flash car, no cash. And all the services – complete collapse. You got the rubbish picked up once in six months, maybe, you were lucky. Next door put their old washer out, thinking the Council'd come for it. It's still there. Bloody thing looked new to me, as well. Got a replacement, anyway, they say...

And then, seeing my Mum and Jimmy with that gear – it all looked out of line. Because we'd never had that kind of stuff, our family. Not ever.

I was watching telly late one night. Did lots of that – safer than drink! – and there's this bloke comes on, smart suit, smart tie, moustache, and copper written through him just like Blackpool rock.

He's talking about counterfeits. Not notes. Fake goods, he says. His face is grim, his lips a thin, straight line. High quality, he says. Fake stuff, so good no-one can tell it from the real.

I wasn't listening much till then. But I thought: fake stuff nobody can tell from real? Well then, it can't be fake, can it?

He yattered on and on. How it was putting people out of work. Wrecking profits. Factories all closed and workers on the dole... All sounded like a big excuse to me, the kind of thing you'd get from any politician's stooge.

Except that, well –

I don't know why it was. I hadn't thought of him for years. But suddenly, he popped into my head just then.

The Man From Mars.

And I reckoned anyone could pull a bottle out of thin air wasn't going to spend his life consorting with the winos and assorted maniacs down in the parks. He'd make a lot of friends, one way or other. And I thought about that smile he'd had. Dead keen to please, he'd been. Dead keen...

I sat there, looking at my Mum's TV. Not at the picture any more. Just at the set. And at the DVD. I reached out and I touched them. Got up close, real close, and stared. I shifted them around, looked at the backs. And it was true: you couldn't tell them from the real thing. They looked normal. They worked normal.

Better than normal, even.

I switched the set off, switched it on again. Changed channels. Changed the colour, changed the brightness, changed the volume.

Perfect.

Beautiful.

It made me queasy all at once. And if I'd still been drinking, I'd have taken one right there and then.

Fast Eddie'd said he was the Man From Mars. But, fat lot Eddie knew. I reckoned he was something more than that. Something divine – or devilish.

I never go to mass, these days. But Mum still has the priest round now and then. I asked him once: "Father, is there a patron saint of worldly goods, like?"

Well, he said that was a question, right enough, and chattered on a while. Not worth repeating, most of it. But he's the only parish priest I've ever met who drives a BMW and wears a Rolex watch. *Two* Rolex watches, it turns out: one set to Greenwich, one to Rome.

And now, he says, he wants a third, soon as they're back down at a 'decent' price again.

He leans up close, gives me a greedy little wink.

"*Jerusalem*," he whispers in my ear. "I'm thinking big, these days, John, just like all of us. We're all thinking that wee bit bigger, now we can afford it, eh?"

Relics

I took the flyer south along the coast, engine coughing on the dingy local fuel. I called it reconnoitring, this trip, though sight-seeing was much nearer the mark. The seagulls wheeled around me, squawking in alarm, as if I were some giant, prehistoric bird of prey, the flyer's frame a skeleton touched magically to life. I frightened them; but as for me, I'd lost none of the thrill I always felt in flight. Red hills rose to a sky of polished blue, plunging as I banked, then shore and sand were rushing past and I was high above the ocean, watching the patterns on the water, great dark splotches of marine weed, white surf rolling over hidden rocks... Was this what I was looking for? A sign, a clue? The key to sunken treasure?

The wind pulled at my hair. The engine hummed and sputtered, hummed again. I swooped so low I could have stuck my feet out and gone walking on the wave-tops, if I'd wanted to.

The water wasn't giving anything away.

A hundred years ago, or so the story went, a starship had come down here. Crashed, sunk, and never been recovered. Too far off the beaten track, too many better pickings elsewhere in the world. The thing was there, alright, I'd had my proof of that; exactly where, though – that was anybody's guess.

I circled, and the sea rose like a wall beside me. Tiny islands floated in the mid-day glare. The water wasn't deep here. Only deep enough.

I turned inland, riding the air over the cliff tops. A solitary goatherd watched me, flock stirring as I dropped towards him. I waved. He didn't move. Faintly annoyed, I swooped in low, scattering the animals, yelling out over the engine noise, but the man stayed stock still, like a statue caught in time. I spun over his head, taunting him, then swung around and sped off north.

My base town, G___ , was so small that it only featured on the map out of default; without it, the whole coast would have been blank for miles. Two low horns of buildings jutted round a harbour far too large for the few fishing boats it held; even the water seemed peculiarly slack and tired, with the tranquillity of absolute old age. Dilapidation was the keynote, houses fixed up with whatever came to hand, including sections of a disused oil refinery a few miles downshore; curved sheets of steel, shining where they hugged the old stone walls and wooden roofs. It gave the place a jumbled, quaint sort of a look, more like a scrapyard than a village; and privately I'd long ago re-christened it 'the Garbage Heap'.

I buzzed the quayside, caught a look from the old men outside the bar, then lifted up over the rooftops to the field where I habitually parked. By the time I landed, half the village children had come out to welcome me. And by the water pump, still some way off, stood Julia.

Her height, her colouring, the way she moved, all marked her out from those around. A passing sailor, merchant or whatever, far off in her ancestry, might have accounted for her looks. Her moods weren't quite so easy to explain. Why now, when I expected her to run to me, why did she hang back, sullen, making me push my way through these excited, dark-skinned kids, smiling, nodding, pretending to be charmed; and all the time, intent on her?

Under the blaring summer light, her eyes were blue, bright silver-blue: eyes like the sky.

They didn't look at me.

"So you came back," she said.

"Course I came back! What d'you think?"

I went to clasp her hand, but she folded her arms, and it wasn't till the evening that her glum phase lifted, and she smiled, and snuggled up, as if it had been she, not I, who'd been away.

*

We lived together all that summer, in my little rented room above the quay. I was the village curiosity, the one old women peeped at from their shadowed rooms, and gossiped over in their own strange, hybrid tongue – or so I fancied, anyway. Yet when I'd first arrived I'd no intention to stay on, not for a day, a night, not even for a single afternoon.

Meeting Julia had changed all that.

I scarcely thought of us as lovers then. I'd never been at ease with women – not the girls back home, at any rate – but Julia, with her quiet, cat-like presence, comical pronunciation, and her table manners which would frankly have appalled my parents – soon helped me relax. She put up with my nervousness, my fumbling at her body, my clumsy efforts to be 'passionate', all with a patience which in any other context would have credited a saint. Even when she laughed at me, or tenderly corrected one of my more amateur caresses, there was never any malice in her – none of that jockeying for status I'd so often seen in couples back at home. The thinness of my arms amused her, and the softness of my hands and feet ('Like a bambino!' she would cry). Her own hands were as tough as crabs, but sensitive enough; I'll vouch for that.

I liked to watch her in the morning, making breakfast, washing in the bucket by the window, delighting in her looks, those high, steep cheekbones, tapered chin, and most of all her eyes, which in the daylight would be icy blue, yet other times reflected almost any colour you could dream of – silver mirrors, meant to hide, not to reveal. I only knew one other person who had eyes like that, and in him, although they fascinated still, they made me wary, too.

I was eighteen then. I'd fled from home, its nagging pressure of careers, exams, the need to get a 'good' job, meet the 'right' people... But she knew nothing about that. I'd try to talk to her, and watch her eyes glaze over, fingers start to fidget. Such things weren't even relevant to her. She'd want to eat, or sleep, make love, or talk about her father's latest exploits. Or show me what she'd brought back from the far bays, across the headland, which she visited from time to time, and which gave her the small income that she had.

She found amazing objects on the beach – alien artefacts, smashed fragments, pieces of machinery – then sold them for a pittance to a trader who came by once a month or so. I told her she was being robbed. She ought to save her finds and take them to the city, sell them there herself, I said. She only shrugged. Life wasn't lived like that. It wasn't done. My efforts to bring enterprise into her tiny world were met with sceptical dismissal. Habit – tradition – was the keynote here. Lose that, she seemed to say, and life would fall apart. Lose that, your dignity went, too.

I'd yet to understand just how much dignity she really had.

*

Her mother had died, ten years earlier, of something she called 'fever'. Her father lived a few miles out of town, on one of the old dirt roads that festooned the hills. He owned some sheep, some goats, he did a little fishing, but the main thing that he liked was getting paralytic drunk, then weeping sentimentally about the past. The first time that we met he greeted me as if I were a long-lost son. He grasped my hand in his big, horny palm and kept repeating the few English words he knew: 'Hello!' 'Bye-bye!' 'Good!' 'London!'. Under the rolls of fat, the sun-burned lines, I still saw traces of the same high cheekbones that I knew so well in Julia, although the eyes were dull, like stones. I saw the family as echoes of her, clumsy mirror-images; and yet her sisters hardly looked like her at all. Only the brother, Juan, was truly of her type – so much so, that, for weeks, I thought they must be twins. His forehead was as broad, his eyes the same bright, liquid silver, and I hoped that I'd become his friend, as if my closeness to his sister would extend to him, as well.

This didn't happen. Rather, he shunned me.

He was the only one among the family who sat apart, like a mistrustful elf, or took my visits as a cue to get on with his farm chores. I tried to show my good intentions, calling out, "Hi, Juan," each time I saw him, but he'd only scowl or turn his back.

Did he resent my being there? Imagine I'd besmirched his sister's honour, say? If so, as I knew even then, I can't have been the first. And would he want some terrible revenge?

Such fantasies were foolish, though. He'd never go against his sister's wishes. As eldest, she'd assumed her mother's role, ruling the family like some stern, benevolent dictator, and nobody – not Juan, her father or her sisters – would even once have dared offend her.

178

That, at least, was plain.

Their poverty seemed quaint and picturesque at first. I loved the smoky little cottage where they crowded with their hens and goats, three rooms for a family of five. It was a lark for me, to squat there on the earthen floor. I couldn't even dream of how it must be through the long, drab winter months, in rooms lit intermittently by oil lamps, cold and draughty, never any privacy... No wonder Julia had come to live with me.

I told her I was short of money. Already I was worried by the cost of fuel. I don't think she believed me – all foreigners had money, after all, and by her standards, I must have been a wealthy man – but, after some confusion, she seemed willing to accept whatever game I might be playing, and to play along.

"I know how to make money," she announced, and soon was making plans which privately I thought were ludicrous, but didn't have the heart to stop.

She roused me in the pre-dawn light. She forced hot coffee down me, waited while I dressed, and then, on foot, we left the town, walked up over the headland – a long walk, three hours and more. She moved with an extraordinary speed, chasing the goat tracks, and more than once I had to call for her to wait. My ankles were soon scratched and bleeding, scraped by thorns and harsh grass. Downhill was worse than up. Once, I slipped and fell, scraping a few yards down the hillside; in a moment, she was with me, though her concern soon turned to laughter when she saw I wasn't hurt.

"You!" she chided. "City boy!"

I grew irritable, sullen. So much of our relationship was founded on my own sense of superiority, the fact I came from somewhere far, far richer, more advanced than she. I could afford to visit her, but she could never, never visit me...

All it took was just an early morning walk to show how frail such notions really were.

I sulked for the remainder of the trip – though not so much I missed the beauty of my first sight of the bay. We topped a rise and there it was before us, a great sheet of sea, all grey, and at the same moment we saw it, so the sun began to rise.

It came up from the waters, tiny, like a pomegranate seed, bright

179

and moving almost visibly, so that my hurt pride, bruised knees and bleeding legs were banished for a moment from my mind. Watching the sea turn pinky-grey, the sun ascending on a spear of light, once more I tried to picture the old ship, concealed under the water, crusted, covered up in weed... Not here, perhaps, but far out, on the horizon, prey to tides and currents, long lost and far from home...

And thinking of it, I was reminded how far I, too, was from home, and felt that early morning sadness come upon me, a fear that I might somehow die in this forsaken place, news of my death unknown to either family or friends...

She called to me. She was a hundred feet below, nimble as a lizard, the empty canvas bag she carried draped across her back.

"On! On!" she called. "What's stopping you?"

Cautiously, I set off after her. I wished I'd brought a camera – wished I owned a camera, as if in one small picture I could hold this mood, this sense of melancholy which, in some peculiar self-indulgent way, I realised I enjoyed.

*

Instinct guided her. I never understood what signs she looked for, how she chose her days, her hunting grounds. We picked our way among the pools, and shoes in hand she danced from rock to rock, light as could be. It took her twenty minutes. Then she yelled out, "Yah!"

I peered into the black silt of the pool bottom. Saw nothing. A swarm of tiny fish swept through the water. Then she knelt, plunged in her hand, and brought up treasure.

It didn't look like treasure. Not at first.

It was a strip, long as her forearm, slightly curved; black with dirt, a slimy seaweed streamer hanging from it.

"There," she said, and held it close up to her face, scratching at it with a thumbnail. She let me see the glint of silver, shining filigree beneath the muck.

"How did you...?"

She shrugged, secretive.

"It doesn't look like anything. How did you see it? How...?"

Two more pieces she produced that day – perhaps two portions of a single thing. Small cylinders, a little thicker than a pencil, one long as my hand, the other smaller. These, too, seemed near invisible among the debris of the pool bottom, yet she went quickly to them, guided by some curious affinity.

She dropped them in her bag. And we went home.

The sun was falling as we came back into town. Over the harbour now, the low, square houses at the promontory's tip were sliced with golden light. Shadows swallowed up the rest. I was tired, scarcely even watching where I went.

I didn't see him, waiting for us. Not till she suddenly cried out and ran ahead.

Juan. My heart sank at the sight of him; not that I feared or even much disliked him, but I was tired and I resented his intrusion here, on what I saw as my home ground. He and Julia began to talk immediately, in hushed tones. As I came near, he seemed to glower at me. "Hi, Juan," I said. He gave a nod. Under his dark brows, his strange eyes almost matched the last gold tips of sunlight on the buildings opposite.

I climbed the outside stairway to my room. At the top, I waited. I could see them, talking in an agitated way, but couldn't understand. She shook her head, as if forbidding something. I was hungry. I wished he'd clear off, go home and leave us on our own. But when he did, it seemed to have left ill-feeling between him and his sister. I asked her what was wrong – bad news about her father, say? – but she said, no, no, her father was just fine, the family was well.

"Your brother doesn't like me very much."

"Juan?"

"Who else d'you think I mean?"

But she placed her hand upon my arm, squeezed hard. "Juan likes you very, very much," she said. "Do not forget."

We made love that night, as was our custom, the tiredness of our bodies giving the act a dream-like quality, urgent yet detached, as if we watched ourselves; and when she came, she cried out – so loudly I was worried that my hosts, down in the room below, might come up and complain.

*

I woke in darkness, and instead of trying to sleep again, I got up, looked out across the harbour, and then up, towards the stars – thousands and thousands of them, unfogged here by pollution or a hint

181

of cloud, the Milky Way a great jewelled river leading God knows where.

And if the stars made up a river, I was standing in its smallest, most forgotten backwater; a ragged little town, here on a planet nobody had bothered with in well over a century.

For twenty years, the aliens had visited our world, had come and gone in all their countless species and designs; had used us as a way station, a home-from-home – even today, their weird 'environments', great geodesic domes, lay scattered over every continent on Earth, each with its set conditions, suitable for this creature or that; now slowly rotting, weakened by the sunlight and the rain, the hostile airs of Earth. Impressive as they were, they hadn't lasted half the time of those crude steel edifices the Victorians put up. But then, as we knew now, they hadn't been intended to.

The aliens' technology had left us flattened, spiritually prostrated by their miracles. We'd marvelled like a backwoods tribe presented with a string of beads, we'd thought the aliens our benefactors, wonder-workers, saviours from the stars. And what did they care, if we'd cadged a few discarded gadgets, picked up a small smattering of knowledge – enough to keep our physicists awake for weeks, plotting the new trajectories of their careers, enough to make the multi-nationals all drool with hunger... Oh, but that was nothing. Throwaways. They kept their greatest secrets from us, I've no doubt. They gave us just a taste.

And then they disappeared.

No explanations. No announcements. One day, the last ship left; and people waited for the next.

It never came.

It was as if they'd all, those diverse creatures, suddenly lost interest in our little portion of the universe. As if we'd fallen out of fashion. We'd had the arrogance to see ourselves as colleagues, allies. But they'd left without a backward glance.

The gifts that still remained we'd put to use, and for a time it seemed their legacy would be a beautiful, Edenic world, a place where – as in some Nineteenth Century fantasy – science really would solve all man's ills.

And yet it was a science it might take millennia to understand. Too much seemed burdened with a built-in obsolescence, like cheap goods left us by a richer and more careless race. Machines wore out. Others relied on elements we simply did not have – and could not synthesise.

Perhaps it was deliberate.

It was notable that, in spite of questioning, the aliens had never shared the secrets of their space flight. Like tourists, they would give us gifts, but wanted us, essentially, to go on just as they first found us – quaint, primitive and charming.

Much of the trouble now in the industrialised world was simply recoil from those boom years – the forced attempt to re-adjust to the technology our forefathers had known. We had become like cargo cultists, propped up by the debris of another's industry; or millenarians, scanning the skies for signs our saviours might return.

Perhaps they would. Who knew? A century must seem like nothing to them, like they'd just stepped out the door.

I thought about the ship under the water. One of countless relics, littering the world, like all the rusting hulks of cars, the broken washing machines, and old, dumped armchairs that I'd seen along the roadside in my travels. An accident, a piece of tragic carelessness...

Were the aliens mere tourists, then? Moving on as trends and crazes changed? It was a tempting thought, but one that didn't fit. It was like reading human motives into animals – no, stranger: into clouds, or trees. The aliens weren't in the least like us. The little lemur creatures had been vaguely recognisable, almost cute; and they'd been popular as a result. I'd seen films of them. But there were others – creatures who could only be described in terms of mathematics, who defied the eye and warped the senses with their presence. Tourists? Not in the sense I understood, at any rate...

*

We made love in the morning, too.

She worked on me, using her fingers and her mouth, her body twisting like a snake. I dreamed she'd swallow me, absorb me utterly, make me a part of her... A frightening, delicious feeling, like sitting in the front seat of the roller coaster.

And when she'd finished, she went straight to her latest artefact, the silver filigree, and held it high up in the sunlight, so it caught the rays and shone.

"Look!" she cried, then, "Beautiful! Beautiful!"

*

We found other relics, as the weeks went by – or she did, anyway. I trudged behind, watching the ground and seeing nothing. It was her, all her. If there was anything to find, she'd find it, eyes as sharp as needles. I made plans to take our treasure trove up north, to find an honest dealer, get a decent price. That's if I could.

And yet there came a time my interest in the project waned. I couldn't help it; it was more a loss of faith than anything. It had been her idea, not mine. Perhaps I'd wanted instant riches, or thought we'd come back from the bay loaded with treasure, rather than these piecemeal relics slowly gathering around us. I was impatient. I looked up at the stars at night, and felt some wonder at the clutter of exotic items we'd amassed, but I no longer saw our fortune there. I no longer believed.

From time to time, I noticed a few clouds pass through the sky, perhaps the harbingers of Julia's much longed-for storm, the tempest which would fill the beaches with fresh plunder. One thing they did remind me of: the season was about to change.

I went to check the flyer. It was sheltered by tarpaulin. The fuel was scarce, the servicing entirely amateur. I reckoned it would take me north just one more time before it had to have a thorough overhaul. Meanwhile, I did my best to keep it clean and shield it from the elements.

The future raced towards me now, after the long, still summer; born on those first few clouds, the cooling breeze that drifted from the mountains, stirring the waves into a frenzy as they battered on the shore.

It was a climate of extremes. The wind and rain were fierce in winter, so the locals said. Snow on the mountains. I'd been surprised, when I'd heard that, but now I could believe it. I began to see just how unwelcoming the place must be in winter, cut off from the world... And what did people eat? I'd read how, in the Middle Ages, winter would mean stored food, resulting in all kinds of vitamin deficiencies; then people would go mad, see visions, suffer religious fits and hypochondria... Suppose that happened here? To me, and those around?

In some part of myself I knew that if I went back to the city, I'd never come back here. It would be much too easy to go on, go somewhere else; too easy to go home.

Julia, as if she sensed my restlessness, tried hard to please. She bought an octopus and simmered it for hours in a stew of herbs, until the flesh was tender and delicious. More than ever, she initiated lovemaking, finding new games, tending to my wants. Yet all the while, unknowingly, she worked against herself. I grew selfish. It was easier, these days, to satisfy my own needs, scarcely bothering with hers. Our lovemaking was frequent, yes, but it was often brief. I don't mean that I cared for her the less. Just that the novelty, the rush of joy we'd had, was gone, and I was unsure what, if anything, replaced it. When our affair began, she'd occupied my thoughts both day and night. Now there were other matters claiming my attention, many far more strongly than did she.

One night a wind came up. It rattled at the shutters, and a door banged intermittently, and she hugged me and she whispered in my ear, "Good finds tomorrow! Good finds!"

*

I never made it to the bay that morning. Crapulous, hung over from the local wine, I told her, "You go – I'll come later."

It was after ten when I woke properly.

My head felt thick. I was alone. I made a coffee, very sweet, and drank it painfully. I downed a pint of water. Then I pushed the shutters back. The light was hard, corrosive, and it shattered on the harbour in a way that hurt my eyes. I told myself she didn't need me in the bay, and wondered why I ever went; I was her porter, nothing more. And I saw then what I should have seen so long ago: that I was just a foreigner, a summer guest, and all my talk of staying on was no more than a sham. I couldn't live in her world, any more than she could live in mine – or, I thought, would want to.

Hangovers are lethal to your self-esteem. But sometimes, in that glazed and almost ego-less condition, you see things with a clarity unknown at any other time.

I fumbled for my cigarettes, lit up, and heard a faint tap at the door. Ignored it. But it came again: *tap-tap, tap-tap...*

Her brother stood there. Juan. He hunched up slightly when he saw me, ducked his head in a peculiar, self-deprecating way, and peered at me with sharp, bright eyes.

*

He was different, here alone; awkward, uncertain of himself, without his sister's presence. His gaze moved round the room, lingered for a moment on the bed, then longer on the pile of artefacts laid out across the floor.

"She's at the bay," I said. "She won't be back for hours..."

Yet I knew already that it wasn't Julia he'd come to see.

I made fresh coffee and he took it, still without a word. His lips peeled back in what was meant to be a smile. Once more he glanced down at the artefacts.

I told him, "Go ahead."

It was a strange thing. I'd seen Juan many times these last few weeks. He'd struck me as a sullen, graceless creature, and his similarities to Julia lacked both her intelligence and wit. Yet now a change seemed to come over him. He squatted on his heels and picked up each object in turn, held it, moved it in the light, ran his fingers over it as if his horny, calloused hands became as sensitive as the most expert jewelsmith's. I watched, almost against my will, so struck now by his transformation. For minutes, he seemed totally absorbed. It was as if all other matters – myself, the room, even the town itself – had faded from his mind.

The last objects he came to were the two dull rods, the fragments we'd brought back that first day, and he picked the longer one, examined it a moment. Then he gripped it in his fist and squeezed it, rhythmically. He stood up, gestured me to pull the shutters closed.

The room in shadow now, he held the rod between his thumb and forefinger. With his other hand, he made a pass around it, like a stage magician, intricate, precise; I seemed to see an after-image where his fingers moved, a geometric web that flickered for a half second in the air, too complex fully to recall.

Next, he touched the tip quite lightly with his forefinger. A tiny, purple light appeared. He moved his finger gently down the rod, from end to end. The small spark followed it. It seemed to be inside, somehow, enclosed within the darker matter, like a firefly in a jar. I stared at it. The rod was just as solid as before, opaque as polished

186

stone. It made no sense.

He grinned. Not the forced smile of his greeting, but a real, wide, gap-toothed grin – a look of sheer delight. He ran his finger back and forth, the small light trailing it. Wonder of wonders. Miracle of miracles.

And then it dimmed.

It took a second or two, fading like an ember.

Disappeared.

The rod was grey, inert again, just as we'd found it.

"No good." He held the end out so that I could see. "Broken," he said.

I agreed; what else was I supposed to say? I asked him how he'd done it, what he'd done, but he just looked away, as if it were a minor matter, much too modest to discuss.

"You've seen these things before," I said.

He grinned then, proudly.

"You know what they were used for?"

"In the ship," he said. "A engine. Or..." He fumbled for the word. "A instrument."

"You know about the ship? You know where it was from? Who brought it here?"

Again, I got a vague response, a quick, dismissive shrug that might mean anything; but what I thought it meant was, 'No, I don't know – but I don't mind you thinking I do.'

He put the rod back on the floor, sat down. I made more coffee, pushed the shutters back. I said, "You know what they were like – the people on the ship? The aliens? Has anything washed up? A picture, maybe, or, or – " 'a body,' I'd been going to say, but stopped myself. "Something like that?"

He laughed. "Spacemen," he said. "Big monsters. Many tentacles. Big teeth!" He pulled a face, sucking his cheeks in, waving his arms around. "Monsters. Eat everyone!"

I looked down at the artefacts, the silver filigree, those other items, all their strength, their delicacy.

"No," I said. "I don't think they were monsters..."

"All dead," he went on. "Ship come down – crash into sea." He mimed it with his hand, coming in too steeply, swerving now over the

187

water... Again, I had the strange impression of precise geometry, as if in some way he were plotting an exact trajectory, the very angle of their flight, repeated here in miniature. He made the motion several times. "Boom," he said. "Boom, boom."

I sat down on the bed, keeping my face out of the sun. My head still ached.

"Well," I said, "maybe Julia'll bring something back this time. She's waiting for a storm..." I nodded to the window. "Won't get one today, though."

Juan sat, legs together, elbows resting on his knees, his fingers interlinked and fidgeting. Then – quickly, as if it took him nerve to ask – he said, "You marry Julia?"

The question startled me. "Oh, well, I, I don't know – and it's up to her..."

"You marry Julia." No query now; nor any threat. He leaned towards me, offering advice. "She very good. Smart, up here." He tapped his head. "She give you children." He smiled, marking their heights out with his hand: a little one, a bigger one, and one as tall as he was, sitting down. He didn't realise that, if any image could have put me off, it was the picture of his sister, transformed into some peasant-hipped brood-mare, another baby-factory like the women on the quayside, waiting for their husbands to come home. My rural idyll was a strictly adolescent one; it didn't involve families.

He said, "You stay. You make much money here."

I shrugged. He frowned.

"You have money, yes?"

"Not a bean," I said. He looked confused. I told him, "No."

He contradicted me. "You have money. Yes. You have money, or your father, or your mother. You bring money here. Many men. You make more money. Me – I show you how."

"So how's that, Juan?"

"I show. But – need boats. Many thing." He mimed, an odd gesture I couldn't place.

"Fishing rods?" I said.

"No – big – big."

"Winches? Cranes?"

"Yes. Cranes. Need cranes. Boats. Men – "he made a diving

motion – "in the water. The ship..." He held his hand out, flat, close to the floor. Then, face creased, mimicking the strain, he raised it slowly, stiffly to the level of his eyes.

He grinned at me.

"You're joking, Juan. You want to raise the ship? It's probably not even in one piece. And if it was worth doing, they'd have done it long ago..."

"One piece," he echoed. "Yes. We can fly. One piece."

He moved his hand around, like a child playing at aeroplanes, though there was nothing childish in his face; it was a look of fierce intensity, something startling: the look of a fanatic.

I'd once believed that he was trying to protect his sister's honour. Now I saw that it was something very different that he wanted to protect – and use me to retrieve.

"I'll have to... think about it," I said cautiously.

He shook his head.

"No think. Do."

"It's going to take a lot of planning. I mean, it needs locating... You know where it is? Exactly? Have you seen it?"

Again, I got that look: perhaps I have, perhaps I've not.

"And then I'd need to talk to people. Back at home. Financial backing. I might... know someone who'd be interested." I was improvising, though; stalling for time. "But then – there's things like salvage rights. If people put up money for it, well, they'll want a good return. You wouldn't get a thing..."

He tipped his head on one side, queried me. I said, "Whoever paid to bring it up would get the ship. You might get wages, but that's all. The ship wouldn't be yours. Or mine. I haven't got the money."

"Yes. You have money."

"No, Juan – "

"You *make* money."

"Maybe when I'm older. But right now... No. Seriously – you've probably got more than me."

It was a heartless thing to say, and obviously untrue. Again, he seemed to fold in on himself, hunched up like a suspicious little goblin. His brief delight over the artefacts was gone. Now he was tense; deep lines like knife-cuts dug into his brows. I tried a little to explain my situation, then, giving up, I told him I was interested, and thought there was a chance we might work something out.

"I'll need to speak to people, first," I said again.

"Alright. You speak. Is good."

And as he left, he did something that took me by surprise. He reached out and, with carefully rehearsed formality, he shook my hand. His eyes held mine. They were so like his sister's eyes – the complex whorls of blue and white – but these were hard and purposeful, like frozen jewels. The eyes of insects.

I watched him go, scuttling down the steps, then off along the street, without even a backward glance.

*

I didn't know how I could stay with her, from that time on. It sounds ridiculous, perhaps, and paranoid, but everywhere we went I felt that I was being followed by a string of little ones – infant Julias and Juans, toddlers and schoolchildren and crabby adolescents, and none of them looked in the least like me.

Their eyes were blue – bright silver blue.

Oh, on the surface, I suppose, our lives went on much as before. We drank down at the harbour bar, we took long walks, made love, made visits... There was a big festivity up in the hills, to celebrate a marriage, with roasted pig and quantities of homemade liquor, and dancing until dawn. It was a glorious, exciting time. And yet my heart just wasn't in it.

Once, when I was sitting, brooding, smoking cigarettes and staring out to sea, she came up and she asked me, "So?"

"So what?" I said, joking, smiling, like I'd missed the real enquiry there.

We made love now with a quiet fury, as if we had to fuck or die; mashing each others' bodies, gouging one another with an energy that left no room for sentiment, as if we were mere animals, helpless creatures, harassed by the onset of the night.

This was no glorious Arcadia, I knew now, no simple world of fisher-folk and goatherds, but something more unsettling, come down from the stars, long, long ago, before it ever came to me. A conspiracy which even the conspirators themselves had failed to comprehend.

Most days now found me working on the flyer. I drained the tank,

190

leaving a patch of stained black earth and poisoned grass. I made sure every plug and contact was at optimum efficiency, each part gleaming like the starmen's jewels up in my room.

And then the weather turned.

Fierce winds blew off the sea, and clouds banked up over the mountains, spilling rain and thunder on the low hills and the town. I knew this was the weather she'd been waiting for, a storm so strong that it would rake the sea floor, dredging up the debris she required.

To me, though, it meant something else.

I couldn't fly in winds like this.

When winter came, then I'd be stuck here. I needed to fly north as soon as possible. To take the first clear day, and make a start.

*

There are forgivable betrayals. Excuses that will just hold up: you were too young, naive, you didn't understand... There are mitigating circumstances. To hold to them will make it possible to go on living.

What damns though, and damns utterly, are all the efforts afterwards to justify yourself. The claims that what you did was right, and fair, even self-sacrificing – these are the real crimes, the real treachery involved.

A few days later, and a hundred miles from Julia, sat in an air-conditioned bar, I wrote to her.

It was a nasty, pious little letter, though at the time it seemed to me the soul of magnanimity: it wasn't her fault, I insisted, it was mine; what we'd had had been as beautiful and fragile as a butterfly in summer, a creature of a season, nothing more; our lives had coincided, briefly, and the parting had, I told her, been inevitable from the start...

I said she meant a lot to me, would always have a place deep in my heart. We'd meet again some day. And in the meantime, if she ever needed help, in any way, she was to contact me immediately. I'd be there for her.

I wrote the note on hotel stationery, and somehow managed to forget to give a permanent address.

Another week, and I was home.

I boasted to my friends, of course. It was expected. I described adventures, crises, insights that had come to me. I talked about the beautiful young native girl I'd lived with all that summer... I returned, brown-skinned and lean, self-confident, and with a certain measure of celebrity. I never told the story as I've told it here, the real story, the one that counts.

*

These days, I think about the starship most of all. I still don't know who flew it, what fatal error brought it down. But I think about its pilots, in their final moments, when they knew they were about to crash. At such a time, it strikes me you'll do anything to save yourself, won't you? Whether you're a man, or whether you're a five-dimensional blob from Planet X. Whatever kind of life you've got, you don't want it to end.

Only I think that Juan was right – they *are* dead, in any terms that we can understand. As individuals. As entities. Their bodies are still down there, trapped beneath the sea. Mangled, crushed, starved; whatever got them in the end.

But I imagine (and this is fancy, speculation, nothing more), I imagine that before they died, there was an element within themselves, an energy, perhaps, a particle or wave, an essence of some kind, that they were able to release (perhaps only with great pain; perhaps only at the point of death, a magic suicide); an element released into the world, to find a new host, a new life... Perhaps a solitary fisherman. Perhaps a goatherd, high up in the hills. Someone, at any rate. And that day, something alien crept into him, inhabited his cells, printing its stamp upon his chromosomes, his very soul.

Later, the man fathered a child.

The child had ice-blue eyes.

This may have happened countless times in human history; an alien soul, blended with ours, changing the texture of our lives, our selves.

It might disappear for decades, a generation, maybe more, resurfacing in grandchildren, like a recessive gene: here and gone, and back again.

And each time, it grows more dilute. Its needs are filtered through the mores and temper of society. It manifests as vague, unsettled feelings, unconsoled ideas, longings that seem wild, irrational, absurd; that have to be explained away, somehow.

I think Juan truly thought raising the ship would make his fortune. What other decent reason could he have? Why else should he be interested? Yet at night he must have dreamed of seeing its great

192

ruptured hull, stripped of its weeds and barnacles, of entering its hidden chambers, sitting once again at its controls...

That's how I tell the story now. That I fled from something sinister and alien, that threatened to consume me.

Yet there's another version, too. One I only tell myself, when I wake up at three or four a.m., feeling depressed and worthless, when it seems the sky's no longer filled with stars but black, and empty, and devoid of any meaning we could ever learn.

Then I imagine it a different way, a story much, much smaller and more personal: a young man, both naive and arrogant, uncertain of himself, secretly scared of everything – who one time knew a girl who genuinely loved him, cared for him, and whom he found a reason to abandon. Not even, when you come to it, a good reason.

But that's a story I tell seldom, and only to myself, and hope, some day, I might forget.

*

A Specialist in Souls

by Ernest Hemingway

edited and prepared for publication by Tim Lees

[The publishers are pleased to present this so-called "lost" or "suppressed" chapter of Mr Hemingway's Paris memoir, A Moveable Feast. How the manuscript came into Mr Lees's possession is a story which his legal counsel will not at present allow him to reveal, though he assures us when the truth comes out, it will make Mr Hemingway's own tales of derring-do look pretty small potatoes in comparison.]

You had to take what company you could when you were new in Paris and had worked hard and were a writer not yet known, or not yet for your writing, anyway. So I found myself one evening in the company of several worthless fellows and their presiding deity, a Dr Dempster, as he called himself in Paris at that time, and I was watching as the light changed, the beautiful Parisian light they don't have any more, which goes from grey to mauve and to a deep mauve-grey the colour of a bruise, when Dr Dempster said, quite loudly in my ear, "Of course, metempsychosis is these days an accepted scientific fact, at least to any educated man."

I told him, "Bull."

"That the soul deserts the body at the point of death, seeking a new and better home has, we know, long been intuited by even the most primitive of peoples, and with modern scientific methods, we can show – "

I told him, 'Poppycock,' which was not the word I used but which will do for this account. Dr Dempster frowned, and raised one perfectly arched eyebrow, a product of the topiarist's art, perhaps.

"My dearest Hem. You have some small objection to my talk?"

"Don't poppycocking *dearest* me," I said. "I've seen more poppycocking death than any dozen of you poppycocking poppycockers, and a great deal more than you have, Dr Poppycock-face. And if you tell me any one of them was letting out his poppycocking soul to find a better home, I'll poppycock your poppycock from here to kingdom poppycocking come."

One of the worthless fellows, to smooth things over, ordered a round of drinks, calling the waiters 'boy', even Miguel, who was the most dignified and beautifully mannered waiter I have ever known.

"There are those who hold that the more violent the death, the more rapidly and more efficiently the soul will be released. To the Vikings, of course, death in battle was the greatest honour; the soul would go directly to Valhalla. In the Christian crusades, and the Mohammedan holy wars, similar dispensations would be granted. Indeed," he giggled, a sound that almost had me reaching for my trousers belt, he was so fervently in need of whipping, "in many ways the worst fate might befall a man is to die peacefully in his sleep. Don't you agree there, Mr Hemingway?"

"For some people it's never too poppycocking soon to die."

"Why so hostile, Hem? Why so... *engagé*?"

The worthless fellows grinned at one another, as if it were a clever trick to use a word of French while here, in France.

I saw Miguel watch as he wiped the zinc counter-top, the kind of counter-top they once had everywhere in Paris, but is now found only in the few, the simplest and the best of bars.

"I'm hostile to a poppycocking poppycock-licker who thinks by talking about things that he knows poppycock about he'll make people impressed enough to buy him the next round of drinks."

One of the worthless fellows started to speak up. I silenced him.

Only Dr Dempster was unruffled. "Hem, Hem, Hem." He put his hands together, steepling his fingers. "Hem, Hem, Hem, Hem." He sounded like a toad with something in its throat. "You dispute clear scientific principles. Why – " he turned to share with his companions, "Cocteau for one is utterly convinced. I spoke to him about it just the other day. He wants to come back as a penguin. Can you believe? He seems to think that sitting on an ice floe eating fish must be the world of heaven. Up there, with the northern lights... Or is it in the Antarctic? Where do penguins live? The Arctic or Antarctic?"

"Cocteau," I said, "is a fine one. He believes in fairies."

"Ah! But so does half of Paris! They simply prefer not to talk about it! And Hem – why – is that a touch of henna in your hair?"

"Poppycock you, poppycocker."

"Oh, I am so tired of that word."

I pushed my chair back and stood up to go.

"You see," said Dempster, "Hemingway is rather smug. As a man of action he can fairly guarantee a violent death. His soul will be literally catapulted into the next life, blown out of his skull... But if not – Hem?"

I didn't answer him.

"Hem, if all else fails, a shotgun in the mouth. Always the safest way."

I went to settle with Miguel. He looked at me with sad brown eyes.

"I am so sorry, Monsieur Ernest. There is nothing I can do."

"It's not your fault, Miguel. I'll be back when the air is fresher."

I put the francs down on the counter-top.

"But Monsieur Ernest, the other gentleman, he has already paid."

"I buy my own drinks, thank you, Miguel."

I handed him the tip.

"Thank you, Monsieur."

When you were new in Paris and not yet known and did not have much money, it hurt to buy your own drinks. But it hurt far more and in a deeper and more lasting way if you did not.

The next time I saw Dempster was at Gertrude's, more than two years later. He had put on weight. He called himself Professor Julius these days and claimed that he was working at a university, but did not say which.

197

"We've met before," I said.

"Oh no. I would remember."

"We have."

"I always remember Americans."

"Professor Julius," said Gertrude, "is here to help Scott with his drinking."

It seemed to me Scott needed no help with his drinking, but when it was explained that Julius was here to stop him drinking, I said, "Easy. Cut off his credit. Cut off his – "

"Please, Hemingway," said Gertrude, "no vulgarity."

" – his royalties," I said, and poured myself a glass of *eau-de-vie*. The talk of stopping drinking had given me a thirst.

Scott was looking pale. His pale hair matched his pale face, and the famous blondness, of which he was so proud, was now the blondness of a *bier blond* at the Dome or Deux Magots.

"Hem," he said.

"Why are you doing this, Scott? Why are you listening to this charlatan?"

Scott was very sad by that stage. "They tell me if I'm sober," he said, "Zelda might come back to me."

When someone has a notion in his head like that and cannot or else will not let it go then there is little that a man can do, and though I swore to do all that I could, I knew defeat would be inevitable. And when Julius began to speak, I knew it three times over, and took refuge in a refilled glass.

"What you have here," he said, "is the soul of a drunkard. It is a common and a sad phenomenon, in which the vices of a past life have survived their transmigration to be reborn in the present. It is a difficult state, to be sure, yet not lacking in hope."

I poured myself another *eau-de-vie*.

"The habits of the old life cling. We may ask ourselves why one fellow likes onions, while another cannot bear them; why this man has a fear of heights, while that can walk a tightrope over the Niagara Falls. There is, of course," he clucked derisively, "a Viennese school which puts all things down to sex. We are, I hope, a little more sophisticated here."

"I hope so, yes," said Scott. He smiled his best ingratiating smile.

I said, "Professor Julius. Are you a Hindoo?"

"I am not."

"Funny. You talk like one."

"The Hindoos, of course, have rather more advanced ideas on these matters than are generally to be found here in the west, Mr, ah, Hammaway, is it? But my own methods are fundamentally scientific, I assure you. Mr Fitzgerald here is suffering an atavism of the spirit, which can be cured by a specialist course of hypnotic therapy, which I am qualified to provide. This will not only rid him of his drinking habits, but also – "

" – of several thousand US dollars. Am I right?"

"I charge a small fee for my work, as does any healer, but the long term benefits will more than – "

My fist took out his right lower incisor, bloodying his face a little, and knocking him to Miss Stein's floor. And if the rift with Gertrude started for me then, at least I have the compensation that I saved the great Fitzgerald fortune, however much was left, and gave Scott the chance to drink it all himself.

"Mr Hemingway," said Julius, getting my name right now despite a swollen lip, "you own a shotgun?"

"Not yet. But you make me want to get one."

"You will. And you'll know when to use it, too."

These days, if you go to Paris, a few people remember Gertrude Stein, but they think of her as the fat American lady with the paintings, and nobody remembers Scott, who was so drunk that he remembers nobody in turn. But everyone recalls the big American with the moustache and later with the beard, who wrote in pencil in the blue-backed notebooks and who could be seen at the Closerie and sometimes other cafés, working with the air of a man alone in the jungle, and later drinking with the air of a man very much not alone, but still in the jungle. And the spring came to Paris, and I worked well and I worked valiantly, and on the best days I could close the notebooks at the end of work and know that what I had was good, and of a quality that there would never be again, although there would be other work and good work but never work like this.

"Hemingway," Gertrude had said to me, that day, "you're drunk."

And I had kissed my knuckles, which were skinned, and lit a

cigarette, preparatory to leaving her. "Miss Stein," I said, "the drunk also rises, does he not?"

Tim Lees is a world-renowned big game hunter, bullfighter and war correspondent. In 1954 he was awarded the Nobel Prize for his novel *That's a Big Fish, Mister, Are You Having It With Chips?*

Ernest Hemingway is best remembered for his science fiction.

Previously from Elastic Press

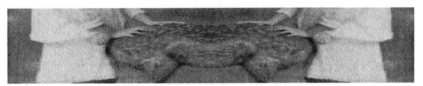

Visits To The Flea Circus by Nick Jackson

Quiet magical realism and poignant character studies go hand in hand in Nick Jackson's first collection of stories. His understated style and meticulous prose lead us into situations from which reality is the only escape.

Enviably lucid...the pictures he paints are potent enough to thrive without metaphor or narrative trickery...the characters live on in the reader's mind - Neil Ayres, author of *Nicolo's Gifts*

Forthcoming from Elastic Press

Trailer Park Fairy Tales by Matt Dinniman

Matt Dinniman combines the mundane with the unusual to fashion twelve intriguing stories where the only certainty is that uncertainty lies ahead. The lives of his characters uniquely exist within a caricaturised America that is simultaneously both frightening yet familiar. Urban fairytales will never be read quite the same way again.

For further information visit:

www.elasticpress.com

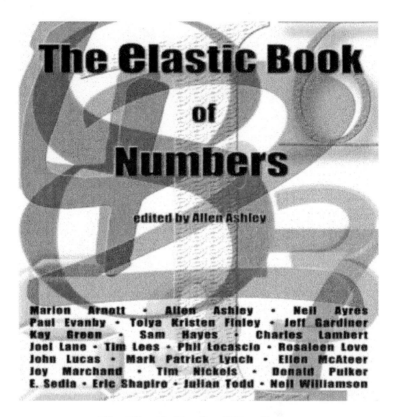

The Elastic Book of Numbers

edited by Allen Ashley

Marion Arnott • Allen Ashley • Neil Ayres
Paul Evanby • Telya Kristen Finley • Jeff Gardiner
Kay Green • Sam Hayes • Charles Lambert
Joel Lane • Tim Lees • Phil Locascio • Rosaleen Love
John Lucas • Mark Patrick Lynch • Ellen McAteer
Joy Marchand • Tim Nickels • Donald Pulker
E. Sedia • Eric Shapiro • Julian Todd • Neil Williamson

The Elastic Book of Numbers
Available Now From Elastic Press

Numbers rule our lives: clocks, calendars and deadlines; salaries and benefits; tax codes and pin numbers; mortgages, bills and credit limits; the FTSE and the Dow Jones; mobiles, land lines and pagers; binary strings of digitised information held for and about us, instantly accessible.

In this unique collection of 21 stories, some of the world's finest fictioneers examine the effect of numbers on humankind's past, present and future. From the rewriting of history through the thrill of the roulette wheel to the codes controlling the starships, each of these tales engages with numbers in innovative, entertaining and meaningful ways.

www.elasticpress.com